LAD
AN

By IDA ASHWORTH TAYLOR

CHAPTER I

The condition of Europe and England—Retrospect—Religious Affairs—A reign of terror—Cranmer in danger—Katherine Howard.

In 1546 it must have been evident to most observers that the life of the man who had for thirty-five years been England's ruler and tyrant—of whom Raleigh affirmed that if all the patterns of a merciless Prince had been lost in the world they might have been found in this one King—was not likely to be prolonged; and though it had been made penal to foretell the death of the sovereign, men must have been secretly looking on to the future with anxious eyes.

Of all the descendants of Henry VII. only one was male, the little Prince Edward, and in case of his death the succession would lie between his two sisters, Mary and Elizabeth, branded by successive Acts of Parliament with illegitimacy, the infant2 Queen of Scotland, whose claims were consistently ignored, and the daughters and grand-daughters of Henry VII.'s younger daughter, Mary Tudor.

The royal blood was to prove, to more than one of these, a fatal heritage. To Mary Stuart it was to bring captivity and death, and by reason of it Lady Jane Grey was to be forced to play the part of heroine in one of the most tragic episodes of the sixteenth century.

The latter part of Henry VIII.'s reign had been eventful at home and abroad. In Europe the three-cornered struggle between the Emperor Charles V., Francis of France, and Henry had been passing through various phases and vicissitudes, each of the wrestlers bidding for the support of a second of the trio, to the detriment of the third. New combinations were constantly formed as the kaleidoscope was turned; promises were lavishly made, to be broken without a scruple whensoever their breach might prove conducive to personal advantage. Religion, dragged into the political arena, was used as a party war-cry, and employed as a weapon for the destruction of public and private foes.

At home, England lay at the mercy of a King who was a law to himself and supreme arbiter of the destinies of his subjects. Only obscurity, and not always that, could ensure a man's safety, or prevent him from falling a prey to the jealousy or hate of those amongst his enemies who had for the moment the ear3 of the sovereign. Pre-eminence in rank, or power, or intellect, was enough to give the possessor of the distinction an uneasy sense that he was marked out for destruction, that envy and malice were lying in wait to seize an opportunity to denounce him to the weak despot upon whose vanity and cowardice the adroit could play at will. Every year added its tale to the long list of victims who had met their end upon the scaffold.

For fifteen years, moreover, the country had been delivered over to the struggle carried on in the name of religion. In 1531 the King had responded to the refusal of the Pope to sanction his divorce from Katherine of Aragon by repudiating the authority of the Holy See and the assertion of his own supremacy in matters spiritual as well as temporal. Three years later Parliament, servile and subservient as Parliaments were wont to be under the Tudor Kings, had formally endorsed and confirmed the revolt.

"The third day of November," recorded the chronicler, "the King's Highness held the high Court of Parliament, in the which was concluded and made many and sundry good, wholesome, and godly statutes, but among all one special statute which authorised the King's Highness to be supreme head of the Church of England, by which the Pope ... was utterly abolished out of this realm."1

4 Since then another punishable crime was added to those, already none too few, for which a man was liable to lose his head, and the following year saw the death upon the scaffold of Fisher and of More. The execution of Anne Boleyn, by whom the match had, in some sort, been set to the mine, came next, but the step taken by the King was not to be retraced with the absence of the motive which had prompted it; and Catholics and Protestants alike had continued to suffer at the hands of an autocrat who chastised at will those who wandered from the path he pointed out, and refused to model their creed upon the prescribed pattern.

In 1546 the "Act to abolish Diversity of Opinion"—called more familiarly the Bloody Statute, and designed to conform the faith of the nation to that of the King—had been in force for seven years, a standing menace to those persons, in high or low place, who, encouraged by the King's defiance of Rome, had been emboldened to adopt the tenets of the German Protestants. Henry had opened the floodgates; he desired to keep out the flood. The Six Articles of the Statute categorically reaffirmed the principal doctrines of the Catholic Church, and made their denial a legal offence. On the other hand the refusal to admit the royal supremacy in matters spiritual was no less penal. A reign of terror was the result.

"Is thy servant a dog?" The time-honoured5 question might have risen to the King's lips in the days, not devoid of a brighter promise, of his youth, had the veil covering the future been withdrawn. "We mark curiously," says a recent writer, "the regular deterioration of Henry's character as the only checks upon his action were removed, and he progressively defied traditional authority and established standards of conduct without disaster to himself." The Church had proved powerless to punish a defiance dictated by passion and perpetuated by vanity and cupidity; Parliaments had cringed to him in matters religious or political, courtiers and sycophants had flattered, until "there was no power on earth to hold in check the devil in the breast of Henry Tudor."2

Such was the condition of England. Old barriers had been thrown down; new had not acquired strength; in the struggle for freedom men had cast aside moral restraint. Life was so lightly esteemed, and death invested with so little tragic importance, that a man of the position and standing of Latimer, Bishop of Worcester, when appointed to preach on the occasion of the burning of a priest, could treat the matter with a flippant levity scarcely credible at a later day.

"If it be your pleasure, as it is," he wrote to Cromwell, "that I shall play the fool after my customary manner when Forest shall suffer, I6 would that my stage stood near unto Forest" (so that the victim might benefit by his arguments).... "If he would yet with heart return to his abjuration, I would wish his pardon, such is my foolishness."3

Yet there was another side to the picture; here and there, amidst the din of battle and the confusion of tongues, the voice of genuine conviction was heard; and men and women were ready, at the bidding of conscience, to give up their lives in passionate loyalty to an ancient faith or to a new ideal. "And the thirtieth day of the same month," June 1540, runs an entry in a contemporary chronicle, "was Dr. Barnes, Jerome, and Garrard, drawn from the Tower to Smithfield, and there burned for their heresies. And that same day also was drawn from the Tower with them Doctor Powell, with two other priests, and there was a gallows set up at St. Bartholomew's Gate, and there were hanged, headed, and quartered that same day"—the offence of these last being the denial of the King's supremacy, as that of the first had been adherence to Protestant doctrines.4

HENRY VIII.

No one was safe. The year 1540 had seen the fall of Cromwell, the Minister of State. "Cranmer and Cromwell," wrote the French ambassador, "do not know where they are."5 Cromwell at least was7 not to wait long for the certainty. For years all-powerful in the Council, he was now to fall a victim to jealous hate and the credulity of the master he had served. At his imprisonment "many lamented, but more rejoiced, ... for they banquetted and triumphed together that night, many wishing that day had been seven years before; and some, fearing that he should escape although he were imprisoned, could not be merry."6 They need not have feared the King's clemency. The minister had been arrested on June 10. On July 28 he was executed on Tower Hill.

If Cromwell, in spite of his services to the Crown, in spite of the need Henry had of men of his ability, was not secure, who could call themselves safe? Even Cranmer, the King's special friend though he was, must have felt misgivings. A married man, with children, he was implicitly condemned by one of the Six Articles of the Bloody Statute, enjoining celibacy on the clergy, and was besides well known to hold Protestant views. His embittered enemy, Gardiner, Bishop of Winchester, vehement in his Catholicism though pandering to the King on the subject of the royal supremacy, was minister; and his fickle master might throw the Archbishop at any moment to the wolves.

One narrow escape he had already had, when in 1544 a determined attempt had been hazarded8 to oust him from his position of trust and to convict him of his errors, and the party adverse to him in the Council had accused the Primate "most grievously" to the King of heresy. It was a bold stroke, for it was known that Henry loved him, and the triumph of his foes was the greater when they received the royal permission to commit the Lord Archbishop to the Tower on the following day, and to cause him to undergo an examination on matters of doctrine and faith. So far all had gone according to their hopes, and his enemies augured well of the result. But that night, at eleven o'clock, when Cranmer, in ignorance of the plot against him, was in bed, he received a summons to attend the King, whom he found in the gallery at Whitehall, and who made him acquainted with the action of the Council, together with his own consent that an examination should take place.

"Whether I have done well or no, what say you, my lord?" asked Henry in conclusion.

Cranmer answered warily. Knowing his master, and his jealousy of being supposed to connive at heresy, save on the one question of the Pope's authority, he cannot have failed to recognise the gravity of the situation. He put, however, a good face upon it. The King, he said, would see that he had a fair trial—"was indifferently heard." His bearing was that of a man secure that justice would be done him. Both he, in his heart, and the King, knew better.

9 "Oh, Lord God," sighed Henry, "what fond simplicity have you, so to permit yourself to be imprisoned!" False witnesses would be produced, and he would be condemned.

Taking his precautions, therefore, Henry gave the Archbishop his ring—the recognised sign that the matter at issue was taken out of the hands of the Council and reserved for his personal investigation. After which sovereign and prelate parted.

When, at eight o'clock the next morning, Cranmer, in obedience to the summons he had received, arrived at the Council Chamber, his foes, insolent in their premature triumph, kept him at the door, awaiting their convenience, close upon an hour. My lord of Canterbury was become a lacquey, some one reported to the King, since he was standing

3

among the footmen and servants. The King, comprehending what was implied, was wroth.

"Have they served my lord so?" he asked. "It is well enough; I shall talk with them by and by."

Accordingly when Cranmer, called at length and arraigned before the Council, produced the ring—the symbol of his enemies' discomfiture—and was brought to the royal presence that his cause might be tried by the King in person, the positions of accused and accusers were reversed. Acting, not without passion, rather as the advocate of the menaced man than as his judge, Henry received the Council10 with taunts, and in reply to their asseverations that the trial had been merely intended to conduce to the Archbishop's greater glory, warned them against treating his friends in that fashion for the future. Cranmer, for the present, was safe.7

Protestant England rejoiced with the Protestant Archbishop. But it rejoiced in trembling. The Archbishop's escape did not imply immunity to lesser offenders, and the severity used in administering the law is shown by the fact that a boy of fifteen was burnt for heresy—no willing martyr, but ignorant, and eager to catch at any chances of life, by casting the blame of his heresy on others. "The poor boy," says Hall, "would have gladly said that the twelve Apostles taught it him ... such was his childish innocency and fear."8 And England, with the strange patience of the age, looked on.

Side by side with religious persecution ran the story of the King's domestic crimes. To go back no further, in the year 1542 Katherine Howard, Henry's fifth wife, had met her fate, and the country had silently witnessed the pitiful and shameful spectacle. As fact after fact came to light, the tale will have been told of the beautiful, neglected child, left to her own devices and to the companionship of maid-servants in the disorderly household of her grandmother, the Duchess of Norfolk, with11 the results that might have been anticipated; of how she had suddenly become of importance when it had been perceived that the King had singled her out for favour; and of how, still "a very little girl," as some one described her, she had been used as a pawn in the political game played by the Howard clan, and married to Henry. Only a few months after she had been promoted to her perilous dignity her doom had overtaken her; the enemies of the party to which by birth she belonged had not only made known to her husband misdeeds committed before her marriage and almost ranking as the delinquencies of a misguided child, but had hinted at more unpardonable misdemeanours of which the King's wife had been guilty. The story of Katherine's arraignment and condemnation will have spread through the land, with her protestations that, though not excusing the sins and follies of her youth—she was seventeen when she was done to death—she was guiltless of the action she was specially to expiate at the block; whilst men may have whispered the tale of her love for Thomas Culpeper, her cousin and playmate, whom she would have wedded had not the King stepped in between, and who had paid for her affection with his blood. "I die a Queen," she is reported to have exclaimed upon the scaffold, "but I would rather have died the wife of Culpeper."9 And it may have been rumoured that12 her head had fallen, not so much to vindicate the honour of the King as to set him free to form fresh ties.

However that might be, Katherine Howard had been sent to answer for her offences, or prove her innocence, at another bar, and her namesake, Katherine Parr, reigned in her stead.

From a photo by W. Mansell & Co. after a painting of the School of Holbein. KATHERINE HOWARD.
13

4

Katherine Parr—Relations with Thomas Seymour—Married to Henry VIII.—
Parties in court and country—Katherine's position—Prince Edward.

It was now three years since Katherine Parr had replaced the unhappy child who
had been her immediate predecessor. For three perilous years she had occupied—with
how many fears, how many misgivings, who can tell?—the position of the King's sixth
wife. On a July day in 1543 Lady Latimer, already at thirty twice a widow, had been raised
to the rank of Queen. If the ceremony was attended with no special pomp, neither had it
been celebrated with the careful privacy observed with respect to some of the King's
marriages. His two daughters, Mary—approximately the same age as the bride, and who
was her friend—and Elizabeth, had been present, as well as Henry's brother-in-law,
Edward Seymour, Earl of Hertford, and other officers of State. Gardiner, Bishop of
Winchester, afterwards her dangerous foe, performed the rite, in the Queen's Closet at
Hampton Court.

Sir Thomas Seymour, Hertford's brother and14 Lord Admiral of England, was not
at Hampton Court on the occasion, having been despatched on some foreign mission.
More than one reason may have contributed to render his absence advisable. A wealthy
and childless widow, of unblemished reputation, and belonging by birth to a race
connected with the royal house, was not likely to remain long without suitors, and Lord
Latimer can scarcely have been more than a month in his grave before Thomas Seymour
had testified his desire to replace him and to become Katherine's third husband. Nor does
she appear to have been backward in responding to his advances.

Twice married to elderly men whose lives lay behind them, twice set free by death
from her bonds, she may fairly have conceived that the time was come when she was
justified in wedding, not for family or substantial reasons, not wholly perhaps, as before,
in wisdom's way, but a man she loved.

Seymour was not without attractions calculated to commend him to a woman
hitherto bestowed upon husbands selected for her by others. Young and handsome,
"fierce in courage, courtly in fashion, in personage stately, in voice magnificent, but
somewhat empty in matter,"10 the gay sailor appears to have had little difficulty in
winning the heart of a woman who, in spite of the learning, the prudence, and the piety
for which she was noted, may have15 felt, as she watched her youth slip by, that she had
had little good of it; and it is clear, from a letter she addressed to Seymour himself when,
after Henry's death, his suit had been successfully renewed, that she had looked forward
at this earlier date to becoming his wife.

"As truly as God is God," she then wrote, "my mind was fully bent, the other time I
was at liberty, to marry you before any man I know. Howbeit God withstood my will
therein most vehemently for a time, and through His grace and goodness made that
possible which seemed to me most impossible; that was, made me renounce utterly mine
own will and follow His most willingly. It were long to write all the processes of this
matter. If I live, I shall declare it to you myself. I can say nothing, but as my Lady of
Suffolk saith, 'God is a marvellous man.'"11

Strange burdens of responsibility have ever been laid upon the duty of obedience to
the will of Providence, nor does it appear clear to the casual reader why the consent of
Katherine to become a Queen should have been viewed by her in the light of a sacrifice
to principle. Whether her point of view was shared by her lover does not appear. It is at

all events clear that both were wise enough in the world's lore not to brave the wrath of the despot by crossing his caprice. Seymour retired16 from the field, and Katherine, perhaps sustained by the inward approval of conscience, perhaps partially comforted by a crown, accepted the dangerous distinction she was offered.

To her brother, Lord Parr, when writing to inform him of her advancement, she expressed no regret. It had pleased God, she told him, to incline the King to take her as his wife, the greatest joy and comfort that could happen to her. She desired to communicate the great news to Parr, as being the person with most cause to rejoice thereat, and added, with a suspicion of condescension, her hope that he would let her hear of his health as friendly as if she had not been called to this honour.12

Although the actual marriage had not taken place until some six months after Lord Latimer's death, no time can have been lost in arranging it, since before her husband had been two months in the grave Henry was causing a bill for her dresses to be paid out of the Exchequer.

It was generally considered that the King had chosen well. Wriothesley, the Chancellor, was sure His Majesty had never a wife more agreeable to his heart. Gardiner had not only performed the marriage ceremony but had given away the bride. According to an old chronicle the new Queen was a woman "compleat with singular humility."13 She17 had, at any rate, the adroitness, in her relations with the King, to assume the appearance of it, and was a well-educated, sensible, and kindly woman, "quieter than any of the young wives the King had had, and, as she knew more of the world, she always got on pleasantly with the King, and had no caprices."14

The story of the marriage was an old one in 1546. Seymour had returned from his mission and resumed his former position at Court as the King's brother-in-law and the uncle of his heir, and not even the Queen's enemies—and she had enough of them and to spare—had found an excuse for calling to mind the relations once existing between the Admiral and the King's wife. Nevertheless, and in spite of the blamelessness of her conduct, the satisfaction which had greeted the marriage was on the wane. A hard task would have awaited Queen or courtier who should have attempted to minister to the contentment of all the rival parties striving for predominance in the State and at Court, and to be adjudged the friend of the one was practically equivalent to a pledge of distrust from the other. Whitehall, like the country at large, was divided against itself by theological strife; and whilst the men faithful to the ancient creed in its entirety were inevitably in bitter opposition to the adherents of the new teachers whose headquarters were in Germany, a third party, more unscrupulous than either, was made up of the middle men who18 moulded—outwardly or inwardly—their faith upon the King's, and would, if they could, have created a Papacy without a Pope, a Catholic Church without its corner-stone.

At Court, as elsewhere, each of these three parties were standing on their guard, ready to parry or to strike a blow when occasion arose, jealous of every success scored by their opponents. The fall of Cromwell had inspired the Catholics with hope, and, with Gardiner as Minister and Wriothesley as Chancellor, they had been in a more favourable position than for some time past at the date of the King's last marriage. It had then been assumed that the new Queen's influence would be employed upon their side—an expectation confirmed by her friendship with the Princess Mary. The discovery that the widow of Lord Latimer—so fervent a Catholic that he had joined in the north-country insurrection known as the Pilgrimage of Grace—had broken with her past, openly displayed her sympathy with Protestant doctrine, and, in common with the King's nieces, was addicted to what was called the "new learning," quickly disabused them of their hopes, rendered the Catholic party at Court her embittered enemies, and lent additional danger to what was already a perilous position by affording those at present in power a motive for removing from the King's side a woman regarded as the advocate of innovation.

19 So far their efforts had been fruitless. Katherine still held her own. During Henry's absence in France, whither he had gone to conduct the campaign in person, she had administered the Government, as Queen-Regent, with tact and discretion; the King loved her—as he understood love—and, what was perhaps a more important matter, she had contrived to render herself necessary to him. Wary, prudent, and pious, and notwithstanding the possession of qualities marking her out in some sort as the superior woman of her day, she was not above pandering to his love of flattery. Into her book entitled The Lamentations of a Sinner, she introduced a fulsome panegyric of the godly and learned King who had removed from his realm the veils and mists of error, and in the guise of a modern Moses had been victorious over the Roman Pharaoh. What she publicly printed she doubtless reiterated in private; and the King found the domestic incense soothing to an irritable temper, still further acerbated by disease.

By other methods she had commended herself to those who were about him open to conciliation. She had served a long apprenticeship in the art of the step-mother, both Lord Borough, her first husband, and Lord Latimer having possessed children when she married them; and her skill in dealing with the little heir to the throne and his sisters proved that she had turned her experience to good account. Her genuine kindness, not only to Mary, who had been20 her friend from the first, but to Elizabeth, ten years old at the time of the marriage, was calculated to propitiate the adherents of each; and to her good offices it was in especial due that Anne Boleyn's daughter, hitherto kept chiefly at a distance from Court, was brought to Whitehall. The child, young as she was, was old enough to appreciate the importance of possessing a friend in her father's wife, and the letter she addressed to her step-mother on the occasion overflowed with expressions of devotion and gratitude. To the place the Queen won in the affections of the all-important heir, the boy's letters bear witness.

From an engraving by F. Bartolozzi after a picture by Holbein.
HENRY VIII. AND HIS THREE CHILDREN.
There is no need to assume that Katherine's course of action was wholly dictated by interested motives. Yet in this case principle and prudence went hand in hand. Henry was becoming increasingly sick and suffering, and, with the shadow of death deepening above him, the gifts he asked of life were insensibly changing their character. His autocratic and violent temper remained the same, but peace and quiet, a soothing atmosphere of submissive affection, the absence of domestic friction, if not sufficient to ensure his wife immunity from peril, constituted her best chance of escaping the doom of her predecessors. To a selfish man the appeal must be to self-interest. This appeal Katherine consistently made and it had so far proved successful. For the rest, whether21 she suffered from terror of possible disaster or resolutely shut her eyes to what might have unnerved and rendered her unfit for the part she had to play, none can tell, any more than it can be determined whether, as she looked from the man she had married to the man she had loved, she indulged in vain regrets for the happiness of which she had caught a glimpse in those brief days when she had dreamed of a future to be shared with Thomas Seymour.

In spite, however, of her caution, in spite of the perfection with which she performed the duties of wife and nurse, by 1546 disquieting reports were afloat.

"I am confused and apprehensive," wrote Charles V.'s ambassador from London in the February of that year, "to have to inform Your Majesty that there are rumours here of a new Queen, although I do not know how true they be.... The King shows no alteration in his behaviour towards the Queen, though I am informed that she is annoyed by the rumours."15

With the history of the past to quicken her apprehensions, she may well have been more than "annoyed" by them. But, true or false, she could but pursue the line of conduct she had adopted, and must have turned with relief from domestic anxieties to any other matters that could22 serve to distract her mind from her precarious future. Amongst the learned ladies of a day when scholarship was becoming a fashion she occupied a foremost place, and was actively engaged in promoting educational interests. Stimulated by her step-mother's approval, the Princess Mary had been encouraged to undertake part of the translation of Erasmus's paraphrases of the Gospels; and Elizabeth is found sending the Queen, as a fitting offering, a translation from the Italian inscribed on vellum and entitled the Glasse of the Synneful Soule, accompanying it by the expression of a hope that, having passed through hands so learned as the Queen's, it would come forth from them in a new form. The education of the little Prince Edward too was pushed rapidly forward, and at six years old, the year of his father's marriage, he had been taken out of the hands of women and committed to the tuition of John Cheke and Dr. Richard Cox. These two, explains Heylyn, being equal in authority, employed themselves to his advantage in their several kinds—Dr. Cox for knowledge of divinity, philosophy, and gravity of manners, Mr. Cheke for eloquence in the Greek and Latin tongues; whilst other masters instructed the poor child in modern languages, so that in a short time he spoke French perfectly, and was able to express himself "magnificently enough" in Italian, Greek, and Spanish.16

23 His companion and playfellow was one Barnaby Fitzpatrick, to whom he clung throughout his short life with constant affection. It was Barnaby's office to bear whatever punishment the Prince had merited—a method more successful in the case of the Prince than it might have proved with a less soft-hearted offender, since it is said that "it was not easy to affirm whether Fitzpatrick smarted more for the default of the Prince, or the Prince conceived more grief for the smart of Fitzpatrick."17

Katherine Parr is not likely to have regretted the pressure put upon her stepson; and the boy, apologising for his simple and rude letters, adds his acknowledgments for those addressed to him by the Queen, "which do give me much comfort and encouragement to go forward in such things wherein your Grace beareth me on hand."

The King's latest wife was, in fact, a teacher by nature and choice, and admirably fitted to direct the studies of his son and daughters, as well as of any other children who might be brought within the sphere of her influence. That influence, it may be, had something to do with moulding the character and the destiny of a child fated to be unhappily prominent in the near future. This was Lady Jane Grey.

24

CHAPTER III

1546

The Marquis of Dorset and his family—Bradgate Park—Lady Jane Grey—Her relations with her cousins—Mary Tudor—Protestantism at Whitehall—Religious persecution.

Amongst the households where both affairs at Court and the religious struggle distracting the country were watched with the deepest interest was that of the Marquis of Dorset, the husband of the King's niece and father of Lady Jane Grey.

Married at eighteen to the infirm and aged Louis XII. of France, Mary Tudor, daughter of Henry VII. and friend of the luckless Katherine of Aragon, had been released by his death after less than three months of wedded life, and had lost no time in choosing a more congenial bridegroom. At Calais, on her way home, she had bestowed her hand upon "that martial and pompous gentleman," Charles Brandon, Duke of Suffolk, who, sent by her brother to conduct her back to England, thought it well to secure his bride and to wait until the union was accomplished before obtaining the King's consent. Of this hurried marriage the eldest child was the25 mother of Jane Grey, who thus derived her disastrous heritage of royal blood.

It was at the country home of the Dorset family, Bradgate Park, that Lady Jane had been born, in 1537. Six miles distant from the town of Leicester, and forming the south-east end of Charnwood Forest, it was a pleasant and quiet place. Over the wide park itself, seven miles in circumference, bracken grew freely; here and there bare rocks rose amidst the masses of green undergrowth, broken now and then by a solitary oak, and the unwooded expanse was covered with "wild verdure."18

The house itself had not long been built, nor is there much remaining at the present day to show what had been its aspect at the time when Lady Jane was its inmate. Early in the eighteenth century it was destroyed by fire, tradition ascribing the catastrophe to a Lady Suffolk who, brought to her husband's home as a bride, complained that the country was a forest and the inhabitants were brutes, and, at the suggestion of her sister, took the most certain means of ensuring a change of residence.

But if little outward trace is left of the place where the victim of state-craft and ambition was born and passed her early years, it is not a difficult matter to hazard a guess at the religious and political atmosphere of her home. Echoes of the fight carried on,26 openly or covertly, between the parties striving for predominance in the realm must have almost daily reached Bradgate, the accounts of the incidents marking the combat taking their colour from the sympathies of the master and mistress of the house, strongly enlisted upon the side of Protestantism. At Lord Dorset's house, though with closed doors, the condition of religious affairs must have supplied constant matter for discussion; and Jane will have listened to the conversation with the eager attention of an intelligent child, piecing together the fragments she gathered up, and gradually realising, with a thrill of excitement, as she became old enough to grasp the significance of what she heard, that men and women were suffering and dying in torment for the sake of doctrines she had herself been taught as a matter of course. Serious and precocious, and already beginning an education said to have included in later years Greek, Latin, Hebrew, Chaldaic, Arabic, French, and Italian, the stories reaching her father's house of the events taking place in London and at Court must have imprinted themselves upon her imagination at an age specially open to such impressions, and it is not unnatural that she should have grown up nurtured in the principles of polemics and apt at controversy.

Nor were edifying tales of martyrdom or of suffering for conscience' sake the only ones to penetrate to the green and quiet precincts of Bradgate. At his niece's house the King's domestic affairs—27a scandal and a by-word in Europe—must have been regarded with the added interest, perhaps the sharper criticism, due to kinship. Henry was not only Lady Dorset's sovereign, but her uncle, and she had a more personal interest than others in what Messer Barbaro, in his report to the Venetian senate, described as "this confusion of wives."19 To keep a child ignorant was no part of the training of the day, and Jane, herself destined for a court life, no doubt had heard, as she grew older, many of the stories of terror and pity circulating throughout the country, and investing, in the eyes of those afar off, the distant city—the stage whereon most of them had been enacted—with the atmosphere of mystery and fear and excitement belonging to a place where martyrs were shedding their blood, or heretics atoning for their guilt, according as the narrators inclined to the ancient or the novel faith; where tragedies of love and hatred and revenge were being played, and men went in hourly peril of their lives.

Of this place, invested with the attraction and glamour belonging to a land of glitter and romance, Lady Jane had glimpses on the occasions when, as a near relation of the King's, she accompanied her mother to Court, becoming for a while a sharer in the life of palaces and an actor, by reason of her strain of royal blood, in the pageant28 ever going forward at St. James's or Whitehall;20 and though it does not appear that she was finally transferred from the guardianship of her parents to that of the Queen until after the death of Henry in the beginning of the year 1547, it is not unlikely that the book-loving child of nine may have attracted the attention of the scholarly Queen during her visits to Court and that Katherine's belligerent Protestantism had its share in the development of the convictions which afterwards proved so strong both in life and in death.

There is at this date little trace of any connection between Jane and her cousins, the King's children. A strong affection on the part of Edward is said to have existed, and to it has been attributed his consent to set his sisters aside in Lady Jane's favour. "She charmed all who knew her," says Burnet, "in particular the young King, about whom she was bred, and who had always lived with her in the familiarity of a brother." For this statement there is no contemporary authority, and, so far as can be ascertained, intercourse between29 the two can have been but slight. Between Edward and his younger sister, on the other hand, the bond of affection was strong, their education being carried on at this time much together at Hatfield; and "a concurrence and sympathy of their natures and affections, together with the celestial bond, conformity in religion,"21 made it the more remarkable that the Prince should have afterwards agreed to set aside, in favour of his cousin, Elizabeth's claim to the succession. It is true that in their occasional meetings the studious boy and the serious-minded little girl may have discovered that they had tastes in common, but such casual acquaintanceship can scarcely have availed to counterbalance the affection produced by close companionship and the tie of blood; and grounds for the Prince's subsequent conduct, other than the influence and arguments of those about him, can only be matter of conjecture.

Of the relations existing between Jane and the Prince's sisters there is little more mention; but the entry by Mary Tudor in a note-book of the gift of a gold necklace set with pearls, made "to my cousin, Jane Gray," shows that the two had met in the course of this summer, and would seem to indicate a kindly feeling on the part of the older woman towards the unfortunate child whom, not eight years later, she was to send to the scaffold.30 Could the future have been laid bare it would perhaps not have been the victim who would have recoiled from the revelation with the greatest horror.

Although what was to follow lends a tragic significance to the juxtaposition of the names of the two cousins, there was nothing sinister about the King's elder daughter as she filled the place at Court in which she had been reinstated at the instance of her step-mother. A gentle, brown-eyed woman, past her first youth, and bearing on her countenance the traces of sickness and sorrow and suffering, she enjoyed at this date so great a popularity as almost, according to a foreign observer, to be an object of adoration to her father's subjects, obstinately faithful to her injured and repudiated mother. But, ameliorated as was the Princess's condition, she had been too well acquainted, from childhood upwards, with the reverses of fortune to count over-securely upon a future depending upon her father's caprice.

Her health was always delicate, and during the early part of the year she had been ill. By the spring, however, she had resumed her attendance at Court, and—to judge by a letter from her little wise brother, contemplating from a safe distance the dangerous pastimes of Whitehall—was taking a conspicuous part in the entertainments in fashion. Writing in Latin to his step-mother, Prince Edward besought31 her "to preserve his dear sister Mary from the enchantments of the Evil One, by beseeching her no longer to attend to foreign dances and merriments, unbecoming in a most Christian Princess"—and least of all in one for whom he expressed the wish, in the course of the same summer, that the wisdom of Esther might be hers.

It does not appear whether or not Mary took the admonitions of her nine-year-old Mentor to heart. The pleasures of court life are not likely to have exercised a perilous fascination over the Princess, her spirits clouded by the memory of her melancholy past and the uncertainty of her future, and probably represented to her a more or less wearisome part of the necessary routine of existence.

Whilst the entertainments the Prince deplored went forward at Whitehall, they were accompanied by other practices he would have wholly approved. Not only was his step-mother addicted to personal study of the Scriptures, but she had secured the services of learned men to instruct her further in them; holding private conferences with these teachers; and, especially during Lent, causing a sermon to be delivered each afternoon for her own benefit and that of any of her ladies disposed to profit by it, when the discourse frequently turned or touched upon abuses in the Church.22

It was a bold stroke, Henry's claims to the32 position of sole arbiter on questions of doctrine considered. Nevertheless the Queen acted openly, and so far her husband had testified no dissatisfaction. Yet the practice must have served to accentuate the dividing line of theological opinion, already sufficiently marked at Court; some members of the royal household, like Princess Mary, holding aloof; others eagerly welcoming the step; the Seymours, Cranmer, and their friends looking on with approval, whilst the Howard connection, with Gardiner and Wriothesley, took note of the Queen's imprudence, and waited and watched their opportunity to turn it to their advantage and to her destruction.

Edward Prince
From an engraving by R. Dalton after a drawing by Holbein.
PRINCE EDWARD, AFTERWARDS EDWARD VI.

Such was the internal condition of the Court. The spring had meanwhile been marked by rejoicings for the peace with foreign powers, at last concluded. On Whit-Sunday a great procession proceeded from St. Paul's to St. Peter's, Cornhill, accompanied by a banner, and by crosses from every parish church, the children of St. Paul's School joining in the show. It was composed of a motley company. Bishop Bonner—as vehement in his Catholicism as Gardiner, and so much less wary in the display of his opinions that his brother of Winchester was wont at times to term him "asse"—carried the Blessed Sacrament under a canopy, with "clerks and priests and vicars and parsons"; the Lord Mayor was there in crimson velvet, the aldermen were in scarlet, and all the crafts33 in their best apparel. The occasion was worthy of the pomp displayed in honour of it, for it was—the words sound like a jest—the festival of a "Universal Peace for ever,"· announced by the Mayor, standing between standard and cross, and including in the proclamation of general amity the names of the Emperor, the King of England, the French King, and all Christian Kings.23

11

If soldiers had for the moment consented to proclaim a truce and to name it, merrily, eternal, theologians had agreed to no like suspension of hostilities, and the perennial religious strife showed no signs of intermission.

"Sire," wrote Admiral d'Annebaut, sent by Francis to London to ratify the peace, "I know not what to tell your Majesty as to the order given me to inform myself of the condition of religious affairs in England; except that Henry has declared himself head of the Anglican Church, and woe to whomsoever refuses to recognise him in that capacity. He has also usurped all ecclesiastical property, and destroyed all the convents. He attends Mass nevertheless daily, and permits the papal nuncio to live in London. What is strangest of all is that Catholics are there burnt as well as Lutherans and other heretics. Was anything like it ever seen?"24

34 Punishment was indeed dealt out with singular impartiality. During the spring Dr. Crome had been examined touching a sermon he had delivered against Catholic doctrine. Two or three weeks later, preaching once more at Paul's Cross, he had boldly declared he was not there for the purpose of denying his former assertions; but a second "examination" had proved more effective, and on the Sunday following the feast of Corpus Christi he eschewed his heresies.25 "Our news here," wrote a merchant of London to his brother on July 2, "of Dr. Crome's canting, recanting, decanting, or rather double-canting, be this."26 The transaction was representative of many others, which, with their undercurrent of terror, struggle, intimidation, menace, and remorse, formed a melancholy and recurrent feature of the day, the victory remaining sometimes with a man's conscience—whatever it dictates might be—sometimes with his fears.

The King was, in fact, still endeavouring to stem the torrent he had set loose. In his speech to Parliament on Christmas Eve, 1545, after commending and thanking Lords and Commons for their loyalty and affection towards himself, he had spoken with severity of the discord and dissension prevalent in the realm; the clergy, by their sermons against each other, sowing debate and discord35 amongst the people.... "I am very sorry to know and hear how unreverently that most precious jewel, the Word of God, is disputed, rimed, sung and jangled in every ale-house and tavern ... and yet I am even as much sorry that the readers of the same follow it in doing so faintly and so coldly. For of this I am sure, that charity was never so faint amongst you, and virtuous and godly living was never less used, nor God Himself amongst Christians was never less reverenced, honoured, and served."27

Delivered scarcely more than a year before his death, Henry's speech was a singular commentary upon the condition of the realm, consequent upon his own policy, during the concluding years of his reign.

36

CHAPTER IV

1546

Anne Askew—Her trial and execution—Katherine Parr's danger—Plot against her—Her escape.

As the months of 1546 went by the measures taken by the King and his advisers to enforce unanimity of practice and opinion in matters of religion did not become less drastic. A great burning of books disapproved by Henry took place during the autumn, preceded in July by the condemnation and execution of a victim whose fate attracted an unusual amount of attention, the effect at Court being enhanced by the fact that the heroine of the story was personally known to the Queen and her ladies. It was indeed reported that one of the King's special causes of displeasure was that she had been the means of imbuing his nieces—among whom was Lady Dorset, Jane Grey's mother—as well as his wife, with heretical doctrines.

Added to the species of glamour commonly surrounding a spiritual leader, more particularly in times of persecution, Anne Askew was beautiful and young—not more than twenty-five at the time37 of her death—and the thought of her racked frame, her undaunted courage, and her final agony at the stake, may well have haunted with the horror of a night-mare those who had been her disciples, and who looked on from a distance, and with sympathy they dared not display.

There were other circumstances increasing the interest with which the melancholy drama was watched. Well born and educated, Anne had been the wife of a Lincolnshire gentleman of the name of Kyme. Their life together had been of short duration. In a period of bitter party feeling and recrimination, it is difficult to ascertain with certainty the truth on any given point; and whilst a hostile chronicler asserts that Anne left her husband in order "to gad up and down a-gospelling and gossiping where she might and ought not, but especially in London and near the Court,"28 another authority explains that Kyme had turned her out of his house upon her conversion to Protestant doctrines. Whatever might have been the origin of her mode of life, it is certain that she resumed her maiden name, and proceeded to "execute the office of an apostle."29

Her success in her new profession made her unfortunately conspicuous, and in 1545 she was committed to Newgate, "for that she was very38 obstinate and heady in reasoning on matters of religion." The charge, it must be confessed, is corroborated by her demeanour under examination, when the qualities of meekness and humility were markedly absent, and her replies to the interrogatories addressed to her were rather calculated to irritate than to prove conciliatory. On this first occasion, for example, asked to interpret certain passages in the Scriptures, she declined to comply with the request on the score that she would not cast pearls among swine—acorns were good enough; and, urged by Bonner to open her wound, she again refused. Her conscience was clear, she said; to lay a plaster on a whole skin might seem much folly, and the similitude of a wound appeared to her unsavoury.30

For the time she escaped; but in the course of the following year her case was again brought forward, and on this occasion she found no mercy. Her examinations, mostly reported by herself, show her as alike keen-witted and sharp-tongued, rarely at a loss for an answer, and profoundly convinced of the justice of her cause. If she was not without the genuine enjoyment of the born controversialist in the opportunity of argument and discussion, she possessed, underlying the self-assertion and confidence natural in a woman holding the position of a religious leader, a fund of indomitable heroism.39 For she must have been fully conscious of her danger. It is possible that, had she not been brought into prominence by her association with those in high places, she might again have escaped; but, apart from the grudge owed her for her influence over the King's own kin, her attitude was almost such as to court her fate. Refusing "to sing a new song of the Lord in a strange land," she replied to the Bishop of Winchester, when he complained that she spoke in parables, that it was best for him that she should do so. Had she shown him the open truth, he would not accept it.

"Then the Bishop said he would speak with me familiarly. I said, 'So did Judas when he unfriendlily betrayed Christ....' In conclusion," she ended, in her account of the interview, "we could not agree."

Spirited as was her bearing, and thrilling as the prisoner plainly was with all the excitement of a battle of words, it was not strange that the strain should tell upon her.

"On the Sunday," she proceeds—and there is a pathetic contrast between the physical weakness to which she confesses and her undaunted boldness in confronting the men bent upon her destruction—"I was sore sick, thinking no less than to die.... Then was I sent to Newgate in my extremity of sickness, for in all my life I was never in such pain. Thus the Lord strengthen us in His truth. Pray, pray, pray."

40 Her condemnation was a foregone conclusion. It followed quickly, with a subsequent visit from one Nicholas Shaxton, who, having, for his own part, made his recantation, counselled her to do the same. He spoke in vain. It were, she told him, good for him never to have been born, "with many like words." More was to follow. If her assertion is to be believed—and there seems no valid reason to doubt it—the rack was applied "till I was nigh dead.... After that I sat two long hours reasoning with my Lord Chancellor upon the bare floor. Then was I brought into a house and laid in a bed with as weary and painful bones as ever had patient Job. I thank my God therefore."

A scarcely credible addition is made to the story, to the effect that when the Lieutenant of the Tower had refused to put the victim to the torture a second time, the Lord Chancellor, Wriothesley, less merciful, took the office upon himself, and applied the rack with his own hands, the Lieutenant departing to report the matter to the King, "who seemed not very well to like such handling of a woman."31 What is certain is the final scene at Smithfield, where Shaxton delivered a sermon, Anne listening, endorsing his41 words when she approved of them and correcting them "when he said amiss."

So the shameful episode was brought to an end. The tale, penetrating even the thick walls of a palace, must have caused a thrill of horror at Whitehall, accentuated by reason of certain events going forward there about the same time.

The King's disease was gaining upon him apace. He had become so unwieldy in bulk that the use of machinery was necessary to move him, and with the progress of his disorder his temper was becoming more and more irritable. In view of his approaching death the question of the guardianship and custody of the heir to the throne was increasing in importance and the jealousy of the rival parties was becoming more embittered. In the course of the summer the Catholics about the Court ventured on a bold stroke, directed against no less a person than the Queen.

Emboldened by the tolerance displayed by the King towards her religious practices and the preachers and teachers she gathered around her, Katherine had grown so daring as to make matters of doctrine a constant subject of conversation with Henry, urging him to complete the work he had begun, and to free the Church of England from superstition.32 Henry appears at first—though he was a man ill to argue with—to have shown singular patience under his wife's admonitions. But daily controversy is not42 soothing to a sick man's nerves and temper, and Katherine's enemies, watching their opportunity, conceived that it was at hand.

Henry's habits had been altered by illness, and it had become the Queen's custom to wait for a summons before visiting his apartments; although on some occasions, after dinner or supper, or when she had reason to imagine she would be welcome, she repaired thither on her own initiative. But perhaps the more as she perceived that time was short, she continued her imprudent exhortations. And still her enemies, wary and silent, watched.

Henry appears—and it says much for his affection for her—to have for a time maintained the attitude of a not uncomplacent listener. On a certain day, however, when Katherine was, as usual, descanting upon questions of theology, he changed the subject abruptly, "which somewhat amazed the Queen." Reassured by perceiving no further signs of displeasure, she talked upon other topics until the time came for the King to bid her farewell, which he did with his customary affection.

The account of what followed—Foxe being, as before, the narrator—must be accepted with reservation. Gardiner, chancing to be present, was made the recipient of his master's irritation. It was a good hearing, the King said ironically, when women were become clerks, and a thing much to his comfort, to come in his old days to be taught by his wife.

43 Gardiner made prompt use of the opening afforded him; he had waited long for it, and it was not wasted. The Queen, he said, had forgotten herself, in arguing with a King whose virtues and whose learnedness in matters of religion were not only greater than were possessed by other princes, but exceeded those of doctors in divinity. For the Bishop and his friends it was a grievous thing to hear. Proceeding to enlarge upon the subject at length, he concluded by saying that, though he dared not declare what he knew without special warranty from the King, he and others were aware of treason cloaked in heresy. Henry, he warned him, was cherishing a serpent in his bosom.

It was risking much, but the Bishop knew to whom he spoke, and, working adroitly upon Henry's fears and wrath, succeeded in obtaining permission to consult with his colleagues and to draw up articles by which the Queen's life might be touched. "They thought it best to begin with such ladies as she most esteemed and were privy to all her doings—as the Lady Herbert, her sister, the Lady Lane, who was her first cousin, and the Lady Tyrwhitt, all of her privy chamber." The plan was to accuse these ladies of the breach of the Six Articles, to search their coffers for documents or books compromising to the Queen, and, in case anything of that nature were found, to carry Katherine by night to the Tower. The King, acquainted with44 the design, appears to have given his consent, and all went on as before, Henry still encouraging, or at least not discouraging, his wife's discourse on spiritual matters.

Time was passing; the bill of articles against the Queen had been prepared, and Henry had affixed his signature to it, whether with a deliberate intention of giving her over to her enemies, or, as some said, meaning to deter her from the study of prohibited literature—in which case, as Lord Herbert of Cherbury observes, it was "a terrible jest."33 That Katherine herself did not regard the affair, as soon as she came to be cognisant of it, in the light of a kindly warning, is plain; for when, by a singular accident, the document containing the charges against her was dropped by one of the council and brought for her perusal, the effect upon her was such that the King's physicians were summoned to attend her, and Henry himself, ignorant of the cause of her illness, and possibly softened by it, paid her a visit, and, hearing that she entertained fears that she had incurred his displeasure, reassured her with sweet and comfortable words, remained with her an hour, and departed.

Though Katherine had played her part well, she must have been aware that she stood on the brink of a precipice, and the ghosts of Anne Boleyn and Katherine Howard warned her how little reliance45 could be placed upon the King's fitful affection. Deciding upon a bold step, she sought his bed-chamber uninvited after supper on the following evening, attended only by her sister, Lady Herbert, and with Lady Lane,34 her cousin, to carry the candle before her. Henry, found in conversation with his attendant gentlemen, gave his wife a courteous welcome, entering at once—contrary to his custom—upon the subject of religion, as if moved by a desire of gaining instruction from her replies. Read in the light of what Katherine already knew, this new departure may well have been viewed by her with misgiving; and she hastened to disclaim the position the King appeared anxious to assign her. The inferiority of women being what it was, she said, it was for man to supply from his wisdom what they lacked. She being a silly poor woman, and his Majesty so wise, how could her judgment be of use to him, in all things her only anchor, and, next to God, her supreme head and governor on earth?

The King demurred. The attitude of submission may have struck him as unfamiliar.

"Not so, by St. Mary," he said. "You are become a doctor, Kate, to instruct us, as we take it, and not to be instructed or directed by us."

The plain charge elicited, it was more easy to reply to it. The King had much mistaken her,46 Katherine humbly declared. It had ever been her opinion that it was unseemly for the woman to instruct and teach her lord and husband; her place was rather to learn of him. If she had been bold to maintain opinions differing from the King's, it had been to "minister talk"—to make conversation, in modern language—to distract him from the thought of his infirmities, as also in the hope of profiting by his learned discourse—with more of the same nature.

Henry, perhaps not sorry to be convinced, yielded to the skilful flattery thus administered.

"Is it even so, sweetheart?" he said, "and tend your arguments to no worse end? Then perfect friends we are now again," adding, as he took her in his arms and kissed her, that her words had done him more good than news of a hundred thousand pounds.

The next day had been fixed for the Queen's arrest. As the appointed hour approached the King sought the garden, sending for Katherine to attend him there. Accompanied by the same ladies as on the night before, the Queen obeyed the summons, and there, under the July sun, the closing scene of the serio-comic drama was played. Amused, it may be, by the anticipation of his counsellors' discomfiture, Henry was in good spirits and "as pleasant as ever he was in his life before," when the Chancellor, with forty of the royal guard,47 appeared, ready to take possession of the culprit. What passed between Wriothesley and his master, at a little distance from the rest of the party, could only be matter of conjecture. The Chancellor's words, as he knelt before the angry King, were not audible to the curious bystanders, but the King's rejoinder, "vehemently whispered," was heard. "Knave, arrant knave, beast and fool," were the epithets applied to the crestfallen official. After which, he was promptly dismissed.

Katherine, whether or not she divined the truth, set herself to plead Wriothesley's cause. Ignorance, not will, was in her opinion the probable origin of what had so manifestly moved Henry to wrath. The advocacy of the intended victim softened the King's heart even more towards her.

"Ah, poor soul," he said, "thou little knowest how ill he deserves this grace at thy hands. On my word, sweetheart, he hath been towards thee an arrant knave, and so let him go."35

For the moment, at least, the danger was averted, and before it recurred the despot was in his grave, and Katherine was safe. It is curious to observe that in the list of contents to the Acts and Monuments the danger of the Queen is pointed out, "and how gloriously she was preserved by her kind and loving Husband the King."

48

CHAPTER V

1546

The King dying—The Earl of Surrey—His career and his fate—The Duke of Norfolk's escape—Death of the King.

The King was dying. So much must have been apparent to all who were in a position to judge. None, however, dared utter their thought, since it had been made an indictable offence—the act being directed against soothsayers and prophets—to foretell his death. Those who wished him well or ill, those who would if they could have cared for his soul and invited him to make his peace with God before taking his way hence, were alike constrained to be mute. Before he went to present himself at a court of justice where king and crossing-sweeper stand side by side, another judicial murder was to be accomplished, and one more victim added to the number of the accusers awaiting him there. This was the poet Earl of Surrey, heir to the Dukedom of Norfolk.

Surrey was not more than thirty. But much had been crowded, according to the fashion of the time, into his short and brilliant life. Brought up during his childhood at Windsor as the companion of the49 King's illegitimate son, the Duke of Richmond—who subsequently married Mary Howard, his friend's sister—Surrey had suffered many vicissitudes of fortune; had been in confinement on a suspicion of sympathy with the Pilgrimage of Grace; and in 1543 had again fallen into disgrace, charged with breaking windows in London by shooting pebbles at them. To this accusation he pleaded guilty, explaining, in a satire directed against the citizens of London, that his object had been to prepare them for the divine retribution due for their irreligion and wickedness:

This made me with a reckless brest,
To wake thy sluggards with my bowe;
A figure of the Lord's behest,
Whose scourge for synne the Scriptures shew.

He can scarcely have expected that the plea would have availed, and he expiated his offence by a short imprisonment, chiefly of importance as accentuating his hatred towards the Seymours, who were held responsible for it.36

In the course of the same year he was more worthily employed in fighting the battles of England abroad, where his conduct elicited a cordial tribute of praise from Charles V. "Our cousin, the Earl of Surrey," wrote the Emperor to Henry, on Surrey's return to England, would supply him with an account of all that had taken place. "We will50 therefore only add that he has given good proof in the army of whom he is the son; and that he will not fail to follow in the steps of his father and forefathers, with si gentil cœur and so much dexterity that there is no need to instruct him in aught, and you will give him no command that he does not know how to execute."37

Two years later Surrey was in command of the English forces at Boulogne, there suffered defeat, and was, though not as an ostensible result of his failure, superseded by his rival and enemy, the Earl of Hertford, brother of the Admiral and head of the Seymour clan.

Such was the record of the man who was to fall a prey to the malice and jealousy of the opposite party in the State. His noble birth, his long descent, and his brilliant gifts, were so many causes tending to make him hated and feared; besides which, even amongst men in whom humility was a rare virtue, he was noted for his pride—"the most foolish, proud boy," as he was once described, "that is in England." When he came to be tried for his life those of his own house came forward to bear witness to the contempt he had displayed towards inferiors in rank, if not in power. "These new men," he had said scornfully—it was his sister who played the part of his accuser—"these new men loved no nobility, and if God called away the King51 they should smart for it."38 None of the King's Council, he was reported to have declared, loved him, because they were not of noble birth, and also because he believed in the Sacrament of the Altar.39

In verse he had likewise made his sentiments clear, comparing himself, much to his advantage, with the men he hated.

17

Behold our kyndes how that we differ farre;
I seke my foes, and you your frendes do threten still with warre.
I fawne where I am fled; you slay that sekes to you;
I can devour no yelding pray; you kill where you subdue.
My kinde is to desire the honoure of the field,
And you with bloode to slake your thirst on such as to you yeld.

It was a natural and inevitable consequence of his attitude towards them that the "new men" hated and sought the ruin of the poet who held them up publicly to scorn; and if his great popularity in the country was in some sort a shield, it was also calculated to prove perilous, by giving rise to suspicion and distrust on the part of a sovereign prone to indulge in these sentiments, and thereby to render the success of his foes more easy.

The Seymours were aware that their time was short. With the King's approaching death the question of the guardianship of the successor to the throne was becoming daily more momentous; and when pride and vanity on the part of the Earl, together with treachery on that of friends and kin, placed a dangerous52 weapon in the hands of his opponents, they were prompt to use it.

During the summer there was nothing to serve as a presage of his fate; and so late as August he took part in the magnificent reception accorded to the French ambassadors, successfully vindicating on that occasion his right to precedence over the Earl of Hertford, with whom he was as usual at open enmity.

A new cause of quarrel had been added to the old. The Duke of Norfolk, developing, as age crept upon him, an unwonted desire for peace and amity, had lately devised a method of terminating the feud between his heir and the Seymour brothers, so powerful, by reason of their kinship to Prince Edward, in the State. Not only had he revived a project for uniting his widowed daughter, the Duchess of Richmond, to Thomas Seymour, Lord Admiral, Katherine Parr's former lover, but had made a further proposal to cement the alliance between the rival houses by marrying three of his grandchildren to Hertford's children.

The old man's scheme was not destined to succeed. Whether or not the Seymours would have consented to forget ancient grudges, Surrey remained irreconcilable, flatly refusing his consent to his father's plan. So long as he lived, he declared, no son of his should ever wed Lord Hertford's daughter; and when his sister—perhaps not insensible to Thomas Seymour's attractions—showed an inclination to53 yield to the Duke's wishes, he addressed bitter taunts to her. Since Seymour was in favour with the King, he told her ironically, let her conclude the farce of a marriage, and play in England the part which had, in France, belonged to the Duchesse d'Étampes, Francis I.'s mistress.

Mary Howard did not marry the Admiral, but, possibly sharing her brother's pride, she never forgot or forgave the insult he had offered her; and, repeating the sarcasm as if it had been advice tendered in all seriousness, did her best to damn the Earl in his day of extremity. In a contemporary Spanish chronicle further particulars, true or false, of the quarrel are added. It is there related that, grieved at the tales that had reached him of his sister's lightness of conduct, Surrey had taken upon himself to administer a brotherly rebuke.

"Sister," he said, "I am very sorry to hear what I do about you; and if it be true, I will never speak to you again, but will be your mortal enemy."40

The Duchess was not a woman to accept the admonition meekly, and it was she who was to prove, in the sequel, the more dangerous foe of the two.

The offence for which Surrey nominally suffered the capital penalty seems trivial enough. According to the story told by contemporary authorities—and it suits well with his overweening pride in54 his ancient blood and royal descent—he caused a painting to be executed wherein the Norfolk arms were joined to those of the royal house, the motto Honi soit qui mal y pense being replaced by the enigmatical device Till then thus, and the whole concealed by a canvas placed above it.

From an engraving by Scriven after a painting by Holbein.
HENRY HOWARD, EARL OF SURREY.

The very fact of the secrecy observed betrays the Earl's consciousness that he had committed an imprudence. He was guilty of a worse when, notwithstanding the terms upon which he stood with his sister, he made her his confidant in the matter. The Duchess, in her turn, informed her father of what had been done, but to the Duke's remonstrances Surrey turned a deaf ear. His ancestors, he replied, had borne these arms, and he was much better than they. Powerless to move him, his father, reiterating his fears that it might furnish occasion for a charge of treason, begged that the affair might be kept strictly private, to which Surrey readily agreed. Both men, however, had reckoned without the woman who was daughter to the one, sister to the other. Whether, as some aver,41 the Duchess took the step of betraying her brother directly to the King, or merely corroborated the accusations preferred against him by others—Sir Richard Southwell, a friend of Surrey's childhood, being the first to denounce him42—the matter soon became known, the55 Earl was examined at length, and by the middle of December was, with his father, lodged in the Tower on the charge of treason, the assumption of the royal arms being viewed as an implied claim to the succession to the throne, and as a menace to the little heir. Hertford and his brother were at hand to exaggerate the peril to be feared from his ambition; and the affection of the populace, who, as he was taken through the city to his place of captivity, made great lamentation,43 was not fitted to allay apprehension. A month later the Earl's trial took place at the Guildhall, crowds filling the streets as he went by. Brought before his judges, he made so spirited a defence that Holinshed admits that "if he had tempered his answers with such modesty as he showed token of a right perfect and ready wit, his praise had been the greater"; and though neither wit nor modesty was likely to avail to save him, it was not without long deliberation that the jury agreed to declare him guilty.

Their verdict was pronounced by his implacable enemy, Hertford; being greeted by the people with "a great tumult, and it was a long while before they could be silenced, although they cried out to them to be quiet."44

The prisoner received what was practically sentence of death in characteristic fashion. His56 enemies might have vanquished him, but he could still despise them, still assert his inborn superiority to his victors.

"Of what have you found me guilty?" he demanded. "Surely you will find no law that justifies you; but I know that the King wants to get rid of the noble blood around him, and to employ none but low people."45

On January 19, not a week after his trial, the poet, King Henry VIII.'s latest victim, was beheaded on Tower Hill. It was not the fault of Henry's advisers that his aged father did not follow him to the grave. To have cleared Surrey out of their path was much; but it was not enough. The Duke's heir gone, there were many eager to share amongst themselves the Norfolk spoils; Henry was ready to send his old servant to join his son; and only the King's death, on the very night before the day appointed for the Duke's execution, saved him from sharing Surrey's fate. On January 28, 1547, nine days after the Earl had been slain, Henry was dead.

19

The end can have taken few people by surprise. Whether it was unexpected by the King none can tell. His will was made—a will paving the way for the misfortunes of one of his kin, and preparing the scaffold upon which Lady Jane Grey was to die; since, tacitly setting aside the claims of his elder sister, Margaret of Scotland, and her heirs, he57 provided that, after his own children, Edward, Mary, and Elizabeth, the descendants of Mary Tudor, of whom Jane was, in the younger generation, the representative, should stand next in the order of succession to the throne. It was the first occasion upon which Lady Jane's position had been explicitly defined, and was the prelude of the tragedy that was to follow. Should the unrepealed statutes declaring the King's daughters illegitimate be permitted in the future to weigh against his present provisions in their favour, his great niece or her mother would, in the event of Prince Edward's death, become heirs to the crown.

For Henry the opportunity of cancelling, had it been possible, the injustices of a lifetime was over. "Soon after the death of the Earl of Surrey," writes the Spanish chronicler, "the King felt unwell; and, as he was a wise man, he called his council together, and said to them, 'Gentlemen, I am unwell, and cannot tell when God may call me, so I wish to put my soul in order, and to reward my servants for what they have done.'"

The writer was probably drawing upon his imagination, and presenting rather a picture of what, in his opinion, ought to have taken place than of what truly happened. It quickly became patent to all that the end was at hand; but, though the physicians represented to those about the dying man that it was fitting that he should be warned of his condition,58 most of them shrank from the task. At length Sir Anthony Denny took the performance of the duty upon himself, exhorting his master boldly to prepare for death, "calling himself to remembrance of his former life, and to call upon God in Christ betimes for grace and mercy."46

What followed must again be largely matter of conjecture, the various accounts being coloured according to the theological views of the narrator. It is possible that, feeling the end near, and calling to mind, as Denny bade him, the life he had led, Henry may have been visited by one of those deathbed repentances so mercilessly described by Raleigh: "For what do they do otherwise that die this kind of well-dying, but say to God as followeth: We beseech Thee, O God, that all the falsehoods, forswearings, and treacheries of our lives past may be pleasing unto Thee; that Thou wilt, for our sakes (that have had no leisure to do anything for Thine) change Thy nature (though impossible) and forget to be a just God; that Thou wilt love injuries and oppressions, call ambition wisdom, and charity foolishness."47 Into the secrets of the deathbed none can penetrate. Some say the King's remorse, for the execution of Anne Boleyn in particular, was genuine; others that he was haunted by visionary fears and terrors. In the Spanish chronicle quoted above, it59 is asserted that, sending for "Madam Mary," his injured daughter, he confessed that fortune—he might have said himself—had been hard against her, that he grieved not to have married her as he wished, and prayed her further to be a mother to the Prince, "for look, he is very little yet."

The same authority has also drawn what one must believe to be an imaginary picture of a final and affecting interview between Katherine and her husband, "when the good Queen could not answer for weeping."48 His account is uncorroborated by other evidence, and it is impossible to believe that she can have felt genuine sorrow for the death of a man whose life was a perpetual menace to her own.

According to Foxe, when Denny, the courageous servant who had warned him of his danger, asked whether he would see no learned divine, the King replied that, were any such to be called, it should be Cranmer, but him not yet. He would first sleep, and then, according as he felt, would advise upon the matter. When, an hour or two later, finding his weakness increasing, he sent for the Archbishop, it was too late for speech. "Notwithstanding ... he, reaching his hand to Dr. Cranmer, did hold him fast," and, desired by the latter to give some token of trust in God, he "did wring his hand in his as hard as he could, and so, shortly after, departed."49

60

CHAPTER VI

1547

Triumph of the new men—Somerset made Protector—Coronation of Edward VI.—Measures of ecclesiastical reform—The Seymour brothers—Lady Jane Grey entrusted to the Admiral—The Admiral and Elizabeth—His marriage to Katherine.

With the death of the King a change, complete and sudden, passed over the face of affairs. So long as Henry drew breath all was uncertain; security there was none. The men who were in favour to-day might be disgraced to-morrow, and with regard to the government of the country and the guardianship of the new sovereign all depended upon the state of mind in which death might find him. Happening when it actually did, it left the "new men," the objects of Surrey's contempt, triumphant. Norfolk was in prison on a capital charge; his son was dead. Gardiner had fallen into disgrace at the same time as the Howards, and, though averting a worse fate by a timely show of submission, had never regained his power, his name being omitted by Henry from the list of his executors, all, with the exception of Wriothesley the Chancellor, adherents of the Seymours and for the61 most part pledged to the support of the Protestant interest. Henry had acted deliberately.

"My Lord of Winchester—I think by negligence—is left out of Your Majesty's will," said Sir Anthony Browne, kneeling by the King's side, and recalling to the dying man the Bishop's long service and great abilities. But Henry refused to reconsider the question.

"Hold your peace," he returned. "I remembered him well enough, and of good purpose have left him out; for surely, if he were in my testament, and one of you, he would cumber you all, and you should never rule him, he is of so troublesome a nature."50

Gardiner removed, there was no one left of sufficient influence to combat the Seymours. Their day was come.

The King's death had taken place on Friday, January 28. The Council, for reasons of their own, kept the news secret until the following Monday, when, amidst a scene of strong emotion, real or simulated, the fact was made known to Lords and Commons, Parliament was dissolved, and the Commons dismissed, the peers staying in London to welcome their new sovereign. On February 1 a fresh and crowning success was scored by the dominant party, and Hertford—Wriothesley's being the sole dissentient voice in the governing body—was made Protector and guardian of the King. That afternoon62 Edward received the homage of the Lords spiritual and temporal, and the new reign was inaugurated.

On the 20th of the same month the coronation took place with all magnificence. On the previous day the nine-year-old King had been brought "through his city of London in most royal and goodly wise" to Westminster, the crafts standing on one side of the streets to see him pass, priests and clerks on the other, with crosses and censers, waiting to cense the new sovereign as he went by. The sword of state was borne by Dorset, as Constable of England, and his daughter, the same age as the King, was probably a witness of the splendid pageant and watched her cousin as, in his gown of cloth of silver embroidered in gold and with his white velvet jerkin and cape, he rode through the city.51

At the coronation on the following day Dorset again occupied a prominent place, standing by the King and carrying the sceptre, Somerset bearing the crown. Cranmer, with no longer anything to fear from his enemies, performed the ceremony and delivered an address that can have left no doubt in the minds of any of his hearers, if such there were, who had clung to the hope that a moderate policy would be pursued in ecclesiastical matters, of what was to be expected from the men who had in their hands the little head of Church and State. As God's63 Vice-regent and Christ's Vicar, Edward Tudor was exhorted to see that God was worshipped, idolatry destroyed, the tyranny of the Bishop of Rome banished, and images removed, the hybrid ceremony being concluded by a solemn high mass, Cranmer acting as celebrant.

Signal success had attended the inauguration of the new régime. Dissentients were almost nonexistent. Wriothesley, now Earl of Southampton, remained the solitary genuine adherent of the old faith belonging to the Council. His lack of caution in putting the great seal into commission without the authority of his colleagues afforded them an excuse for ousting him from his post of Chancellor; he was compelled to resign his office, and received orders to confine himself to his house, whilst Hertford, become Duke of Somerset, took advantage of his absence to obtain letters patent by which he became virtually omnipotent in the State.

The earlier months of his government were chiefly devoted to carrying through drastic measures of ecclesiastical reform, in which he was aided by conviction in some, and cupidity in others, of his colleagues, eager to benefit by the spoliation of the Church. With the education of the King in the hands of the Protector, they could count upon immunity when he should come to an age to execute justice on his own account, and the work went swiftly forward. Gardiner, it was true, offered a64 determined opposition. If he had pandered to his old master, he vindicated his character for courage by braving the resentment of the men now in power, and paid for his boldness by imprisonment.

By September the internal affairs of the kingdom were on a sufficiently settled footing to allow the Protector to turn his attention to Scotland. Crossing the border with an army of twenty thousand men, he conducted in person a short campaign ending with the victory of Pinkie, after which, to the surprise of those who expected to see him follow up his success, he hurried home.

His hasty retreat was ascribed to different causes. Some supposed him eager to be again at his post, with the prestige of his victory still fresh. By others it was imagined that he feared the intrigues of his enemies, and in especial of his brother the Admiral. Nor would such uneasiness have been without justification. So long as their combined strength was necessary to enable them to stand against their enemies, the two had made common cause. Somerset was popular in the country; the nobles preferred the Admiral. For both a certain distrust was entertained by those who felt that "their new lustre did dim the light of men honoured with ancient nobility.52" The consciousness of insecurity kept them at one with each other. Become all-powerful in the State, jealousy and passion sundered them.65 Ambitious, proud, and resentful of the Duke's assumption of undivided authority, Seymour had quickly shown an intention of undermining his brother's position in the country, with his hold upon the King, and the Protector may reasonably have felt that it was neither safe nor politic, so far as his personal interest was concerned, to remain too long at a distance from the centre of government.

To the jealousies natural to ambitious men other causes of dissension had been added. These were due to the position achieved by Seymour some months previous to the Scotch campaign by his marriage with the King's widow.

The conduct of Katherine at this juncture is allowed by her warmest partisans to furnish matter for regret. Little information is forthcoming concerning her movements at the time of the King's death; nor does any blame attach to her if she regarded that event in the light of a timely release, an emancipation from a condition of perpetual unrest and anxiety. In any case the age was not one when overmuch time was squandered in mourning, real or conventional, for the dead; and, judging by the sequel, it is possible that, even before the final close was put to her married life, she may have been contemplating the recovery of her lost lover. It is said that when the Lord Admiral paid her his formal visit of condolence she not only received him in private, but candidly confessed how66 slight was her reason to regret a man who had done her the wrong of appropriating her youth.53

If the conversation is correctly reported, Seymour would augur well of the Queen's willingness, so far as was possible, to make up for lost time. But he was not himself inclined to be hurried. Intent upon securing every means within his power to assist him in the coming struggle for pre-eminence, he did not at once convince himself that it was his best policy to become the husband of the King's step-mother, and that a more advantageous alliance was not within his grasp.

Other matters were also occupying his attention; and it was now that Lady Jane Grey, unfortunately a factor of importance in the political world, was brought prominently forward and that her small figure comes first into view in connection with the competition for power and influence.

Although allied with the royal house, and in a position to share in some sort Surrey's contempt for the parvenu nobility of whom the Seymours were representative, Dorset and the King's uncles, agreed upon the crucial matter of religion, were on good terms; and Henry was no sooner dead than it occurred to the Admiral that he might steal a march upon his brother and secure to himself a point of vantage in the contest between them, by obtaining the custody for the present, and the disposal in the future, of the marquis's eldest daughter.

67 He lost no time in attempting to compass his purpose. Immediately after the late King's death—according to statements made when, at a later date, Seymour had fallen upon evil times—Lord Dorset received a visit from a dependant of the Admiral's, named Harrington, and the negotiations ending in the transference of the practical guardianship of the child to Seymour were set on foot.

Harrington was, it would seem, the bearer of a letter from his master, containing the proposal that Lady Jane should be committed to his care; and found the Marquis, on this first occasion, "somewhat cold" in the matter. The messenger, however, proceeded to urge the wishes of his principal, supporting them by arguments well calculated to appeal to an ambitious man. He reported that he had heard Seymour say "that Lady Jane was as handsome as any lady in England, and that, if the King's Majesty, when he came of age, would marry within the realm, it was as likely he would be there as in any other place, and that he [the Admiral] would wish it."54

Such was Harrington's deposition. Dorset's account of the interview is to much the same effect. Visiting him at his house at Westminster "immediately after the King's death," he stated that Seymour's envoy had advised him to be68 content that his daughter should be with the Admiral, assuring him that he would find means to place her in marriage much to his comfort.

23

"With whom?" demanded Dorset, plainly anxious to obtain an explicit pledge.

"Marry," answered Harrington, "I doubt not you shall see him marry her to the King."

As a consequence of this conversation Dorset called upon the Admiral at Seymour House a week later, and as the two walked in the garden an agreement was arrived at, and her father was won over to send for the child, who thereafter remained in the Admiral's house "continually" until the death of the Queen.55

It was a strange arrangement; the more so that it was evidently concluded before the marriage of the late King's widow to Seymour, a man one would imagine to have been in no wise fit to be entrusted with the sole guardianship of the little girl. But Dorset was ambitious; the favour of the King's uncle, with the possibility of securing the King himself as a son-in-law, was not lightly to be forgone; and the sacrifice of Jane was made, not for the last time, to her father's interest.

To the child herself the change from the Bradgate fields and parks to the London home of her new guardian must have been abrupt. Yet, though she may have felt bewildered and desolate in her new69 surroundings and separated from her two little sisters, her training at home had not been of a description to cause her overmuch regret at a parting from those responsible for it. It has been said that every child should dwell for a time within an Eden of its own, and with many men and women the recollection of the unclouded irrational joy belonging to a childhood surrounded by love and tenderness may have constituted in after years a pledge and a guarantee that happiness is possible, and that, in spite of sin and sorrow and suffering, the world is still, as God saw it at creation, very good. The garden in which little Jane's childhood was passed was one of a different nature. "No lady," says Fuller pitifully, "which led so many pious, lived so few pleasant days, whose soul was never out of the nonage of affliction till Death made her of full years to inherit happiness, so severe her education." Her father's house was to her a house of correction.56

Such being the case, the less regret can have mingled with the natural excitement of a child brought into wholly new conditions of life, and treated perhaps for the first time as a person of importance. Nor was it long before circumstances provided her with a home to which no exception could be taken. By June Seymour's marriage with the Queen-Dowager had been made public.

In the interval, short though it was, that elapsed70 between the King's death and the union of his widow and the Admiral, Seymour had had time, before committing himself to a renewal of his suit to Katherine, to attempt a more brilliant match. Henry had been scarcely a month dead before he addressed a letter, couched in the correct terms of conventional love-making, to the Princess Elizabeth, now fourteen. He wished, he wrote, that it were possible to communicate to the missive the virtue of rousing in her heart as much favour towards him as his was full of love for her, proceeding to pay the customary tribute to the beauty and charm, together with "a certain fascination I cannot resist," by which he had been subjugated.

Elizabeth, at fourteen, was keen-witted enough to estimate aright the advantages offered by a marriage with the uncle of the reigning sovereign. Nor was she, perhaps, judging by what followed, indifferent to the personal attractions of this, her first suitor. Though a certain impression of vulgarity is conveyed, in spite of his magnificent voice and splendid appearance, by the Lord Admiral, a child twenty years younger than himself was not likely to detect, in the recognised Adonis of the Court, the presence of this somewhat indefinable attribute. In her eyes he was doubtless a dazzling figure; and though she replied by a polite refusal to entertain his addresses, it is said that she afterwards owed her step-mother a grudge for having discouraged71 her from accepting them. Her answer was, however, a model of maidenly modesty. She had, she stated, neither age nor inclination to think of marriage, and would never have believed that the subject would have been broached so soon after her father's death. Two years at least must be passed in mourning, nor could she decide to become a wife before she had reached years of discretion.57

That problematical date would not be patiently awaited by a man intent upon building up without delay the fabric of his fortunes; and, denied the late King's daughter, Seymour promptly fell back upon his wife. A graphic account of the beginning of his courtship is supplied by the Spanish chronicle, and, if not reliable for accuracy, the narrative no doubt represents what was believed in London, where the writer was resident. The question of the marriage had been, according to him, first mooted to the Council by the Protector, and though other authorities assert that the Duke was opposed to the match, both facts may be true. It is not inconceivable that, whilst he would have preferred that his brother should have looked less high for a wife, the possibility that Seymour might have obtained the hand of the King's sister may have caused the Protector to regard with favour an arrangement putting a marriage with the Princess out of the question.

72 At the Council Board it is said that the proposal received the approbation of the Chancellor. Cranmer, though characterising it as an act of disrespect to the memory of the late King, promised to interpose no obstacle. Paget, the Secretary, went further, engaging that his wife, in attendance on the Queen, should push the matter to the best of her ability.

After dinner one day, accordingly—to continue the narrative of the Spaniard—when the Queen, with all her ladies, was in the great hall of the palace, and the Lord Admiral entered, "looking so handsome that every one had something to say about him," Lady Paget, taking her opportunity, made a whispered inquiry to the Queen as to her opinion of Seymour's appearance. To which the Queen answered that she liked it very much— "oh, how changeable," sighs the chronicler, "are women in that country!" Encouraged by Katherine's reply, Lady Paget ventured to go further, and to hint at a marriage; answering, when the Queen replied by demurring on the score of her superior rank as Queen-Dowager, that to win so pretty a man you might well stoop. Katherine would, she added, continue to retain her royal title.58

The Queen did not prove difficult to persuade. If it is true that she had been cognisant of Seymour's attempt to obtain the hand of her step-daughter, the fact might have warned her of the nature of the love73 he was offering to herself. But a woman in her state of mind is not accessible to reason. A little more than a month after Henry's death the betrothal took place, the marriage following upon it in May, and the haste displayed giving singular proof of how far the Queen's old passion had mastered prudence and discretion. The world was scandalised, and the King's daughters in particular were strong in their disapproval; Mary, the more energetic of the two on this occasion, summoning her sister to visit her, that together they might devise means of preventing the impending insult to their father's memory, or concert a method of making their attitude clear.

Elizabeth, though her objections to the match were probably, on personal grounds, stronger than those of her sister, was more cautious than Mary. The girl, or her advisers, may have been aware of the fact that opposition to the King's uncle would be a dangerous course to be pursued by any one whose future was as ill assured as her own; and, in answer to her sister, she pointed out, though expressing her grief at the affair, that their sole consolation would lie in submission to the will of Providence, since neither was able to offer practical resistance to the project. Dissimulation, under these circumstances, would be their best policy. Mary might decline to visit the Queen, but in Elizabeth's subordinate position she would herself be compelled74 to do so, her step-mother having shown her so much kindness.59

Despite public censure, despite the blame and disapproval of critics whose disapproval would carry more weight, Katherine may not at this time have regretted her defiance of conventional propriety; and those spring weeks, passed at her jointure palace in Chelsea, were probably the happiest of her life. The nightmare sense of insecurity, which can never have been wholly laid to rest so long as Henry lived, was removed; the price exacted for her royal dignity had been paid, to the uttermost farthing; and she was a free woman. Her old love for Seymour had re-awakened in full force, and she believed it was returned. Pious and prudent, Katherine had forgotten to be wise. Disillusionment might come later, but at present the future smiled upon her; and she may fairly have counted upon it to pay, at long last, the debts of the past.

Her letters, light and tender, grave and gay, indicate her mood as she awaited the day when she would take her place before the world as Seymour's wife. Whether a marriage had already taken place, though kept private as a concession to public opinion, or whether it was still to come, there were secret meetings in the early spring mornings by the river, when the town was scarcely awake, the more welcome, it may be, because of the sense that they were stolen.

75 "When it shall be your pleasure to repair hither," wrote Kateryn the Quene—her invariable signature—to her lover, "ye must take some pains to come early in the morning, that ye may be gone again by seven o'clock; and so I suppose ye may come hither without suspect. I pray you let me have knowledge over-night at what hour ye will come, that your portress [herself] may wait at the gate of the fields for you.... By her that is, and shall be, your humble, true, and loving wife during her life."

Poor, learned Katherine had fallen an unresisting victim, like any other common woman, to the gifts and attractions of the man who was to prove so unsatisfactory a husband!

By May 17, if not before, it is clear that the marriage had taken place, though the secret had been so closely kept that it was a surprise to the bridegroom to discover that it was known to the Queen's own sister, Lady Herbert. On visiting the latter, he told Katherine in a letter of this date, she had charged him "touching my lodging with your Highness at Chelsea," the Admiral stoutly maintaining that he had done no more than pass by the garden on his way to the house of the Bishop of London; "till at last she told me further tokens, which made me change colour," and he had arrived at the conclusion that Lady Herbert had been taken into her sister's confidence.

76 Meantime the inconvenience of the present condition of things was evident; and to Mary—curiously enough, since her disapproval of the projected marriage had been so pronounced—Seymour applied for help which should enable him to put an end to it. Although he preserved the attitude of a mere suitor for the Queen's hand, it may be that the Princess suspected that she was being consulted after the event. Her answer was not encouraging. Had the matter concerned her nearest kinsman and dearest friend it would, she told the Admiral, stand least with her poor honour than with any other creature to meddle in the affair, considering whose wife the Queen had lately been.

"If the remembrance of the King's Majesty my father ... will not suffer her to grant your suit, I am nothing able to persuade her to forget the loss of him who is, as yet, very rife in mine own remembrance." If, however, the Princess refused the assistance he

26

begged, she assured him that, "wooing matters apart, wherein, being a maid, I am nothing cunning," she would be ready in other things to serve him.

The young King, to whom recourse was next had, was found more accommodating; and indeed appears to have been skilfully convinced that it was by his persuasions that his step-mother had been induced to bestow her hand upon his uncle, writing to thank the Queen for her gentle acceptation77 of his suit. The boy, after Katherine's death and her husband's disgrace, gave an account of the methods used to obtain his intervention:

"The Lord Admiral came to me ... and desired me to write a thing for him. I asked him what. He said it was none ill thing; it is for the Queen's Majesty. I said if it were good the Lords would allow it; if it were ill I would not write on it. Then he said they would take it in better part if I would write. I desired him to let me alone in that matter. Cheke said afterwards to me, 'Ye were best not to write.'"60

The boy's letter to the Queen proves that he had subsequently yielded to his uncle's request; and in June the fact of the marriage became public property.

The progress of the love-affair will have been watched with interest by the curious and jealous eyes of Elizabeth, the half-grown girl, who, placed by the Council under her step-mother's care at Chelsea, had ample opportunities of forming her conclusions. Lady Jane Grey may, not improbably, have been likewise a spectator of what was going forward. There is no evidence to show whether it was before or after the public avowal of the marriage that she took up her residence under the Queen's roof. But, having obtained his point and gained her custody, it is not unreasonable to imagine that the Admiral may have found a child of ten an encumbrance78 in his household, and have taken the earliest opportunity of consigning her to Katherine's care.

A passive asset as she was in the political reckoning, the debates concerning her guardianship must have done something to bring home to her mind the consciousness of her importance; and she had doubtless been made well aware of her title to consideration by the time that she became an honoured inmate of the Lord Admiral's house. But concerning the details of her existence at this date history is dumb, and we can but guess at her attitude as, fresh from her country home, she watched, under the roof of her new guardian in Seymour Place, the life of the great city around; or within the more tranquil precincts of Chelsea Palace, with the broad river flowing past, shared in the studies and pursuits of her cousin Elizabeth, ready-witted, full of vitality, and already displaying some of the traits marking the Queen of future years.

Did the shadow of predestined and early death single little Jane out from her companions? Like the comrades of whom Maeterlinck tells, "children of precocious death," possessing no friends amongst the playmates who were not about to die, did she stand in some sort apart and separate, regarding those around her with a grave smile? We build up the unrecorded days of childhood from the79 few short years that followed; and reading backwards, and fitting the fragments of a life into its place, we find it difficult to believe that Jane Grey's laughter rang like that of other undoomed children through the pleasant Chelsea gardens, that she shared with a whole heart in the games of her playfellows, or that the strange seriousness of her youth did not envelope the small, sedate figure of the child.

80

CHAPTER VII

1547-1548

Katherine Parr's unhappy married life—Dissensions between the Seymour brothers—The King and his uncles—The Admiral and Princess Elizabeth—Birth of Katherine's child, and her death.

The belated idyll of love and happiness enjoyed by "Kateryn the Quene" was of pitifully short duration. During the first days of September 1548, some fifteen months after the stolen marriage at Chelsea, a funeral procession left Sudeley Castle, and the body of the wife of the Lord Admiral was carried forth to burial, Lady Jane Grey, his ward, then in her twelfth year, acting as chief mourner.61

Jane had good cause to mourn, in other than an official capacity. It is hard to believe that, had Katherine Parr been living, the child she had cared for and who had made her home under her roof, would not have been saved from the doom destined to overtake her not six years later.

Katherine's dream had died before she did, and the period of her marriage, short though it was,81 must have been a time of rapid disillusionment. It could scarcely, taking the circumstances into account, have been otherwise. Seymour was not the man to make the happiness of a wife touching upon middle age, studious, learned, and devout, "avoiding all occasions of idleness, and contemning vain pastimes."62 His love, if indeed it had been ever other than disguised ambition, was short-lived, and Katherine's awakening must have come all too swiftly.

Nor was the revelation of her husband's true character her only cause of trouble. Minor vexations had, from the first, attended her new condition of life, and she had been made to feel that the wife of the Protector's younger brother could not expect to enjoy the deference due to a Dowager-Queen. To Katherine, who clung to her former dignity, the loss of it was no light matter, and her sister-in-law, the Duchess of Somerset, and she were at open war.

Contemporary and early writers are agreed as to the nature of the woman with whom she had to deal. "The Protector," explains the Spanish chronicler, giving the popular version of the affair, "had a wife who was prouder than he was, and she ruled the Protector so completely that he did whatever she wished, and she, finding herself in such great state, became more presumptuous than Lucifer."63 Hayward attributes the subsequent disunion between the brothers, in the first place,82 to "the unquiet vanity of a mannish, or rather a devilish woman ... for many imperfections intolerable, but for pride monstrous";64 whilst Heylyn represents the Duchess as observing that, if Mr. Admiral should teach his wife no better manners, "I am she that will."65

The struggle for precedence carried on between the wives could scarcely fail to have a bad effect upon the relationship of the husbands, already at issue upon graver questions; and Warwick, Somerset's future rival, was at hand to foment the strife between Protector and Admiral, and, "secretly playing with both hands," paved the way for the fall of the younger brother and the consequent weakening of the forces which barred the way to the attainment of his personal ambitions.

From a photo by W. Mansell & Co. after an engraving.
KATHERINE PARR.
Nor can there be any doubt that, apart from the ill offices of those who desired to separate the interests of the brothers, the Protector had good reason to stand upon his guard. When Seymour was tried for his life during the winter of 1548-9, dependants and equals alike came forward to bear witness to his intriguing propensities, their evidence going far to prove that, whatever may be thought of Somerset's conduct as a brother in sending him to the scaffold, as head of the State and responsible for the government of the realm, he was not without83 justification. It is clear that from the first the Admiral,

jealous of the position accorded to the Duke by the Council, had been sedulously engaged in attempting to undermine his power, and had not disguised his resentment at his appropriation of undivided authority. Never had it been seen in a minority—so he informed a confidant66—that the one brother should bear all rule, the other none. One being Protector, the other should have filled the post of Governor to the King, so he averred; although, on another occasion, contradicting himself, he declared he would wish the earth to open and swallow him rather than accept either post. There was abundant proof that he had done his utmost, whenever opportunity was afforded him, to rouse the King to discontent. It was a disagreeable feature of the day that men were in no wise slack in accusing their friends in times of disgrace, thereby seeking to safeguard their reputations; and Dorset came forward later to testify that Seymour had told him that his nephew had divers times made his moan, saying that "My uncle of Somerset dealeth very hardly with me, and keepeth me so straight that I cannot have money at my will." The Lord Admiral, added the boy, both sent him money and gave it to him.67

Perhaps the most significant testimony brought against the Admiral was that of the little King84 himself, who asserted that Seymour had charged him with being "bashful" in his own affairs, asking why he did not speak to bear rule as did other Kings. "I said I needed not, for I was well enough," the boy replied on this occasion. At another time, according to his confession, a conversation took place the more grim from the simplicity of the language in which it is recorded.

"Within these two years at least," said Edward, now eleven years old, "he said, 'Ye must take upon yourself to rule, and then ye may give your men somewhat; for your uncle is old, and I trust he will not live long.' I answered it were better that he should die."68

It was scarcely possible that the Protector should not have been cognisant of a part at least of his brother's machinations; and he naturally, so far as was possible, kept his charge from falling further under the influence of his enemies. The young King's affection for his step-mother had been a cause of disquiet to her brother-in-law and his wife, care being taken to separate him from her as much as was possible. So long as Katherine remained in London it had been Edward's habit to visit her apartments unattended, and by a private entrance. Familiar intercourse of this kind terminated when she removed to a distance; and, so far as the Lord Protector could ensure obedience,85 little communication was permitted between the two during the short time the Queen had to live. The boy, however, was constant to old affection, and used what opportunities he could to express it.

"If his Grace could get any spare time," wrote one John Fowler, a servant of the royal household, to the Admiral, "his Grace would write a letter to the Queen's Grace, and to you. His Highness desires your lordship to pardon him, for his Grace is not half a quarter of an hour alone. But in such leisure as his Grace has, his Majesty hath written (here enclosed) his commendations to the Queen's Grace and to your lordship, that he is so much bound to you that he must remember you always, and, as his Grace may have time, you shall well perceive by such small lines of recommendations with his own hand."69

The scribbled notes, on scraps of paper, written by stealth and as he could find opportunity, by the King, testify to the closeness of the watch kept upon him; their contents show the means by which the Admiral strove to maintain his hold upon his nephew.

"My lord," so runs the first, "send me, per Latimer, as much as ye think good, and deliver it to Fowler." The second note is one of thanks.

29

An attempt was made by the Admiral to obtain86 a letter from the King which, complaining of the Protector's system of restraint, should be laid before Parliament; but the intrigue was discovered, the Admiral summoned to appear before the Council, and, though he was at first inclined to bluster, and replied by a defiance, a hint of imprisonment brought him to reason, and some sort of hollow reconciliation between the brothers followed.

The King, the unfortunate subject of dispute, was probably lonely enough. For his tutor, Sir John Cheke, and for his school-mate, Barnaby Fitzpatrick, he appears to have entertained a real affection; but for his elder uncle and guardian he had little liking, nor was the Duchess of Somerset a woman to win the heart of her husband's ward. From his step-mother and the Admiral he was practically cut off; and his sisters, for whom his attachment was genuine, were at a distance, and paid only occasional visits to Court. Mary's influence, as a Catholic, would naturally have been feared; and Elizabeth, living for the time under the Admiral's roof, would be regarded likewise with suspicion. But the happiness of the nominal head of the State was not a principal consideration with those around him, mostly engaged in a struggle not only to secure present personal advantages, but to ensure their continuance at such time as Edward should have attained his majority.

The relations between the Seymour brothers being87 that of a scarcely disguised hostility, the Admiral had the more reason to congratulate himself upon having obtained the possession and disposal of the person of Lady Jane Grey—third, save for her mother, in the line of succession to the throne. Should her guardian succeed in effecting her marriage with the King the arrangement might prove of vital importance. On the other hand, Somerset's matrimonial schemes for the younger members of the royal house were of an altogether different nature. He would have liked to marry the King to a daughter of his own, another Lady Jane, and to have obtained the hand of Lady Jane Grey for his son, young Lord Hertford.

Such projects, however, belonged to the future. Nothing could be done for the present, nor does it appear that, when Somerset's scheme afterwards became known to the King, it met with any favour in his eyes; since, noting it in his journal, he added his private intention of wedding "a foreign princess, well stuffed and jewelled."

So far as Katherine was concerned, her domestic affairs were probably causing her too much anxiety to leave attention to spare for those of King or kingdom, except as they were gratifying, or the reverse, to her husband. Since the May day when she had given herself, rashly and eagerly, into the keeping of the Lord Admiral, she had been sorrowfully enlightened as to the nature of the88 man and of his affection; and, if she still loved him, her heart must often have been heavy. The presence of the Princess Elizabeth under her roof had been disastrous in its consequences; and, though it was at first the interest of all to keep the matter secret, the inquisition made at the time of the Admiral's disgrace into the circumstances of his married life affords an insight into his wife's wrongs.

In a conversation held between Mrs. Ashley, Elizabeth's governess, and her cofferer, Parry, after the Queen's death, the possibility of a marriage between the widower and the Princess was discussed, Parry raising objections to the scheme, on the score that he had heard evil of Seymour as being covetous and oppressive, and also "how cruelly, dishonourably, and jealously he had used the Queen."

Ashley, from first to last eager to forward the Admiral's interests, brushed the protest aside.

"Tush, tush," she replied, "that is no matter. I know him better than ye do, or those that do so report him. I know he will make but too much of her, and that she knows well enough."70

The same witness confessed at this later date that she feared the Admiral had loved the Princess too well, and the Queen had been jealous of both—an avowal corroborated by Elizabeth's admissions, when she too underwent examination concerning the89 relations which had existed between herself and her step-mother's husband.

"Kat Ashley told me," she deposed, "after the Lord Admiral was married to the Queen, that if my lord might have had his own will, he would have had me, afore the Queen. Then I asked her how she knew that. Then she said she knew it well enough, both from himself and from others."71

If the correspondence quoted in a previous page is genuine,72 Elizabeth, though she may have had reason to keep her knowledge to herself, can have been in no doubt as to the Admiral's sentiments at the time of her father's death. With a governess of Mrs. Ashley's type, a girl of fifteen such as Elizabeth was shown to be by her subsequent career, and a man like Seymour, it would not have been difficult to prophesy trouble. That the Admiral was in love with his wife's charge may be doubted; in the same way that ambition, rather than any other sentiment, may be credited with his desire to obtain her hand a few months earlier. What was certain was that he amused himself, after his boisterous fashion, with the sharp-witted girl to an extent calculated to cause both uneasiness and anger to the Queen. That no actual harm was intended may be true—he could scarcely have been blind to the consequences had he dared to deal otherwise with the daughter and sister of Kings; and the whole story,90 when it subsequently came to light, reads like an instance of coarse and vulgar flirtation, in harmony with the nature of the man and the habits of the times. What is less easy to account for is Katherine's partial connivance, in its earlier stages, at the rough horse-play, if nothing worse, carried on by her husband and her step-daughter. A scene, for example, is described as taking place at Hanworth, where the Admiral, in the garden with his wife and the Princess, cut the girl's gown, "being black cloth," into a hundred pieces; Elizabeth replying to Mrs. Ashley's protests by saying that "she could not strive with all, for the Queen held her while the Lord Admiral cut the dress." Nor was this the only occasion upon which Katherine appears to have looked on without disapproval whilst her husband treated her charge in a fashion befitting her character neither as Princess nor guest.

The explanation may lie in the fact that the unfortunate Queen was attempting to adapt her taste and her manners to those of the man she had married. But the condition of the household could not last. A crisis was reached when one day Katherine, coming unexpectedly upon the two, found Seymour with the Princess in his arms, and decided, none too soon, that an end must be put to the situation. It was not long after that the households of Queen and Princess were parted, "and as I remember," explained Parry the cofferer, "this was the cause why she was91 sent from the Queen, or else that her Grace parted from the Queen. I do not perfectly remember whether of both she [Ashley] said she went of herself or was sent away."73

There can be little doubt, one would imagine, that it was Katherine who determined to disembarrass herself of her visitor. A letter from Elizabeth, evidently written after their separation, appears to show that farewell had been taken in outwardly friendly fashion, although the promise she quotes Katherine as making has an ambiguous sound about it. The Princess wrote to say that she had been replete in sorrow at leaving the Queen, "and albeit I answered little, I weighed it more deeply when you said you would warn me of all evils that you should hear of me; for if your Grace had not a good opinion of me, you would not have offered friendship to me that way, that all men judge the contrary."74

It is not difficult to detect the sore feeling underlying Elizabeth's acknowledgments of a promise of open criticism. Katherine must have breathed more freely when the Princess and her governess had quitted the house.

Meantime, in spite of disappointment and anger and care, the winter was to bring the Queen one genuine cause of rejoicing. Thrice married without children, she was hoping to give Seymour an heir,92 and the prospect was hailed with delight by husband and wife alike. In her gladness, and the chief cause of dissension removed, her just grounds of complaint were forgotten; her letters continued to be couched in terms as loving as if no domestic friction had interrupted her wedded happiness, and she ranged herself upon Seymour's side in his recurrent disputes with his brother with a passionate vehemence out of keeping with her character.

"This shall be to advertise you," she wrote some time in 1548, "that my lord your brother hath this afternoon made me a little warm. It was fortunate we were so much distant, for I suppose else I should have bitten him. What cause have they to fear having such a wife! It is requisite for them continually to pray for a dispatch of that hell. To-morrow, or else upon Saturday ... I will see the King, where I intend to utter all my choler to my lord your brother, if you shall not give me advice to the contrary."75

Another letter, also indicating the strained relations existing between the brothers, is again full of affection for the man who deserved it so ill.

"I gave your little knave your blessing," she tells the Admiral, alluding to the unborn child neither parent was to see grow up, "... bidding my sweetheart and loving husband better to fare than myself."76

93 A few months more, and hope and fear and love and disappointment were alike to find an end. Sudeley Castle, where the final scene took place, was a property granted to the Admiral on the death of the late King, from which he took his title as Lord Seymour of Sudeley. It was a question whether those responsible for the government had the right of alienating possessions of the Crown during the minority of a sovereign, and the tenure upon which the place was held was therefore insecure, Katherine asserting on one occasion that it was her husband's intention to restore it to his nephew when he should come of age. In awaiting that event Seymour and his wife had the enjoyment of the beauty for which the old building had long been noted.

"Ah, Sudeley Castle, thou art the traitor, not I!" said one of its former lords as, arrested by the orders of Henry IV. for treason, and taken away to abide his trial, he cast a last look back at his home—a possession worthy of being coveted by a King, and by the attainder of its owner forfeited to the Crown.

Here, during the summer of 1548—the last Katherine was to see—a motley company gathered round the Queen. Jane Grey, "the young and early wise," was still a member of her household, and the repudiated wife of Katherine's brother, the Earl of Northampton—placed, it would seem, under some species of restraint—was in the keeping of her94 sister-in-law. Her true and tried friend, Lady Tyrwhitt, described by her husband as half a Scripture woman, kept her company, as she had done in her perilous days of royal state. Learned divines, living with her in the capacity of chaplains, were inmates of the castle, charged with the duty of performing service twice each day—exercises little to the taste of the master of the house, who made no secret of his aversion for them.

"I have heard say," affirmed Latimer, in the course of one of the sermons, preached after Seymour's execution, in which the Bishop took occasion again and again to revile the dead man, "I have heard say that when the good Queen that is gone had ordained daily prayer in her house, both before noon and after noon, the Admiral getteth him out of the way, like a mole digging in the earth. He shall be Lot's wife to me as long as I live."77

To Sudeley also had repaired, in the course of the summer, Lord Dorset, possibly desirous of assuring himself that all was well with his little daughter. He may have had other objects in view. According to his subsequent confession, Seymour had discussed with him the methods to be pursued in order to gain popularity in the country, making significant inquiries as to the formation of the marquis's household.

95 Learning that Dorset had divers gentlemen who were his servants, the Admiral admitted that it was well. "Yet," he added shrewdly, "trust not too much to the gentlemen, for they have something to lose"; proceeding to urge his ally to make much of the chief yeomen and men of their class, who were able to persuade the multitude; to visit them in their houses, bringing venison and wine; to use familiarity with them, and thus to gain their love. Such, he added, was his own intention.78

Another inmate had been received at Sudeley not more than a few weeks before Katherine's confinement. This was the Princess Elizabeth, who appears, by a letter she addressed to the Queen when the visit had been concluded, to have been at this time again on terms of friendship and affection with her step-mother, since writing to Katherine with very little leisure on the last day of July, she returned humble thanks for the Queen's wish that she should have remained with her "till she were weary of that country." Yet in spite of the hospitable desire, she can scarcely have been a welcome guest, and it must have been with little regret that her step-mother saw her depart.

Meantime, the birth of the Queen's child was anxiously expected. Seymour characteristically desired a son who "should God give him life to live as long as his father, will avenge his wrongs"—the96 problematical wrongs of a man who had risen to his heights. Elizabeth, who had done her best to wreck the Queen's happiness and peace, was "praying the Almighty God to send her a most lucky deliverance"; and Mary, more sincere in her friendship, wrote a letter full of affection to her step-mother. The preparations made by Katherine for the new-comer equalled in magnificence those that might have befitted a Prince of Wales; and though the birth of a girl, on August 30, must have been in some degree a disappointment, she received a welcome scarcely less warm than might have been accorded to the desired son. A general reconciliation appears to have taken place on the occasion, and the Protector responded to the announcement of the event in terms of cordial congratulation, regarding the advent of so pretty a daughter in the light of a "prophesy and good hansell to a great sort of happy sons."

Eight days after the rejoicings at the birth Katherine was dead.

Into the circumstances attending her illness and death close inquisition was made at a time when it had become an object to throw discredit upon the Admiral, and foul play—the use of poison—was suggested. The charge was probably without foundation; the facts elicited nevertheless afford additional proof of the unsatisfactory relations existing between husband and wife, and throw a97 melancholy light upon the closing scene of the union from which so much had been hoped.

It was deposed by Lady Tyrwhitt, one of the principal witnesses, that, upon her visiting the chamber of the sick woman one morning, two days before her death, Katherine had asked where she had been so long, adding that "she did fear such things in herself that she was sure she could not live." When her friend attempted to soothe her by reassuring words, the Queen went on to say—holding her husband's hand and being, as Lady Tyrwhitt thought, partly delirious—"I am not well handled; for those that be about

33

me care not for me, but stand laughing at my grief, and the more good I will to them the less good they will to me."

The words, to those cognisant of the condition of the household, must have been startling. The Queen may have been wandering, yet her complaint, as such complaints do, pointed to a truth. Others besides Lady Tyrwhitt were standing by; and Seymour made no attempt to ignore his wife's meaning, or to deny that the charge was directed against himself.

"Why, sweet heart," he said, "I would do you no hurt."

"No, my lord, I think not," answered Katherine aloud, adding, in his ear, "but, my lord, you have given me many shrewd taunts."

"These words," said Lady Tyrwhitt in her98 narrative, "I perceived she spake with good memory, and very sharply and earnestly, for her mind was sore disquieted."

After consultation it was decided that Seymour should lie down by her side and seek to quiet her by gentle words; but his efforts were ineffectual, the Queen interrupting him by saying, roundly and sharply, "that she would have given a thousand marks to have had her full talk with the doctor on the day of her delivery, but dared not, for fear of his displeasure."

"And I, hearing that," said the lady-in-waiting, "perceived her trouble to be so great, that my heart would serve me to hear no more."79

Yet on that same day the dying Queen made her will and, "being persuaded and perceiving the extremity of death to approach her," left all she possessed to her husband, wishing it a thousand times more in value than it was.80

Whether pressure was used, or whether, in spite of all, her old love awakened and stirred her to kindness towards the man she was leaving, there is nothing to show. But the names of the witnesses—Robert Huyck, the physician attending her, and John Parkhurst, her chaplain, afterwards a Bishop—would seem a guarantee that the document, dictated but not signed—no uncommon case—was genuine.

99 For the rest, Seymour was coarse and heartless, a man of ambition, and intent upon the furtherance of his fortunes. It is not unlikely that, when his wife lay dying, his thoughts may have turned to the girl to whom he had in his own way already made love; who, of higher rank than the Queen, might serve his interests better, and whom her death would leave him free to win as his bride. And Katherine, with the memories of the last two years to aid her and with the intuitions born of love and jealousy, may have divined his thoughts. But of murder, or of hastening the end by actual unkindness, there is no reason to suspect him. The affair was in any case sufficiently tragic, and one more mournful recollection to be stored in the minds of those who had loved the Queen.

100

CHAPTER VIII

1548

Lady Jane's temporary return to her father—He surrenders her again to the Admiral—The terms of the bargain.

One of the secondary but immediate effects of the Queen's death was to send Lady Jane Grey back to her parents. It was indeed to Seymour, and not to his wife, that the care of the child had been entrusted; but in his first confusion of mind after what he termed his great loss, the Admiral appears to have recognised the difficulty of providing a home for a girl in her twelfth year in a house without a mistress, and to have offered to relinquish her to her natural guardians.

Having acted in haste, he was not slow to perceive that he had committed a blunder, and quickly reawakened to the importance of retaining the possession and disposal of the child. On September 17, not ten days after Katherine's death, he was writing to Lord Dorset to cancel, so far as it was possible, his hasty suggestion that she should return to her father's house, and begging that she might be permitted to remain in his hands. In his101 former letter, he explained, he had been partly so amazed at the death of the Queen as to have small regard either to himself or his doings, partly had believed that he would be compelled, in consequence of it, to break up his household. Under these circumstances he had suggested sending Lady Jane to her father, as to him who would be most tender of her. Having had time to reconsider the question, he found that he would be in a position to maintain his establishment much on its old footing. "Therefore, putting my whole affiance and trust in God," he had begun to arrange his household as before, retaining the services not only of the gentlewomen of the late Queen's privy chamber, but also her inferior attendants. "And doubting lest your lordship should think any unkindness that I should by my said letter take occasion to rid me of your daughter so soon after the Queen's death, for the proof both of my hearty affection towards you and good will towards her, I mind now to keep her until I shall next speak to your lordship ... unless I shall be advertised from your lordship of your express mind to the contrary." His mother will, he has no doubt, be as dear to Lady Jane as though she were her daughter, and for his part he will continue her half-father and more.81

It was clear that the Admiral would only yield the point upon compulsion. Dorset, however, was not102 disposed to accede to his wishes. Developing a sudden parental anxiety concerning the child he had been content to leave to the care of others for more than eighteen months, he replied, firmly though courteously negativing the Admiral's request.

"Considering," he said, "the state of my daughter and her tender years wherein she shall hardly rule herself as yet without a guide, lest she should, for lack of a bridle, take too much the head and conceive such opinion of herself that all such good behaviour as she heretofore have learned by the Queen's and your most wholesome instruction, should either altogether be quenched in her, or at the least much diminished, I shall in most hearty wise require your lordship to commit her to the governance of her mother, by whom, for the fear and duty she owes her, she shall be most easily ruled and framed towards virtue, which I wish above all things to be most plentiful in her." Seymour no doubt would do his best; but, being destitute of any one who should correct the child as a mistress and monish her as a mother, Dorset was sure that the Admiral would think, with him, that the eye and oversight of his wife was necessary. He reiterated his former promise to dispose of her only according to Seymour's advice, intending to use his consent in that matter no less than his own. "Only I seek in these her young years, wherein she now standeth either to make or mar (as the common saying is) the addressing103 of her mind to humility, soberness, and obedience."82

It was the letter of a model parent, anxious concerning the welfare, spiritual and mental, of a beloved child, and Dorset, as he sealed and despatched it, will have felt that policy and conscience were for once in full accord. Lady Dorset likewise wrote, endorsing her husband's views.

"Whereas of a friendly and brotherly good will you wish to have Jane, my daughter, continuing still in your house, I give you most hearty thanks for your gentle offer, trusting, nevertheless, that for the good opinion you have in your sister [by courtesy, meaning herself] you will be content to charge her with her, who promiseth you not only to be ready at all times to account for the ordering of your dear niece, but also to use your counsel and advice on the bestowing of her, whensoever it shall happen. Wherefore, my good brother, my request shall be, that I may have the oversight of her with your good will, and thereby I shall have good occasion to think that you do trust me in such wise as is convenient that a sister be trusted of so loving a brother."

The singular humility of the language used by a king's grand-daughter in demanding restitution of her child is proof of the position held by the Admiral in the eyes of those as well fitted to judge of it as Dorset and his wife, only six months before104 he was sent to the scaffold. It was none the less plain that they were determined to regain possession of their daughter, and, though not abandoning the hope of moving her parents from their purpose, Seymour yielded provisionally to their will and sent Lady Jane home. A letter from the small bone of contention, dated October 1, thanking him for his great goodness and stating that he had ever been to her a loving and kind father, proves that her removal had taken place by that time. The same courier probably conveyed a letter from her mother, making her acknowledgments for Seymour's kindness to the child, and his desire to retain her, and adding an ambiguous hope that at their next meeting both would be satisfied.83

The Admiral, at all events, intended to obtain satisfaction. Where his interest was concerned he was an obstinate man. Notwithstanding his apparent acquiescence, he meant to retain the custody of Lord Dorset's daughter, and he did so. Even his household understood that the concession made in sending her home was but temporary; and, in a conversation with another dependant, Harrington—the same who had served his master as go-between before—observed that he thought the maids were continuing with the Admiral in the hope of Lady Jane's return.

A visit paid by Seymour to Dorset decided the105 question. "In the end"—it is the latter who speaks—"after long debating and much sticking of our sides, we did agree that my daughter should return." The Admiral had come to his house, and had been so earnest in his persuasions that he could not resist him. The old bait had been once again held out—Lady Jane, if Seymour could compass it, was to marry the King. Her mother was wrought upon till her consent was gained to a second parting; and when this was the case, observed the marquis, throwing, according to precedent, the responsibility upon his wife, it was impossible for him to refuse his own. He added a pledge that, "except the King," he would spend life and blood for Seymour. Thus the alliance between the two was renewed and cemented. A further item in the transaction throws an additional and unpleasant light upon the means taken to ensure the Lord Marquis's surrender.

The Admiral was a practical man, and knew with whom he had to deal. He had not confined himself to vague pledges, which Dorset knew as well as he did that he might never be in a position to fulfil. He had accompanied his promises by a gift of hard cash. "Whether, as it were, for an earnest penny of the favour that he would show unto him when the said Lord Marquis had sent his daughter to the said Lord Admiral, he sent the said Lord Marquis immediately £500, parcel of £2,000 which he106 promised to lend unto him and would have asked no bond of him at all for it, but only to leave the Lord Marquis's daughter for a gage."84

Five hundred golden arguments, and more to follow, were found irresistible by the needy Dorset. The pressing necessity that Jane should be under her mother's eye disappeared; the bargain was struck, and the guardianship of the child bought and sold.

The Admiral was triumphant. It was not only the point of vantage implied by the possession of the little ward which he had feared to forfeit, but that his loss might be the gain of his brother and rival. There would be much ado for my Lady Jane, he told his brother-in-law, Northampton, and my Lord Protector and my Lady Somerset would do what they could to obtain her yet for my Lord of Hertford, their son. They should not, however, prevail therein, for my Lord Marquis had given her wholly to him, upon certain covenants between them two. "And then I asked him," said Northampton, describing the conversation, "what he would do if my Lord Protector, handling my Lord Marquis of Dorset gently, should obtain his good will and so the matter to lie wholly in his own neck? He answered he would never consent thereto."85

Thus Lady Jane was, for the first time, made an instrument of obtaining that of which her father107 stood in need. On this occasion it was money; on the next her life was to be staked upon a more desperate hazard. In future she appears and disappears, now in sight, now passing behind the scenes, against the dark background of intrigue and hatred and bloodshed belonging to her times.
108

CHAPTER IX

1548-1549

Seymour and the Princess Elizabeth—His courtship—He is sent to the Tower—Elizabeth's examinations and admissions—The execution of the Lord Admiral.

The matter of Jane's guardianship satisfactorily settled, Seymour turned his attention to one concerning him yet more intimately. He was a free man, and he meant to make use of his freedom. As after the death of Henry, so now when fate rendered the project once more possible, he determined to attempt to obtain the Princess Elizabeth as his wife. The history of the autumn, as regarding him, is of his continued efforts to increase his power and influence in the country and to win the hand of the King's sister. Again the contemporary Spanish chronicler supplies a popular summary of the affair which, inaccurate as it is, is useful in showing how his scheme was regarded by the public.

According to this dramatic account of his proceedings, the Admiral went boldly before the Council; observed that, as uncle to the King, it was fitting that he should marry honourably; and that, having109 formerly been husband to the Queen, it would not be much more were he to be accorded Madam Elizabeth, whom he deserved better than any other man. Referred by the Lords of the Council to the Protector, he is represented as approaching the Duke with the modest request that he might be granted not only Elizabeth as his bride, but also the custody of the King.

"When his brother heard this, he said he would see about it." Calling the Council together, he repeated to them the demand made by the Admiral that his nephew should be placed in his hands; continuing, as the Lords "looked at each other," that the matter must be well considered, since in his opinion his brother could have no good intent in asking first for the Princess, and then for the custody of the King. "The devil is strong," said the Protector. "He might kill the King and Madam Mary, and then claim the crown."86

Whilst this was the version of the Admiral's project current in the street, there is no doubt that his desire to obtain a royal princess for his wife was calculated to accentuate the distrust with which he was regarded by the Protector and his friends. He was well known to aspire to at least a share in the government. As Elizabeth's husband his position would be so much strengthened that it might be difficult to deny it to him, or to maintain110 the right of Somerset to retain supreme power. His proceedings were therefore watched with jealous vigilance, his designs upon the King's sister becoming quickly matter of public gossip. It was not a day marked by an over-scrupulous observance of respect for the dead, and Katherine was hardly in her grave before the question of her successor was freely canvassed amongst those chiefly concerned in it.

"When I asked her [Ashley] what news she had from London," Elizabeth admitted when under examination at a later date, "she answered merrily 'They say that your Grace shall have my Lord Admiral, and that he will shortly come to woo you.'"87

The woman, an intriguer by nature and keen to advance Seymour's interests, would have further persuaded her mistress to write a letter of condolence to comfort him in his sorrow, "because," as Elizabeth explained, "he had been my friend in the Queen's lifetime and would think great kindness therein. Then I said I would not, for he needs it not."

The blunt sincerity prompting the girl's refusal did her credit. It must have been patent to all acquainted with the situation, and most of all to Elizabeth, that the new-made widower stood in no need of consolation. But, in spite of her refusal111 to open communications with him, and though a visit proposed by Seymour was discouraged "for fear of suspicion," he can have felt little doubt that in a struggle with Protector and Council he would have the Princess on his side.

In Seymour's household, naturally concerned in his fortunes, the projected marriage was a subject of anxious debate; and it was recognised by its members that their master was playing a perilous game. In a conversation between two of his dependants, Nicholas Throckmorton and one Wightman, both shook their heads over the risk he would run should he attempt to carry his plan into effect.

Beginning with the conventional acknowledgment of the Admiral's great loss, they wisely decided that it might after all turn to his advantage, in "making him more humble in heart and stomach towards my Lord Protector's Grace." It was also hoped that, Katherine being dead, the Duchess of Somerset might forget old grudges and, unless by his own fault, be once again favourable towards her husband's brother. The two men nevertheless agreed that the world was beginning to speak evil of Seymour, and, discussing the chances of his attempt to match with one of the Princesses, they determined, as they loved him, to do their best to prevent it, Wightman in especial engaging to do all he could to "break the dance."88

112 If Seymour was going to his ruin it was not to be for lack of warnings. Sleeping at the house of Katherine's friends, the Tyrwhitts, one night soon after her death, the question of a marriage with a sister of the King's was mooted; when, although Seymour's aspirations were not definitely mentioned, Sir Robert spoke in a fashion frankly discouraging to any scheme of the kind on the part of his guest.

Conversing after supper with his hostess, Seymour called to her husband as he passed by, saying jestingly that he was talking with my lady his wife in divinity—or divining of the future; that he had told her he wished the crown of England might be in as good a surety as that of France, where it was well known who was heir. So would it be in England were the Princesses married.

Tyrwhitt answered drily. Whosoever married one of them without the consent of King or Council, he said he would not wish to be in his place.

"Why so?" asked the Admiral. If he, for instance, had married thus, would it not be surety for the King? Was he not made by the King? Had he not all he had by the King? Was he not most bound to serve him truly?

Tyrwhitt refused to be convinced, reiterating that the man who married either Princess had better be stronger than the Council, for "if they catch hold of him, they will shut him up."89

113 Lord Russell, the Lord Privy Seal, spoke no less openly to the adventurer of the danger he was running. The two were riding together to Parliament House in the

Protector's train, when Russell opened the subject by observing that certain rumours were abroad which he was very sorry to hear, and that if the Admiral were seeking to marry either of the King's sisters—the special one being left discreetly uncertain—"ye seek the means to undo yourself and all those who shall come of you."

Seymour replied carelessly that he had no such thought, and the subject dropped. A few days later, however, he himself re-introduced it, demanding what reason existed to prevent him, or another man, wedding one of the late King's daughters? Again Russell reiterated his warning. The marriage, he declared, would prove fatal to him who made it, proceeding to point out—knowing that the argument would have more weight with the man with whom he had to do than recommendations to caution and prudence—that from a pecuniary point of view the match would carry with it no great advantage, a statement vehemently controverted by the Admiral, who throughout neither felt nor feigned any indifference to the financial aspect of the affair.

During the ensuing months he was busily engaged in the prosecution of his scheme. He may have had a genuine liking for the girl to whom his attentions had already proved compromising; he could114 scarcely doubt that he had won her affections. But by a clandestine marriage Elizabeth would, under the terms of her father's will, have forfeited her right to the succession, and she was therefore safeguarded from any attempt on her suitor's part to induce her to dispense with the consent of the lawful authorities. Forced to proceed with circumspection, he made use of any opportunity that offered for maintaining a hold upon her, aided and abetted by the partisanship of her servants. A fortnight before Christmas he proffered the loan of his London house as a lodging when she should pay her winter visit to the capital, adding to her cofferer, through whom the suggestion was made, that he would come and see her Grace; "which declaration," reported to her by Parry, "she seemed to take very gladly and to accept it joyfully." Observing, moreover, that when the conversation turned upon Seymour, and especially when he was commended, the Princess "showed such countenance that it should appear she was very glad to hear of him," the cofferer was emboldened to inquire whether, should the Council approve, she would marry him.

"When that time comes to pass," answered Elizabeth, in the language of the day, "I will do as God shall put in my mind."

Notwithstanding her refusal to commit herself, it was not difficult for those about her to divine after what fashion she would, in that case, be moved to115 act. Yet she retained her independence of spirit, and when told that the Admiral advised her to appeal to the Protector through his wife for certain grants of land, as well as for a London residence, she turned upon those who had played the part of his mouthpiece in a manner indicating no intention of becoming his passive tool.

"I dare say he did not so," she replied hotly, refusing to credit the suggestion he was reported to have made that she, a Tudor, should sue to his brother's wife in order to obtain her rights, "nor would so."

Parry adhered to his statement.

"Yes," he answered, "by my faith."

"Well, I will not do so," returned his mistress, "and so tell him. I will not come there, nor begin to flatter now."

If the Admiral possessed partisans in the members of Elizabeth's household, it was probably no less owing to hostility towards the Somersets than to liking for himself; a passage of arms having taken place between Mrs. Ashley and the Duchess, who had found fault with the governess, on account of the Princess having gone on a barge on the Thames by night, "and for other light parts," observing—in which she was undoubtedly right—that Ashley was not worthy to have the charge of the daughter of a King. Such home-truths were not unfitted to quicken the culprit's zeal in the cause of the 116 Admiral, and Ashley was always at hand to push his interests.

It was, nevertheless, necessary that the Princess's dependants should act with caution; and, discussing with Lord Seymour the question of a visit he desired to pay her, Parry declined to give any opinion on the subject, professing himself unacquainted with his mistress's pleasure. The Admiral answered with assumed indifference. It was no matter, he said, "for there has been a talk of late ... they say now I shall marry my Lady Jane," adding, "I tell you this but merrily, I tell you this but merrily."90

The gossip may have been repeated in the certainty that it would reach Elizabeth's ears and in the hope of rousing her to jealousy. But had it suited his plans, there is no reason to doubt that Seymour would not have hesitated to gain permanent possession of the ward who had been left him "as a gage." Elizabeth was, however, nearer to the throne, and was, beside her few additional years, better suited to please his taste than the quiet child who dwelt under his roof.

As it proved he was destined to further his ambitious projects neither by marriage with Jane nor her cousin. By the middle of January the Protector had struck his blow—a blow which was to end in fratricide. Charged with treason, in conspiring117 to change the form of government and to carry off the person of the King, Seymour was sent on January 16 to the Tower—in those days so often the ante-room to death.

Though he had long been suspected of harbouring designs against his brother's administration, the specific grounds of his accusation were based upon the confessions of one Sherrington, master of the mint at Bristol; who, under examination, and in terror for his personal safety, had declared, truly or falsely, that he had promised to coin money for the Admiral, and had heard him boast of the number of his friends, saying that he thought more gentlemen loved him than loved the Lord Protector. The same witness added that he had heard Seymour say that, for her qualities and virtues, Lady Jane Grey was a fit match for the King, and he would rather he should marry her than the daughter of the Protector.

Many of great name and place in England must have been disquieted by the news of the arrest of the man who stood so near the King, and who, if any one, could have counted upon being safeguarded by position and rank from the consequences of his rashness. His assertion that he was more loved than his brother amongst his own class was true, and not a few nobles will have trembled lest they should be implicated in his fall. Loyalty to a disgraced friend was not amongst the customs of 118 a day when the friendship might mean death, and most men were anxious, on these occasions, to dissociate themselves from a former comrade.

Elizabeth was not one of those with least to fear, and it is the more honourable to her that she showed no inclination to follow the example of others, or to abandon the cause of her lover. She was in an embarrassing, if not a dangerous situation. No one knew to what extent she had been compromised, morally or politically, and the distrust of the Government was proved by the arrest of both Ashley and Parry, and by the searching examination to which the Princess, as well as her servants, was subjected.

Sir Robert Tyrwhitt, placed in charge of the delinquent, with directions to obtain from her all the information he could, found it no easy task.

"I do assure your Grace," he wrote to Somerset, "she hath a good wit, and nothing is to be got from her but by great policy."

She would own to no "practice" with regard to Seymour, either on her part or that of her dependants. "And yet I do see in her face," said Sir Robert, "that she is guilty, and yet perceive she will abide more storms before she will accuse Mrs. Ashley."

Whatever may be thought of Elizabeth's former conduct, she displayed at this crisis no less staunchness and fidelity in the support of those she loved119 than a capacity and ability rare in a girl of fifteen, practically standing alone, confronted with enemies, and without advisers to direct her course. Writing to the Protector on January 28, she thanked him for the gentleness and good will he had displayed; professed her readiness to declare the truth in the matter at issue; gave an account of her relations with the Admiral, asserting her innocence of any intention of marrying him without the sanction of the Council; and vindicated her servants from blame.

"These be the things," she concluded, "which I declared to Master Tyrwhitt, and also whereof my conscience beareth witness, which I would not for all earthly things offend in anything, for I know I have a soul to be saved as well as other folks have; wherefore I will, above all things, have respect unto the same." One request she made, namely, that she might come to Court. Rumours against her honour were afloat, accusing her with being with child by the Lord Admiral; and upon these grounds, that she might show herself as she was, as well as upon a desire to see the King, she based her demand.

Tyrwhitt shook his head over the composition. The singular harmony existing between Elizabeth's story and the depositions extracted from her dependants in the Tower struck him as suspicious, and as pointing to a preconcerted tale.

"They all sing one song," he wrote, "and so, I120 think, they would not, unless they had set the note before"; and he continued to watch his charge narrowly, and to report her demeanour at headquarters, assisted in his office by his wife, who had been sent to replace the untrustworthy Ashley as governess to the Princess.

"She beginneth now a little to droop," he wrote, "by reason she heareth that my Lord Admiral's houses be dispersed. And my wife telleth me she cannot hear him discommended, but she is ready to make answer thereto."91

Put as brave a face as she might upon the matter, Elizabeth was in a position of singular loneliness and difficulty. Her lover was in prison on a capital charge, her friend and confidant removed from her, her reputation tarnished. Nor was she disposed to accept in a humble spirit the oversight of the duenna sent her by the Council. As the close friend of the step-mother whose kindness the Princess had so ill requited, Lady Tyrwhitt, for her part, would not in any case have been prejudiced in favour of her charge, or inclined to take an indulgent view of her misdemeanours; and the reception accorded her when she arrived to assume her thankless post was not such as to promote good feeling. Mrs. Ashley, the girl told the new-comer, was her mistress, and she had not so conducted herself that the Council should give her another.

121 Lady Tyrwhitt, no more inclined than she to conciliation, retorted that, seeing the Princess had allowed Mrs. Ashley to be her mistress, she need not be ashamed to have any other honest woman in that place, and so the intercourse of governess and pupil was inaugurated.

That Lady Tyrwhitt's taunt was undeniably justified did not the more soften the Princess towards her, and it was duly reported to the authorities in London that she had taken "the matter so heavily that she wept all that night and lowered all the next day.... The love," it was added, "she yet beareth [Ashley] is to be wondered at."

Tact and discretion might in time have availed to reconcile the Princess to the change in her household; but the methods employed by the Tyrwhitts do not appear to have been judicious. Sir Robert, taking up his wife's quarrel, told her significantly that if she considered her honour she would rather ask to have a mistress than to be left without one; and, complaining to his superiors that she could not digest his advice in any way, added vindictively, "If I should say my phantasy, it were more meet she should have two than one."92

So the days went by, no doubt uncomfortably enough for all concerned. Regarding Tyrwhitt and his wife in the capacity of gaolers, charged with the duty of eliciting her confessions, it was not122 with them that Elizabeth would take counsel as to the best course open to her. The revelations attained by cross-examination from her imprisoned servants as to the relations upon which she had stood during the Queen's lifetime with Katherine's husband, were sufficiently damaging to lend additional colour to the scandalous reports in circulation, and her spirited demand that her fair fame should be vindicated by a proclamation forbidding the propagation of slanders concerning the King's sister was fully in character with the woman she was to become. Though not without delay, her request was granted, and the circumstantial fable of a child born and destroyed may be supposed to have been effectually suppressed.

Whilst this had been Elizabeth's condition during the spring, the man to whom her troubles were chiefly due had been undergoing alternations of hope and fear. It may have seemed impossible that his brother should proceed to extremities. But there were times when, in the silence and seclusion of the prison-house, his spirits grew despondent. On February 16, when his confinement had lasted a month, and his fate was still undecided, his keeper, Christopher Eyre, reported that on the previous Friday the Lord Admiral had been very sad.

"I had thought," he said, upon Eyre remarking on his depression, "before I came to this place123 that my Lord's Grace, with all the rest of the Council, had been my friends, and that I had as many friends as any man within this realm. But now I think they have forgotten me," proceeding to declare that never was poor knave more true to his Prince than he; nor had he meant evil to his brother, though he had thought he might have had the custody of the King.93

There is something pathetic in the dejection of the Admiral, arrogant, proud, vain and ambitious, thus deserted by all upon whose friendship he had imagined himself able to count. It is impossible to avoid the conviction that, in spite of a surface boldness, the nobles of his day were apt to turn craven where personal danger was in question. On the battlefield valour was common enough, and when once hope was over men had learnt—a needful lesson—to meet death on the scaffold with dignity and courage. But so long as a chance of life remained, it was their constant habit to abase themselves in order to escape their doom. We do not hear of a single voice raised in Seymour's defence. The common people, when Somerset in his turn had fallen a victim to jealousy and hate, made no secret of their sorrow and their love; but the nobles who had been his brother's supporters were silent and cowed, or went to swell the number of his accusers.

124 By March 20 hope and fear were alike at an end. A Bill of Attainder had been brought into the House of Lords, after an examination of the culprit before the Council, when his demand to be confronted with his accusers had been refused. The evidence against him was reiterated by certain of the peers; the bill was passed without a division; and, in spite of the opposition of the Commons, who supported his claim to be heard in his own defence, the Protector cut the matter short by a message from the King declaring it unnecessary that the demand should be conceded. His doom was sealed.

Was he innocent or guilty? Dr. Lingard, after an examination of the facts, believes that he was unjustly condemned; that, if he had sought a portion of the power vested in the Protector, and might have been dangerous to the authority of his brother, the charge for which he was condemned—a design to carry off the King and excite a civil war—is unproved.

125 Innocent or guilty, he was to die. In the words of Latimer—who, in sermons preached after the execution, made himself the apologist of the Council by abuse levelled at the dead man—he perished "dangerously, irksomely, horribly.... Whether he be saved or no, I leave it to God. But surely he was a wicked man, and the realm is well rid of him."94

125 Thus Thomas Seymour was done to death by a brother, and cursed by a churchman. Sherrington, who had supplied the principal part of the evidence against him, received a pardon and was reinstated in his office.

Of regret upon the part of friends or kinsfolk there is singularly little token. As they had fallen from his side in life, so they held apart from him in death. If Elizabeth mourned him she was already too well versed in the world's wisdom to avow her grief, and is reported to have observed, on his execution, that a man had died full of ability (esprit) but of scant judgment.95 Whether or not the Lord Protector was troubled by remorse, he was not likely to make the public his confidant; and Katherine, the woman who had loved him so devotedly, was dead.

126

CHAPTER X

1549-1550

The Protector's position—Disaffection in the country—Its causes—The Duke's arrogance—Warwick his rival—The success of his opponents—Placed in the Tower, but released—St. George's Day at Court.

The Protector's conduct with regard to his brother does much to alienate sympathy from him in his approaching fall, in a sense the consequence and outcome of the fratricide. He "had sealed his doom the day on which he signed the warrant for the execution of his brother."96 If the Admiral, having crossed his will, was not safe, who could believe himself to be so? Yet the fashion of the accomplishing of his downfall, the treachery and deception practised towards him by men upon whom he might fairly have believed himself able to count, lend a pathos to the end it might otherwise have lacked.

For the present his power and position showed no signs of diminution. The Queen, his wife's rival, was dead. The Admiral, who had dared to measure his strength against his brother's, would127 trouble him no more, unless as an unquiet ghost, an unwelcome visitant confronting him in unexpected places. During his Protectorate he had added property to property, field to field, and was the master of two hundred manors. If the public finances were low, Somerset was rich, and during this year the building of the house destined to bear his name was carried on on a scale of splendour proportionate to his pretensions. Having thrown away the chief prop of his house, says Heylyn, he hoped to repair the ruin by erecting a magnificent palace.

The site he had chosen was occupied by three episcopal mansions and one parish church; but it would have been a bold man who would have disputed the will of the all-powerful Lord Protector, and the owners submitted meekly to be dispossessed in order to make room for his new abode. Materials running short, there were rough-and-ready ways of providing them conveniently near at hand; and certain "superstitious buildings" close to St. Paul's, including one or two chapels and a "fair charnel-house" were demolished to supply what was necessary, the bones of the displaced dead being left to find burial in the adjacent fields, or where they might. As the great pile rose, more was required, and St.

Margaret's, Westminster, was to have been destroyed to furnish it, had not the people, less subservient than the Bishops, risen to protect their128 church, and forcibly driven away the labourers charged with the work of destruction. St. Margaret's was saved, but St. John's of Jerusalem, not far from Smithfield, was sacrificed in its stead, being blown up with gunpowder in order that its stone-work might be turned to account.

The Protector pursued his way unconscious of danger. The Earl of Warwick, his future supplanter, looked on and bided his time. The condition of the country had become such as to facilitate the designs of those bent upon a change in the Government. Into the course of public affairs, at home and abroad, it is impossible to enter at length; a brief summary will suffice to show that events were tending to create discontent and to strengthen the hands of Somerset's enemies.

The victory of Pinkie Cleugh, though gratifying to national pride, had in nowise served the purpose of terminating the war with Scotland. Renewed with varying success, the Scots, by means of French aid, had upon the whole improved their position, and the hopes indulged in England of a union between the two countries, to be peacefully effected by the marriage of the King with the infant Mary Stuart, had been disappointed, the little Queen having been sent to France and affianced to the Dauphin. In the distress prevailing amongst the working classes of England, more pressing cause for dissatisfaction and agitation was found.129 Partly the result of the depreciation of the currency during the late reign, it was also due to the action of the new owners who, enriched by ecclesiastical property, had enclosed portions of Church lands heretofore left open to be utilised by the labourers for their personal profit. Pasturage was increasing in favour compared with tillage; less labour was required, and wages had in consequence fallen.

To material ills and privations, other grievances were added. Associated in the minds of the people with their condition of want were the changes lately enforced in the sphere of religion. The new ministers were often ignorant men, who gave scandal by their manner of life, their parishioners frequently making complaints of them to the Bishops.

"Our curate is naught," they would say, "an ass-head, a dodipot [?], a lack-latin, and can do nothing. Shall I pay him tithe that doth us no good, nor none will do?"97

In some cases the fault lay with patrons, who preferred to select a man unlikely to assert his authority. Economy on the part of the Government was responsible for other unfit appointments, and capable Churchmen being permitted to hold secular offices, they were removed from their parishes and their flocks were left unshepherded. Against this practice Latimer protested in a sermon at St. Paul's, on the occasion of a clergyman having been130 made Comptroller of the Mint. Who controlled the devil at home in his parish, asked the rough-tongued preacher, whilst he controlled the Mint?

The condition of things thus produced was not calculated to commend the innovations it accompanied to the people, and the introduction of the new Prayer-book was in particular bitterly resented in country districts. In many parts of England, interest and religion joining hands, fierce insurrections broke out, and the measures taken by "the good Duke" to allay popular irritation, by ordering that the lands newly enclosed should be re-opened, had the double effect of stirring the people, thus far successful, to yet more strenuous action in vindication of their rights, and of increasing the dislike and distrust with which his irresponsible exercise of authority was regarded by the upper classes.

Upon domestic troubles—Ket's rebellion in Norfolk, one of large dimensions in the west, and others—followed a declaration of war with France, certain successes on the part of the enemy serving to discredit the Protector and his management of affairs still further.

Whilst rich and poor were alike disaffected in the country at large, the Duke had become an object of jealousy to the members of the Council Board who were responsible for having placed him in the position he occupied. To a man with the sagacity to look ahead and take account of the131 forces at work, it must have been plain that the possession of absolute and undivided power on the part of a subject was necessarily fraught with danger, and that the Duke's astonishing success in obtaining the patent conferring upon him supreme and regal authority contained in itself the seed and prophecy of ruin. But, besides more serious causes of offence, his bearing in the Council-chamber, far from being adapted to conciliate opposition, further exasperated his colleagues against him. Cranmer and Paget were the last to abandon his cause, but on May 8—not two months after his brother's execution—the latter wrote to give him frank warning of the probable consequences of his "great cholerick fashions." It is evident that a stormy scene had taken place that afternoon, and that Paget must have been strongly convinced of the need for interference before he addressed his remonstrance to the despotic head of the Government.

"Poor Sir Richard a Lee," he wrote, "this afternoon, after your Grace had very sore, and much more than needed, rebuked him, came to my chamber weeping, and there complaining, as far as became him, of your handling of him, seemed almost out of wits and out of heart. Your Grace had put him clean out of countenance." After which he proceeded to warn the Duke solemnly, "for the very love he bore him," of the consequences should he not change his manner of conduct.98

132 Paget's love was quickly to grow cold. During the summer the various rebellions in different parts of the country were suppressed, the Earl of Warwick playing an important part in the operations. On September 25 the Protector was, to all appearance, still in fulness of power and authority. By October 13 he was in the Tower.

The Spanish spectator again supplies an account of the view taken by the man in the street of the initiation of the quarrel which led to the Duke's disgrace and fall. Returned to London, Warwick, accompanied by the captains, English and foreign, who had served under him against the rebels, is said to have come to Court to demand for his soldiers the rewards he considered their due. Met by a refusal on the part of the Protector of anything over and above their ordinary wages, his indignation found vent. If money was not to be had, it was because of the sums squandered by the Duke in building his own palace. The French forts were already lost. If the Protector continued in power he would end by losing everything.

From a photo by Emery Walker after a painting in the National Portrait Gallery. WILLIAM, LORD PAGET, K.G.

Somerset replied with no less heat. He deserved, he said, that Warwick should speak as he had spoken, by the favour he had shown him. Warwick having retorted that it was with himself and his colleagues that the fault lay, since they had bestowed so much power on the Protector, the two parted. Of what followed Holinshed gives a description.133 "Suddenly, upon what occasion many marvelled but few knew, every lord and councillor went through the city weaponed, and had their servants likewise weaponed ... to the great wondering of many; and at the last a great assembly of the said Council was made at the Earl of Warwick's lodging, which was then at Ely Place, in Holborn, whither all the confederates came privily armed, and finally concluded to possess the Tower of London."99

As a counterblast, Somerset issued a proclamation in the King's name, summoning all his subjects to Hampton Court for his defence and that of his "most entirely beloved uncle." Open war was declared.

So far the Archbishop and Paget, both resident with the Court, together with the two Secretaries, had adhered to the Protector. Upon Cranmer, if upon any one, Somerset, who had done more than any other person to establish religion upon its new basis, should have been able to count, if not for support, for a loyal opposition. But fear is strong and—again it must be repeated—fidelity to the unfortunate was no feature of the times; and by both Archbishop and Paget the cause of the falling man was abandoned. Not only did they secretly embrace the cause of the party headed by Warwick, but private directions were furnished by Paget as to the means to be employed in seizing the person of the Duke.

134 Meantime, Hampton Court being judged insufficiently secure, Somerset, with a guard of five hundred men, had removed the King, at dead of night, to Windsor, a graphic account of the journey being given by the chronicler.

"As he went along the road the King was all armed, and carried his little sword drawn, and kept saying to the people on the way:

"'My vassals, will you help me against the people who want to kill me?'

"And everybody cried out, 'Sir, we will all die for you.'"100

Windsor reached, the defence of the Castle and of the sovereign was wisely entrusted, in the first instance, to men upon whom the Duke could depend. But the Council was successful in lulling any apprehensions of violent action to rest. Sir Philip Hoby, according to some authorities,101 was despatched from London with open, as well as secret, letters, wherein it was declared that no harm was intended to the Duke; order was merely to be taken for the Protectorship. Somerset had by this time yielded so far to the forces arrayed against him as to recognise the necessity of consenting to some change in the government; and at the reassuring terms of the communication all present gave way to135 emotion; wept with joy, after the fashion of the times; thanked God, and prayed for the Lords; Paget, in particular, clasping the Duke about the knees, and crying with tears, "O my Lord, ye see what my lords be!"

The Protector's ruin had been assured. Trusting to the declarations of the Council, he fell an easy prey into their hands. Yielding to the representations of Cranmer and Paget, to whose "diligent travail" his enemies gratefully ascribed their success, he permitted his trusty followers to be replaced in the defence of the Castle by the usual royal guard; on October 11 he had been seized and placed in safe keeping, and it was reported that the King had a bad cold, and "much desireth to be hence, saying that 'Methinks I am in prison. Here be no galleries nor no gardens to walk in.'"102 The young sovereign had also, with a merry countenance and a loud voice, asked how their Lordships of the Council were, and when he would see them, saying that they should be welcome whensoever they came.

It was plain that objections to a transference of his guardianship were not to be expected from the nephew of the Lord Protector, and the Duke was removed from Windsor to the Tower, followed by three hundred lords and gentlemen, "as if he had been a captive carried in triumph." It would, however, have been more difficult to induce the136 boy to consent to the execution of another of his closest kin, and there may have been some fraction of truth in the report which gained currency that the King had not been made acquainted with the fact that his uncle was actually a prisoner until he learnt it from the Duchess. He then sent for the Archbishop and questioned him on the subject.

"Godfather," he is made to say, "what has become of my uncle, the Duke?" The explanation furnished him by Cranmer—to the effect that, had God not helped the Lords, the country would have been ruined, and it was feared that the Protector might have slain the King himself—did not appear to commend itself to the young sovereign. The Duke, he said, had never done him any harm, and he did not wish him to be killed.

A King's wishes, even at thirteen, have weight, and Warwick suddenly discovered that good should be returned for evil; and that since it was the King's desire, and the first thing he had asked of his Council, the Duke must be pardoned.103

From a photo by W. Mansell & Co. after a painting by Holbein.
EDWARD VI.

What is more certain is that, on condition of an unqualified acknowledgment of his guilt, accompanied by forfeiture of offices and property, it was decided that Somerset should be set at liberty. Self-respect or dignity was not in fashion, and in the eyes of some the submission of the late Lord Protector assumed the character of an "abjectness."137 For the moment it purchased for him safety, and he was gradually permitted to regain a certain amount of influence and power. Some portion of his wealth was restored to him, and he was at length readmitted to the Council and to a limited share in the government. To sanguine eyes all seemed to have been placed on a satisfactory footing; but jealousy, distrust, and hatred take much killing. The position of the man who was the King's nearest of kin amongst his nobles, and had lately been all-powerful in the State, was a difficult one. Warwick was rising, and meant to rise; Somerset was not content to remain fallen and discredited. What seemed a peace was merely an armistice.

Meantime Warwick and his friends were no more successful than his rival in maintaining the national honour, and the peace with France concluded during the spring was regarded by the nation as a disgrace. Boulogne was surrendered to its natural owners, and in magniloquent terms war was once more stated to be at an end for ever between the two countries.

Court and courtiers troubled themselves little with such matters, and on St. George's Day a brilliant company of Lords of the Council and Knights of the Garter kept the festival at Greenwich; when a glimpse of the thirteen-year-old King is to be caught, in a more boyish mood than usual.

Coming out from the discourse preached in138 honour of the day, in high spirits and in the argumentative humour fostered by sermons, the "godly and virtuous imp" turned to his train.

"My Lords," he demanded, "I pray you, what saint is St. George, that we here so honour him?"

The sudden attack was unexpected, and, the Lords of the Council being "astonied" by it, it was the Treasurer who made reply.

"If it please Your Majesty," he said, "I did never read in any history of St. George, but only in Legenda Aurea, where it is thus set down, that St. George out with his sword and ran the dragon through with his spear."

The King, when he could not a great while speak for laughing, at length said:

"I pray you, my Lord, and what did he do with his sword the while?"

"That I cannot tell Your Majesty," said he.104

Poor little King! poor "godly imp"! It is seldom that his laughter rings out through the centuries. Perhaps some of the grave Councillors or divines present may have looked askance, considering that it was not with the weapon of ridicule that the patron saint of England should be most fitly attacked, but with the more legitimate one of theological

47

criticism. But to us it is satisfactory to find that there were times when even the modern Josiah could not speak for laughing.

139

CHAPTER XI

1549-1551

Lady Jane Grey at home—Visit from Roger Ascham—The German divines—Position of Lady Jane in the theological world.

Whilst these events had been taking place Jane Grey had been once more relegated to the care of her parents, to whose house she had been removed upon the imprisonment of her guardian, the Admiral, in January, 1549. To the helpless and passive plaything of worldly and political exigencies, the change from Seymour Place and Hanworth, where she had lived under Seymour's roof, to the quiet of her father's Leicestershire home, must have been great.

Nor was the difference in the moral atmosphere less marked. Handsome, unprincipled, gay, magnificent, one imagines that the Admiral, in spite of the faults to which she was probably not blind, must have been an imposing personage in the eyes of his little charge; and self-interest—the interest of a man who did not guess that the future held nothing for him but a grave—as well as natural kindliness towards a child dependent upon him, will have led him to play the part of her "half-140father" in a manner to win her affection. Was she not destined, should his schemes prosper, to fill the place of Queen Consort? or, failing that, might it not be well to turn into earnest the "merry" possibility he had mentioned to Parry, and, if Elizabeth was denied him, to make her cousin his wife? In any case, so long as she lived in his house, Jane was a guest of importance, of royal blood, to be treated with consideration, cared for, and flattered.

But now the ill-assorted house-mates had parted. Seymour had taken his way to the Tower, as a stage towards the scaffold; and Jane had returned—gladly or sorrowfully, who can tell?—to the shelter of the parental roof, and to the care of a father and mother determined upon neutralising by their conduct any ill-effects produced by her two years of emancipation from their control. Once more she was an insignificant member of her father's family, the eldest of his three children, subjected to the strictest discipline and, whatever the future might bring forth, of little consequence in the present.

It is possible that Lord Dorset's fears, expressed at the time when he was attempting to regain possession of his daughter, had been in part realised; and that Jane, "for lack of a bridle," had "taken too much the head," and conceived an unduly high opinion of herself—it would indeed have been a natural outcome of the position she held both in her guardian's house and, as will be seen, in141 the estimation of divines. If this was the case, her mother and he were to do their best to "address her mind to humility, soberness, and obedience." The means taken to carry out their intentions were harsh.

Of the year following upon Jane's return to Bradgate little is known; but in the summer of 1550, a picturesque and vivid sketch is afforded by Roger Ascham of the child of thirteen105 upon whom so many hopes centred and so many expectations were built. In the description given in his Schoolmaster106 of the visit paid by the great scholar to Bradgate, light is thrown alike upon the system of training pursued by Lord Dorset, upon the character of his daughter, and upon the spirit she displayed in conforming to the manner of life enforced upon her.

Ascham, in his capacity of tutor to her cousin Elizabeth, had known Jane intimately at Court—so he states in a letter to Sturm, another of the academic brotherhood—and had already received learned letters from her. Before starting on a diplomatic mission to Germany in the summer of 1550, he had visited some friends in Yorkshire, and on his way south turned aside to renew his acquaintance with Lady Jane, and to pay his respects to her father, who stood high in the estimation of the religious[142] party to which Ascham belonged. To this visit we owe one of the most distinct glimpses of the girl that we possess.

By a fortunate chance he found "that most noble Lady Jane Grey, to whom I was exceeding much beholden," alone. Lord and Lady Dorset, with all their household, were hunting in the park, and Jane, in the seclusion of her chamber, was engaged in studying the Phaedo of Plato, "with as much delight as some gentlemen would read a merry tale in Boccaccio," when Ascham presented himself to her.

The conversation between the scholar and the student places Lady Jane's small staid figure in clear relief. Notwithstanding Plato's Phaedo, notwithstanding, too, the sun outside, the sounds of horns, the baying of hounds, and all the other allurements she had proved able to resist, there is something very human and unsaintly in her fashion of unburthening herself to a congenial spirit concerning the wrongs sustained at the parental hands. To Ascham, with whom she had been so well acquainted under different circumstances, she opened her mind freely when, "after salutation and duty done," he inquired how it befell that she had left the pastimes going forward in the Park.

After an engraving.
LADY JANE GREY.
"I wis," she answered smiling—the smile, surely, of conscious and complacent superiority—"all their sport in the Park is but a shadow to the pleasure that I find in Plato. Alas, good folk, they never felt what true pleasure meant."

143 "And how came you, Madame," asked Ascham, "to this deep knowledge of pleasure, and what did chiefly allure you to it, seeing not many women, but very few men, have attained thereto?"

Jane, nothing loath to satisfy her guest's curiosity, did so at length.

"I will tell you," she answered, "and tell you a truth, which perchance you will marvel at. One of the greatest benefits that ever God gave me is that He sent me so sharp and severe parents and so gentle a schoolmaster. For when I am in presence either of father or mother, whether I speak, keep silence, sit, stand, or go, eat, drink, be merry or sad, be sewing, playing, dancing, or doing anything else, I must do it, as it were, in such weight, measure, and number, even so perfectly as God made the world, or else I am so sharply taunted, so cruelly threatened, yea presently sometimes with pinches, nips, and bobs, and other ways, which I will not name for the honour I bear them, so without measure disordered, that I think myself in hell, till time come that I must go to Mr. Elmer, who teacheth me so gently, so pleasantly, with such fair allurements to learning, that I think all the time nothing whiles I am with him. And when I am called away from him I fall on weeping, because, whatever I do else but learning is full of grief, trouble, fear, and whole misliking unto me. And thus my book hath been so much my pleasure, and144 bringeth daily to me more pleasure and more, that in respect of it all other pleasures in very deed be but trifles and troubles to me."107

Jane's recital of her wrongs, if correctly reported—and Ascham says he remembers the conversation gladly, both because it was so worthy of memory, and because it was the last time he ever saw that noble and worthy lady—proves that her command of the vernacular was equal to her proficiency in the dead languages, and that she cherished a very natural resentment for the treatment to which she was subjected. There is something

49

irresistibly provocative of laughter in the thought of the two scholars, old and young, and of the lofty compassion displayed by the chidden child towards the frivolous tastes and amusements of the parents to whom she doubtless outwardly accorded the exaggerated respect and reverence demanded by custom. Few would grudge the satisfaction derived from a sympathetic listener to the girl whose pleasures were to be so few and days for enjoying them so short.

When Ascham took leave he had received a promise from Jane to write to him in Greek, provided that he would challenge her by a letter from Germany. And so they parted, to meet no more.

It may be that Lady Jane's sense of the harshness and severity of her treatment at home was accentuated by the tone adopted with regard to her by many145 of the leading Protestant divines. To these men—men to whom Mary was Jezebel, Gardiner that lying and subtle Cerberus,108 and by whom persons holding theological views at variance with their own were freely and unreservedly handed over to the devil—Jane was not only wise, learned, and saintly beyond her years, but to her they turned their eyes, hoping for a future when, at the King's side, she might prove the efficient protectress and patroness of the reformed Church. Her name was a household word amongst them, and whilst it can have been scarcely possible that she was indifferent to the incense offered by those to whom she had been instructed to look up, it may have rendered the system of repression adopted by her parents more unendurable than might otherwise have been the case.

Bradgate was a centre of strong and militant Protestantism. In conjunction with Warwick, the Marquis of Dorset was regarded by the German school of theologians as one of the "two most shining lights of the Church;"109 and the many letters sent from England to Henry Bullinger at Zurich—some of them dated from Bradgate itself—abound in allusions to the family, and throw a useful light upon this part of Lady Jane's life. In these epistles her father's name recurs again and again, always in terms of extravagant eulogy, and as that of a munificent patron of needy divines. Thus he146 had bestowed a pension at first sight upon Ulmis, a young disciple of Bullinger's, doubling it some months later; and his grateful protégé, striving to make what return is possible, impresses upon the foreign master the advisability of dedicating one of his works to the generous Marquis, anxiously sending him, when his request has been granted, the full title to be used in so doing. "He told me, indeed," he adds, "that he had the title of Prince, but that he would not wish to be so styled by you, so you must judge for yourself whether to keep it back or not."110 Bullinger is likewise urged to present a copy of one of his books to the Marquis's daughter, "and, take my word for it, you will never repent having done so." A most learned and courteous letter would thereby be elicited from her. She had already translated into Greek a good part of Bullinger's treatise on marriage, put by Ulmis himself into Latin, and had given it to her father as a New Year's gift.111 In May, 1551, another letter records that two days had been very agreeably passed at Bradgate with Jane, my Lord's daughter, and those excellent and holy persons Aylmer, her tutor, and Haddon, chaplain to the Marquis. "For my own part, I do not think there ever lived any one more deserving of respect than this young lady, if you regard her family; more learned, if147 you consider her age; or more happy, if you consider both. A report has prevailed, and has begun to be talked of by persons of consequence, that this most noble virgin is to be betrothed and given in marriage to the King's majesty. Oh, if that event should take place, how happy would be the union, and how beneficial to the church!"112

A letter despatched by Ulmis on the same day to another of his brethren in the faith, Conrad Pellican, craves his advice on behalf of Lady Jane with regard to the best means of acquiring Hebrew, a language she was anxious to study. She had written to consult

Bullinger on the subject, but Bullinger was a busy man, and all the world knew how perfect was Pellican's acquaintance with the subject. Pellican may argue that he might seem lacking in modesty should he address a young lady, the daughter of a nobleman, unknown to him personally. But he is besought by Ulmis to entertain no fears of the kind, and his correspondent will bear all the blame if he ever repents of the deed, or if Lady Jane does not most willingly acknowledge his courtesy. "In truth," he adds, "I do not think that amongst the English nobility for many ages past there has arisen a single individual who, to the highest excellences of talent and judgment, has united so much diligence and assiduity in the cultivation of every liberal pursuit.... It is148 incredible how far she has advanced already, and to what perfection she will advance in a few years; for I well know that she will complete what she has begun, unless perhaps she be diverted from her pursuits by some calamity of the times.... If you write a letter to her, take care, I pray you, that it be first delivered to me."113

The letter is dated from the house of the daughter of the Marquis. Her mother, it is true, seems to have been at home, though Dorset was in Scotland; but it is a curious fact that the grand-daughter of Henry VII., through whom Jane's royal blood was transmitted to her, appears to have been by common consent tacitly passed over, as a person of no consequence in comparison with her daughter.114

Quite a budget of letters were entrusted to the courier who left Bradgate on May 29, and was the bearer of the missives addressed by Ulmis to his master and his friend. Both John Aylmer, tutor to Lord Dorset's children and afterwards Bishop of London, and Haddon, the Marquis's chaplain, had taken the opportunity of writing to Bullinger, doubtless stimulated to the effort by his young disciple.

The preceptor who compared so favourably in149 Lady Jane's eyes with her parents, was a young Norfolk man, of about twenty-nine, and singularly well learned in the Latin and Greek tongues.115 On James Haddon, Bishop Hooper, writing from prison when, three years later, the friends of the Reformation had fallen on evil days, pronounced a eulogy in a letter to Bullinger. Master James Haddon, he said, was not only a friend and very dear brother in Christ, but one he had always esteemed on account of his singular erudition and virtue. "I do not think," he added, "that I have ever been acquainted with any one in England who is endued either with more sincere piety towards God or more removed from all desire of those perishing objects desired by foolish mortals."116 From Bishop Hooper the panegyric is evidence that Haddon belonged to the extreme party in theological matters, in which Aylmer was probably in full accord with him. On this particular day in May both these devoted and conscientious men were sending letters to the great director of souls in Zurich, that of Haddon being written to a man to whom he was personally unknown, and with the sole object of opening a correspondence and offering a tribute of respect.

Aylmer's case was a different one. Though also a stranger, he wrote at some length, chiefly in the character of the preceptor entrusted with Lady150 Jane's education, making due acknowledgments for the letters and advice which had been of so much use in keeping his patron and his patron's family in the right path, and begging Bullinger to continue these good offices towards the pupil, just fourteen, concerning whom it is strange to find the young man entertaining certain fears and misgivings.

"At that age," he observes, "as the comic poet tells us, all people are inclined to follow their own ways, and, by the attractiveness of the objects and the corruptions of nature, are more easily carried headlong in pleasure ... than induced to follow those studies that are attended with the praise of virtue." The time teemed with many disorders; discreet physicians must therefore be sought, and to tender minds there should not be wanting the counsel of the aged nor the authority of grave and influential men. Aylmer accordingly entreats that Bullinger will minister, by letter and advice, to the improvement of his charge.

An epistle from Jane, dated July 1551, shows that the German theologian responded at once to the appeal, since in it she acknowledges the receipt of a most eloquent and weighty letter, and mentioning the loss she had sustained in the death of Bucer, who appears to have taken his part in her theological training, congratulates herself upon the possession of a friend so learned as Bullinger, so151 pious a divine, and so intrepid a champion of true religion. Bereaved of the "pious Bucer ... who unweariedly did not cease, day and night, and to the utmost of his ability, to supply me with all necessary instructions and directions for my conduct in life, and who by his excellent advice promoted and encouraged my progress and advancement in all virtue, godliness, and learning," she proceeds to beg Bullinger to fill the vacant place, and to spur her on if she should loiter and be disposed to delay. By this means she will enjoy the same advantages granted to those women to whom St. Jerome imparted instruction, or to the elect lady to whom the epistle of St. John was addressed, or to the mother of Severus, taught by Origen. As Bullinger could be deemed inferior to none of these teachers, she entreats him to manifest a like kindness.117 It is plain that Lady Jane, in addressing this "brightest ornament and support of the whole Church," is determined not to be outdone in the art of pious flattery; and in her correspondence with men who both as scholars and divines held a foremost place in the estimation of those by whom she was surrounded, she indemnified herself for the mortifications inflicted upon her at home.

The reformers, for their part, were keeping an anxious watch upon the course of events in England; and to strengthen and maintain their influence over152 one who might have a prominent part to play in future years was of the first importance. A letter from Ascham, who was still abroad, dated some months later, supplies yet another example of the incense offered to the child of fourteen, and of fulsome adulation by which an older head might have been turned. Nothing, he told her, in his travels, had raised in him greater admiration than had been caused when, on his visit to Bradgate, he had found one so young and lovely—so divine a maid—engaged in the study of Plato whilst friends and relations were enjoying field sports. Let her proceed thus, to the honour of her country, the delight of her parents, her own glory, the praise of her preceptor, the comfort of her relations and acquaintances, and the admiration of all. O happy Aylmer, to have a like scholar!

From a photo by W. Mansell & Co. after a painting by G. Fliccius in the National Portrait Gallery.

ARCHBISHOP CRANMER.

It would be easy to multiply quotations which indicate the place accorded to Lord Dorset's daughter in the estimation of the leaders of the extreme party of Protestantism, in whose eyes Cranmer was regarded as a possible trimmer. Allowing to him "right views," Hooper, in writing to Bullinger, adds: "we desire nothing more for him than a firm and manly spirit."118 "Contrary to general expectation," Traheron writes, the Archbishop had most openly, firmly, and learnedly maintained the opinion of the German divine upon the153 Eucharist; and Ulmis, alluding to him in terms of praise, repeats that he had unexpectedly given a correct judgment on this point. Even the youngest of the German theologians felt himself competent to weigh in the balances the head of Protestant England.

Protestant England was itself keeping a wary eye upon its Primate. "The Archbishop of Canterbury," wrote Hooper to Bullinger, "to tell the truth, neither took much note of your letter nor of your learned present. But now, as I hope, Master Bullinger and Canterbury entertain the same opinion." "The people ... that many-headed monster," he wrote again, "is still wincing, partly through ignorance, and partly persuaded by the inveiglements of the Bishops and the malice and impiety of the mass-priests."119

154

CHAPTER XII

1551-1552

An anxious tutor—Somerset's final fall—The charges against him—His guilt or innocence—His trial and condemnation—The King's indifference—Christmas at Greenwich—The Duke's execution.

Aylmer had been so far encouraged by the success of his appeal to Henry Bullinger on behalf of his pupil that he is found, some seven months later, calling the Swiss churchman again into council. He was possibly over-anxious, but the tone of his communication makes it clear that Lady Jane Grey had been once more causing her tutor disquiet. Responding, in the first place, to Bullinger's congratulations upon his privilege in acting as teacher to so excellent a scholar, and in a family so well disposed to learning and religion, he proceeds to request that his correspondent will, in his next letter, instruct Lady Jane as to the proper degree of embellishment and adornment of the person becoming in young women professing godliness. The tutor is plainly uneasy on this subject, and it is to be feared that Jane had been developing an undue love of dress. Yet the example of the Princess Elizabeth might be fitly adduced, observes Aylmer,155 furnishing the monitor with arguments of which he might, if he pleased, make use. She at least went clad in every respect as became a young maiden, and yet no one was induced by the example of "a lady in so much gospel light to lay aside, much less look down upon, gold, jewels, and braidings of the hair." Preachers might declaim, but no one amended her life. Moreover, and as a less important matter, Aylmer desires Bullinger to prescribe the amount of time to be devoted to music. If he would handle these points at some length there would probably be some accession to the ranks of virtue.

One would imagine that it argued ignorance of human nature on the part of Lady Jane's instructor to believe that the admonitions of an old man at a distance would have more effect than those of a young man close at hand; nor does it appear whether or not Bullinger sent the advice for which Aylmer asked. But that his pupil's incipient leaning towards worldly vanities was successfully checked would appear from her reply, reported by himself, when a costly dress had been presented to her by her cousin Mary. "It were a shame," she is said to have answered, in rejecting the gift, "to follow my Lady Mary, who leaveth God's Word, and leave my Lady Elizabeth, who followeth God's Word."

It might have been well for Jane had she practised greater courtesy towards a cousin at this time out of favour at Court; but no considerations of policy or156 of good breeding could be expected to influence a zealot of fifteen, and Mary, more than double her age, may well have listened with a smile.

When Aylmer's letter was written, the Grey family had left Bradgate and were in London. The Marquis had, some two months earlier, been advanced to the rank of Duke of Suffolk, upon the title becoming extinct through the death of his wife's two half-brothers, and the tutor may have had just cause for disquietude lest the world should make good its claims upon the little soul he was so carefully tending. In November 1551

Mary of Lorraine, Queen-Dowager of Scotland, had applied for leave to pass through England on her way north. It had not only been granted, but she had been accorded a magnificent reception, Lady Jane, with her mother, taking part in the ceremony when the royal guest visited the King at Whitehall. Two days later she was amongst the ladies assembled to do the Queen honour at her departure for Scotland. It may be that this participation in the pomp and splendour of court life had produced a tendency in John Aylmer's charge to bestow overmuch attention upon worldly matters, nor can it be doubted that his heart was sore at the contrast she had presented to Elizabeth, "whose plainness of dress," he says, still commending the Princess, "was especially noticed on the occasion of the visit of the Queen-Dowager of Scotland."

157 Perhaps, too, the master looked back with regret to the quiet days of uninterrupted study. The Dorset household, when not in London itself, were now to be chiefly resident at Sheen, within reach of the Court. Jane, too, was growing up; Aylmer was young; and to the "gentle schoolmaster" the training of Lord Dorset's eldest daughter may have had an interest not wholly confined to scholarship or to theology. It is nevertheless impossible to put back the clock, and the days when his pupil could be expected to devote herself exclusively to her studies were irrevocably past.

Meantime the hollow treaty of amity between the two great competitors for supremacy in the realm was to end. In the spring of 1551 Somerset and Warwick were on terms of outward cordiality, and a marriage between the Duke's daughter and the eldest son of his rival, which took place with much magnificence in the presence of the King, might have been expected to cement their friendship. But by October "carry-tales and flatterers," says one chronicler, had rendered harmony—even the semblance of harmony—impossible; or, as was more probable, Warwick, suspicious of the intention on the part of the Duke of regaining the direction of affairs, had determined to free himself once for all from the rivalry of the King's uncle. Somerset had again been lodged in the Tower, to leave it, this time, only for the scaffold.

158 On the question of his innocence or guilt there has been much discussion amongst historians, nor is it possible to enter at length into the question. The crimes of which he stood accused were of the blackest dye. "The good Duke," as the people still loved to call him, was charged with plotting to gain possession of the King's person, of contriving the murder of Warwick, now to be created Duke of Northumberland, of Northampton and Herbert, and was to be tried for treason and felony.

Many and various are the views taken as to the guilt of the late Protector. Mr. Tytler, most conscientious of historians, after a careful comparison of contemporary evidence, has decided in his favour. Others have come to a different conclusion. The balance of opinion appears to be on his side. His bearing throughout the previous summer had been that of an innocent man, who had nothing to fear from justice. But justice was hard to come by. His enemy was strong and relentless—"a competent lawyer, known soldier, able statesman"—and in each of these capacities he was seeking to bring a dangerous competitor to ruin. It was, says Fuller, almost like a struggle between a naked and an armed man.120 Yet, open-hearted and free from distrust as he is described, Somerset must have been aware of some part of his danger. His friends amongst the upper classes had ever been few and cold.159 The reformers, for whom he had done so much, had begun to indulge doubts of his zeal. Become possibly weary of persecution, he had tried to make a way for Gardiner to leave the prison in which he was languishing, and, alone of the Council, had been in favour of permitting to Mary the exercise of her religion. These facts were sufficient, in the eyes of many, to justify the assertion made by Burgoyne to Calvin that he had grown lukewarm, and had scarcely anything less at heart than religion.

He was naturally the last to hear of the intrigues against him, and of the accusations brought in his absence from the Council-chamber. An attempt, it is true, was made to warn him by Lord Chancellor Rich, by means of a letter containing an account of the proceedings which had taken place; but, carelessly addressed only "To the Duke," it was delivered, by a blunder of the Chancellor's servant, to Norfolk, Somerset's enemy. Surprised at the speedy return of his messenger, Rich inquired where he had found "the Duke."

"In the Charter House," was the reply, "on the same token that he read it at the window and smiled thereat."

"But the Lord Rich," adds Fuller, in telling the story, "smiled not"; resigning his post on the following day, on the plea of old age and a desire to gain leisure to attend to his devotions, and thereby escaping the dismissal which would have160 resulted from a betrayal of the secrets of the Council.121

By October 14 the Duke was cognisant to some extent of the mischief that was a-foot, for it is stated in the King's journal that he sent for the Secretary Cecil "to tell him that he suspected some ill. Mr. Cecil answered that, if he were not guilty, he might be of good courage; if he were, he had nothing to say but to lament him." It was not an encouraging reply to an appeal for sympathy and support, and must have been an earnest of the attitude likely to be adopted towards the Duke by the rest of his colleagues. Two days later Edward's journal notes his apprehension.

The issue of the struggle was nevertheless uncertain. In spite of his unpopularity amongst the nobles, and though, to judge by the entries in the royal diary, the course of events was followed by his nephew with cold indifference, Somerset was not without his partisans. Constant to their old affection, the attack upon him was watched by the common people with breathless interest, accentuated by the detestation universally felt for the man who had planned his destruction. Hatred for Northumberland joined hands with love for Somerset to range them on his side. The political atmosphere was charged with excitement. Could it be true that the "good Duke" had designed the murder of his rival,161 who, whatever might be thought of him in other respects, was one of the chief props of Protestantism? Had the King, as some alleged, been in danger? The trial would show; and when it became known that the prisoner had been acquitted of treason, and the axe was therefore, according to custom, carried out of court, his cause was considered to be won; a cry arose that the innocence of the popular favourite had been established, and the applause of the crowd testified to their rejoicing. It had been premature. Acquitted of the principal offence with which he stood charged, he was found guilty of felony, and sentenced to death.

The verdict was received with ominous murmurs, and, in a letter to Bullinger, Ulmis states that, observing the grave and sorrowful aspect of the audience, the Duke of Northumberland was wary enough to take his cue from it, and to attempt to propitiate in his own favour the discontented crowd.

"O Duke of Somerset," he exclaimed from his seat, "you see yourself brought into the utmost danger, and that nothing but death awaits you. I have once before delivered you from a similar hazard of your life; and I will not now desist from serving you, how little soever you may expect it." Let Somerset appeal to the royal clemency, and Northumberland, forgiving him his offences, would do all in his power to save him.122

162 Northumberland's tardy magnanimity fails to carry conviction. But, besides his victim's popularity in the country, it was reported that the "King took it not in good part," and it was thought well to delay the execution, by which means his supplanter might gain credit for exercising his generosity by an attempt to avert his doom. Christmas

was at hand, and it was arranged that the Duke should remain in prison, under sentence of death, whilst the feast was celebrated at Court.

In spite of the assertion that the young King had not been unaffected by a tragedy that should have touched him closely, there is nothing in his own words to indicate any other attitude than that of the indifferent spectator—an attitude recalling unpleasantly the callousness shown by his father as the women he had loved and the statesmen he had trusted and employed were successively sent to the block. Though, in justice to Edward, it should be remembered that he had never loved his uncle, there is something revolting in his casual mention of the measures adopted against him.

"Little has been done since you went," he wrote to Barnaby Fitzpatrick, the comrade of his childish days, now become his favourite, "but the Duke of Somerset's arraignment for felonious treason and the muster of the newly erected gendarmery;"[123] and the journal wherein he traces the progress of the[163] trial, varying the narrative by the introduction of other topics, such as the visit of the Queen-Dowager of Scotland and the festivities in her honour, conveys a similar impression of coldness. "And so he was adjudged to be hanged," he records in conclusion, noting, with no expression of regret, the result of the proceedings.

"It were well that he should die," Edward had told the Duke's brother in those earlier childish days when incited by the Admiral to rebel against the strictness of the discipline enforced by the Protector. But, under the mask of indifference, it may be that misgivings awoke and made themselves apparent to those who, watching him closely, feared that ties of blood might vindicate their strength, and that at their bidding, or through compassion, he might interpose to avert the fate of one of the only near relations who remained to him. It appears to have been determined that the King's mind must be diverted from the subject; and whilst the prisoner was awaiting in the Tower the execution of his sentence, special merry-makings were arranged by the men who had the direction of affairs at Greenwich, where the court was to keep Christmas. Thus it was hoped to "remove the fond talk out of men's mouths," and to recreate and refresh the troubled spirits of the young sovereign. A Lord of Misrule was accordingly appointed, who, dubbed the Master of the King's Pastimes, took order for the general[164] amusement, though conducting himself more discreetly than had been the wont of his predecessors, and the festival was gaily observed. By these means, says Holinshed, the minds and ears of murmurers were well appeased, till it was thought well to proceed to the business of executing judgment upon the Duke.

In whatever light the ghastly contrast between the uncle awaiting a bloody death in the Tower and the noisy merry-making intended to drown the sound of the passing-bell in the nephew's ears may strike students of a later day, it is likely that there was nothing in it to affect painfully those who joined in the proceedings. Life was little considered. Men were daily accustomed to witness violent reverses of fortune. The Duke had aimed over-high; he was a danger to rivals whose turn it was to rise; he must make way for others. He had moreover been too deeply injured to forgive; and, to make all safe, he must die. The reign of the Seymours was at an end; that of Northumberland was beginning. Two more years and their supplanter, with Suffolk and his other adherents, would in their turn have paid the penalty of a great ambition, and, "with the sons of the Duke of Somerset standing by," would have followed the Lord Protector to the grave.

There was none to prophesy their fate. Had it been otherwise, it is not probable that a warning[165] would have turned them from their purpose. For they were reckless gamblers, and to foretell ruin to a man who is staking his all upon a throw of the dice is to speak to deaf ears.

So the merry Christmas passed, Jane—third in succession to the throne—occupying a prominent position at Court. And Aylmer, fearful lest the fruits of his care should be squandered, looked on helplessly, and besought Bullinger, on that 23rd of December, to set a limit, for the benefit of a pupil in danger, to the attention lawfully to be bestowed on the world and its vanities; a letter from Haddon, the Duke's chaplain, following fast and betraying his participation in the anxieties of his colleague by an entreaty that, from afar, the eminent divine would continue to exercise a beneficent influence upon his master's daughter.

Meantime the day had arrived when it was considered safe to carry matters against the King's uncle to extremities, and on January 23, six weeks after his trial, the Duke of Somerset was taken to Tower Hill, to suffer death in the presence of a vast crowd there assembled.

Till the last moment the throng had persisted in hoping against hope that the life of the man they loved might even now, at the eleventh hour, be spared; and at one moment it seemed that they were not to be disappointed. The Duke had taken his place upon the scaffold, and had begun166 his speech, when an interruption occurred, occasioned, as it afterwards proved, by an accidental collision between the mass of spectators and a body of troops who had received orders to be present at the execution, and, finding themselves late, had ridden hard and fast to make up for lost time. This was the simple explanation of the occurrence; but, to the excited mob gathered together, every nerve strained and full of pity and fear and horror, the sound of the thundering hoofs seemed something supernatural and terrible. Was it a sign of divine interposition?

"Suddenly," recounts an eye-witness, "suddenly came a wondrous fear upon the people ... by a great sound which appeared unto many above in the element as it had been the sound of gunpowder set on fire in a close house bursting out, and by another sound upon the ground as it had been the sight of a great number of great horses running on the people to overrun them; so great was the sound of this that the people fell down one upon the other, many with bills; and other ran this way, some that way, crying aloud, 'Jesus, save us! Jesus, save us!' Many of the people crying, 'This way they come, that way they come, away, away.' And I looked where one or other should strike me on the head, so I was stonned [stunned?]. The people being thus amazed, espies Sir Anthony Brown upon a little nag riding towards the scaffold, and therewith167 burst out crying in a voice, 'Pardon, pardon, pardon!' hurling up their caps and cloaks with these words, saying, 'God save the King! God save the King!' The good Duke all the while stayed, and, with his cap in his hand, waited for the people to come together."124

Whatever had been Sir Anthony's errand, it had not been one of mercy; and when the excitement following upon the panic was calmed the doomed man and the crowd were alike aware that the people had been misled by hope, and that no pardon had been brought. It is at such a moment that a man's mettle is shown. With admirable dignity Somerset bore the blow. As for a moment he had participated in the expectation of the cheering throng the colour had flickered over his face; but, recovering himself at once, he resumed his interrupted speech.

"Beloved friends," he said, "there is no such matter as you vainly hope and believe." Let the people accept the will of God, be quiet as he was quiet, and yield obedience to King and Council. A few minutes more and all was over. Somerset, in the words of a chronicler, had taken his death very patiently—with the strange patience in which the victims of injustice scarcely ever failed; the crowd, true to the last to their faith, pressing forward to dip their handkerchiefs in his blood, as in that of a martyr.

168 The laconic entry in the King's journal, to the effect that the Duke of Somerset had had his head cut off on Tower Hill, presents a sharp contrast to the popular emotion and grief. The deed was, at all events, done; Northumberland had cleared his most formidable competitor from his path, and had no suspicion that the tragedy of that winter's day was in truth paving the way for his own ultimate undoing.

From a photo by Emery Walker after a painting in the National Portrait Gallery.
EDWARD SEYMOUR, DUKE OF SOMERSET, K.G.
169
CHAPTER XIII
1552
Northumberland and the King—Edward's illness—Lady Jane and Mary—Mary refused permission to practise her religion—The Emperor intervenes.

For the moment master of the field, Northumberland addressed himself sedulously to the task of strengthening and consolidating the position he had won. In the Council he had achieved predominance, but the King's minority would not last for ever, and the necessity of laying the foundation of a power that should continue when Edward's nominal sovereignty should have become a real one was urgent.

The lad was growing up; nor were there wanting moments causing those around him to look on with disquietude to the day when the nobles ruling in his name might be called upon to give an account of their stewardship. A curious anecdote tells how, as Northumberland stood one day watching the King practising the art of archery, the boy put a "sharp jest" upon him, not without its significance.

"Well aimed, my liege," said the Duke merrily, as the arrow hit the white.

170 "But you aimed better," retorted the lad, "when you shot off the head of my uncle Somerset."125

It was a grim and ominous pleasantry, and in the direct charge it contained of responsibility for the death of Edward's nearest of kin another shaft besides the arrow may have been sent home. The Tudors were not good at forgiving. Even had the King seen the death of the Duke's rival and victim without regret, it was possible that he would none the less owe a grudge to the man to whom it was due; nor was Northumberland without a reason for anticipating with uneasiness the day when Edward, remembering all, should hold the reins of Government in his own hands.

Under these circumstances it was clearly his interest to commend himself to the young sovereign, and the system he pursued with regard to his education and training were carefully adapted to that purpose. Whilst the Protector had had the arrangement of affairs, his nephew had been kept closely to his studies; Northumberland, "a soldier at heart and by profession, had him taught to ride and handle his weapons," the boy welcoming the change, and, though not neglecting his books, taking pleasure in every form of bodily exercise;126 not without occasional pangs of conscience, when171 more time had been spent in pastime than he "thought convenient."

"We forget ourselves," he would observe, finding fault with himself sententiously in royal phrase, upon such occasions, "that should not lose substantia pro accidente."127

It had been the Protector's custom to place little money at his nephew's disposal, thus rendering him comparatively straitened in the means of exercising the liberality befitting his position; and part of the boy's liking for the Admiral had been owing to the gifts contrasting with the niggardliness of the elder brother. Profiting by his predecessor's mistakes, Northumberland's was a different policy. He supplied Edward freely with gold, encouraged him to make presents, and to show himself a King; acquainting him besides with public business, and flattering him by asking his opinion upon such matters.128

The Duke might have spared his pains. It was not by Edward that he was to be called to account. But at that time there were no signs to indicate how futile was the toil of those who were seeking to build their fortunes upon his favour. A well-grown, handsome lad, his health had given no special cause for anxiety up to the spring of 1552. In the March of that year,172 however, a sharp and complicated attack of illness laid him low and sowed the seeds of future delicacy.

"I fell sick of the smallpox and the measles," recorded the boy in his diary. "April 15th the Parliament broke up because I was sick and unable to go abroad."

To us, who read the laconic entry in the light thrown upon it by future events, it marks the beginning of the end—not only the end of the King's short life, but the beginning of the drama in which many other actors were to be involved and were to meet their doom. As yet none of the anxious watchers suspected that death had set his broad arrow upon the lad; and in the summer he had so far recovered as to be sending a blithe account to Barnaby Fitzpatrick, then in France, of a progress he had made in the country, and its attendant enjoyments. Whilst his old playfellow had been occupied in killing his enemies, and sore skirmishing and divers assaults, the King had been killing wild beasts, having pleasant journeys and good fare, viewing fair countries, and seeking rather to fortify his own than to spoil another man's129—so he wrote gaily to Fitzpatrick.

Meantime his illness, with the dissolution of Parliament consequent upon it, had probably emptied London; the Suffolk family, with others, returning to their country home. In July Lady173 Jane was on a visit to her cousin, the Princess Mary, at Newhall; when, once more, an indiscreet speech—a scoff, on this occasion, directed against the outward tokens of that Catholic faith to which Mary was so vehemently loyal—may, repeated to her hostess, have served to irritate her towards the offender against the rules of courtesy and good taste. Under other circumstances, it might have been passed over by the older woman with a smile; but subjected to annoyance and petty persecution by reason of her religion and saddened and embittered by illness and misfortune, the trifling instance of ill-manners on the part of a malapert child of fifteen may have had its share in accentuating a latent antagonism.

In the course of the previous year a controversy had reached its height which had been more or less imminent since the statute enjoining the use of the new Prayer-book had been passed, a work said to have afforded the King—then eleven years of age— "great comfort and quietness of mind." From that time forward—the decree had become law in 1549—there had been trouble in the royal family, as might be expected when opinion on vital points of religion, the burning question of the day, was widely and violently divergent, and friends and advisers were ever at hand to fan the flame of discord in their own interest or that of their party.

174 No one could be blind to the fact that the ardent Catholicism of the Princess Mary, next in succession to the throne, constituted a standing menace to the future of religion as recently by law established, and to the durability of the work hastily carried through in creating a new Church on a new basis. Furthermore it was considered that her present attitude of open and determined opposition to the decree passed by Parliament was a cause of scandal in the realm. It was certainly one of annoyance to the King and Council.

Cranmer would probably have liked to keep the peace. An honest man, but no fanatic and holding moderate views, he might have been inclined, having got what he personally wanted, to adopt a policy of conciliation. Affairs had gone well with him; his friends were in power; and, if he failed to inspire the foreign divines and their English disciples with entire trust, it was admitted in 1550 by John Stumpius, of that school, that things had been put upon a right footing. "There is," he added, "the greatest hope as to religion, for the Archbishop of Canterbury has lately married a wife."130

Matters being thus comfortably arranged, Cranmer, if he had had his way, might have preferred to leave them alone. But what could one man do in the interests of peace, when Churchmen and laity were175 alike clamouring for war, when the King's Council were against the concession of any one point at issue, and the King himself had composed, before he was twelve years old, and "sans l'aide de personne vivant," a treatise directed against the supremacy of the Pope? To the honour of the King's counsellors, few victims had suffered the supreme penalty during his reign on account of their religious opinions;131 but Gardiner and Bonner, as well as Bishops Day and Heath, were in prison, and if the lives of the adherents of the ancient faith were spared, no other mitigation of punishment or indulgence was to be expected by them.

Under pressure from the Emperor the principal offender had been at first granted permission to continue the practice of her religion. But when peace with France rendered a rupture with Charles a less formidable contingency than before, it was decided that renewed efforts should be made to compel the Princess Mary to bow to the fiat of King and Council. Love of God and affection for his sister forbade her brother, he declared, to tolerate her obstinacy longer, the intimation being accompanied by an offer of teachers who should instruct her ignorance and refute her errors.

Mary was a match for both King and Council. In an interview with the Lords she told them that176 her soul was God's, and that neither would she change her faith nor dissemble her opinions; the Council replying by a chilling intimation that her faith was her own affair, but that she must obey like a subject, not rule like a sovereign. The Princess, however, had a card to play unsuspected by her adversaries. The dispute had taken place on August 18. On the 19th the Council was unpleasantly surprised by a strong measure on the part of the imperial ambassador, in the shape of a declaration of war in case his master's cousin was not permitted the exercise of her religion.

The Council were in a difficulty. War with the Emperor, at that moment, and without space for preparation, would have been attended with grave inconvenience. On the other hand Edward's tender conscience had outrun that of his ministers, and had become so difficult to deal with that all the persuasions of the Primate and two other Bishops were needed to convince the boy, honest and zealous in his intolerance, that "to suffer or wink at [sin] for a time might be borne, so all haste possible was used."

A temporising answer was therefore returned to the imperial ambassador, "all haste possible" being made in removing English stores from Flanders, so that, in case of a rupture, they might not fall into Charles's hands. This accomplished, fresh and stringent measures were taken177 to compel the Princess's obedience; her chief chaplain was committed to the Tower, charged with having celebrated Mass in his mistress's house, and three of the principal officers of her household were sent to join him there as a punishment for declining to use coercion to prevent a recurrence of the offence.

An interview followed between Mary and a deputation of members of the Council, who visited her with the object of enforcing the King's orders. The Princess received her guests with undisguised impatience; requested them to be brief; and, having listened to what they had to say, answered shortly that she would lay her head upon a block—no idle rhetoric in those days—sooner than use any other form of service than that in use at her father's death; when her brother was of full age she was ready to obey his commands, but at present—good, sweet King!—he could not be a judge in such matters. Her chaplains, for the rest, could do as they pleased in the matter of saying Mass, "but none of your new service shall be used in my house, or I will not tarry in it."

Thus the controversy practically ended. The Council dared not proceed to extremities against the Emperor's cousin, and tacitly agreed to let her alone, having supplied her with one more bitter memory to add to the account which was to be lamentably settled in the near future.

178

CHAPTER XIV

1552

Lady Jane's correspondence with Bullinger—Illness of the Duchess of Suffolk—Haddon's difficulties—Ridley's visit to Princess Mary—the English Reformers—Edward fatally ill—Lady Jane's character and position.

The removal of the two Seymour brothers, whilst it had left Northumberland predominant, had also increased the importance of the Duke of Suffolk. Both by reason of the position he personally filled, and owing to his connection, through his wife, with the King, he was second to none in the State save the man to whom Somerset's fall was due and who had succeeded to his power. He shared Northumberland's prominence, as he was afterwards to share his ruin; and, as one of the chief props of Protestantism, he and his family continued to be objects of special interest to the divines of that persuasion, foreign and English.

Lady Jane, as before, was in communication with the learned Bullinger, and in the same month—July 1552—that her visit had been paid to the Princess Mary she was sending him another letter, dated from Bradgate, expressing her gratitude for the "great friendship he desired to establish between them, and acknowledging his many favours." After179 a second perusal of his latest letter—since a single one had not contented her—the benefit derived from it had surpassed that to be obtained from the best authors, and in studying Hebrew she meant to pursue the method he recommended.

In August more pressing interests must have taken the place of study, for at Richmond in Surrey her mother was attacked by a sickness threatening at one time to prove fatal.

"This shall be to advertise you," wrote the Duchess's husband, hastily summoned from London, to Cecil, "that my sudden departing from the Court was for that I had received letters of the state my wife was in, who I assure you is more liker to die than to live. I never saw a sicker creature in my life than she is. She hath three diseases.... These three being enclosed in one body, it is to be feared that death must needs follow. By your most assured and loving cousin, who, I assure you, is not a little troubled."

His anxiety was soon relieved. The Duchess was not only to outlive, but, in her haste to replace him, was to show little respect for his memory. She must quickly have got the better of her present threefold disorder, for in the course of the same month a letter was sent from Richmond by James Haddon, the domestic chaplain, to Bullinger, making no mention of any cause of uneasiness as to the physical condition of his master's wife. He was preoccupied by other matters, disquieted by scruples180 of conscience, and glad to unburthen himself to the universal referee with regard to certain difficulties attending his position in the Duke's household.

It was true that he might have hesitated to communicate the fears and misgivings by which he was beset to a guide at so great a distance, had not John ab Ulmis—who, as portrayed by these letters, was somewhat of a busybody, eager to bring all his friends into personal relations, and above all to magnify the authority and importance of his master in spiritual things—just come in and encouraged him to write, stating that it would give Bullinger great satisfaction to be informed of the condition of religion in England, and likewise—a more mundane curiosity—of that of the Suffolk household. Entering into a description of both, therefore, in a missive containing some three thousand words, Haddon fully detailed the sorrows and perplexities attending the exercise of the office of chaplain, even in the most orthodox and pious of houses.

After dealing with the first and important subject of religion at large, he proceeded to treat of the more complicated question—the condition of the ducal household, and especially the duties attaching to his own post.

Of the general regulation of the house, Ulmis, he said, was more capable than he of giving an account. It was rather to be desired that Bullinger should point out the method he would recommend. But[181] upon one point Haddon was anxious to obtain the advice of so eminent a counsellor, and he went on to explain at length the case of conscience by which he had been troubled. This was upon the question of the lawfulness or unlawfulness of conniving, by silence, at the practice of gambling.

The situation was this. The Duke and Duchess had strictly forbidden the members of their household to play at cards or dice for money. So far they had the entire approval of their chaplain. But—and here came in Haddon's cause of perplexity—the Duke himself and his most honourable lady, with their friends—perhaps, too, their daughter, though there is no mention of her—not only claimed a right to play in their private apartments, but also to play for money. The divergence between precept and practice— common in all ages—was grievous to the chaplain, weighted with the responsibility for the spiritual and moral welfare of the whole establishment, from his "patron" the Duke, down to the lowest of the menials. At wearisome and painstaking length he recapitulated the arguments he was wont to employ in his remonstrances against the gambling propensities he deplored, retailing, as well, the arguments with which the offenders met them. "In this manner and to this effect," he says, "the dispute is often carried on."

During the past months matters had reached a climax. As late as up to the previous Christmas he[182] had confined himself to administering private rebukes; but, perceiving that his words had taken no effect, he had forewarned the culprits that a public reprimand would follow a continued disregard of his monitions. Upon this he had been relieved to perceive that there had been for a time a cessation of the reprehensible form of amusement, and had cherished a hope that all would be well. It had been a vain one. Christmas had come round—the season marked by mummeries and wickedness of every kind, when persons especially served the devil in imitation, as it seemed, of the ancient Saturnalia; and though this was happily not the case in the Suffolk family, Duke and Duchess had joined in the general backsliding to the extent of returning to their old evil habit. Such being the case, Haddon had felt that he had no choice but to carry out his threat.

In his Christmas sermon he had taken occasion to administer a reproof as to the general fashion of keeping the feast, including in his rebuke, "though in common and general terms," those who played cards for money. No one in the household was at a loss to fix upon the offenders at whom the shaft was directed. The Duke's servants, if they followed his example, took care never to be detected in so doing; and, accepting the reprimand as addressed to themselves, the Duke and Duchess took it in bad part, arguing that Haddon would have performed all that duty required of him by a private remonstrance.[183] From that time, offence having been given by his plain speech, the chaplain had returned to his old custom of administering only private rebukes; thus conniving, in a measure, at the practice he condemned, lest loss of influence in matters of greater moment should follow. "I bear with it," he sighed, "as a man who holds a wolf by the ears." Conscience was, however, uneasy, and he begged Bullinger to advise in the matter and to determine how far such concessions might be lawfully made.

Looking impartially at the question, it says much for the Duke's good temper and toleration that the worthy Haddon continued to fill his post, and that when, a few months later, he was promoted to be Dean of Exeter, he wrote that the affection between himself and his master was so strong that the connection would even then not be altogether severed.132 His attitude is a curious and interesting example of the position and status of a chaplain in his day, being wholly that of a dependant, and yet carrying with it duties and rights strongly asserted on the one side and not disallowed upon the other.

The Duchess, having recovered from her illness, had taken her three daughters to visit their cousin Mary, and when the younger children were sent home Jane remained behind at St. John's, Clerkenwell, the London dwelling of the Princess, until her father came to fetch wife and daughter away. That the184 whole family had been thus entertained indicates that they were at this time on a friendly footing with the Princess. But though the Duke of Suffolk was doubtless alive to the necessity of maintaining amicable relations, so far as it was possible, with his wife's cousin and the next heir to the crown, it must have been no easy matter, at a time when party spirit ran so high, for one of the chief recognised supporters of Protestantism to continue on terms of cordiality with the head and hope of the Catholic section of the nation. Mary was not becoming more conciliatory in her bearing as time went on, and an account of a visit paid her by Ridley, now Bishop of London in place of Bonner, deprived and in prison, is illustrative of her present attitude.

From a photo by Emery Walker after a painting by Joannes Corvus in the National Portrait Gallery.
PRINCESS MARY, AT THE AGE OF TWENTY-EIGHT.

It was to Hunsdon that, in the month of September, Ridley came to pay his respects to the King's sister, cherishing, it may be, a secret hope that where King and Council had failed, he might succeed; and his courteous reception by the officers of her household was calculated to encourage his sanguine anticipations. Mary too, when, at eleven o'clock, he was admitted to her presence, conversed with her guest right pleasantly for a quarter of an hour, telling him that she remembered the time when he had acted as chaplain to her father, and inviting him to stay to dinner. It was not until after the meal was ended that the Bishop unfolded the true object of his visit.185 It was not one of simple courtesy; he had come, he said, to do his duty by her as her diocesan, and to preach before her on the following Sunday.

If Mary prepared for battle, she answered at first with quiet dignity. It was observed that she flushed; her response, however, was merely to bid him "make the answer to that himself." When, refusing to take the hint, the Bishop continued to urge his point, she spoke more plainly.

"I pray you, make the answer (as I have said) to this matter yourself," she repeated, "for you know the answer well enough. But if there be no remedy but I must make you answer, this shall be your answer: the door of the parish church adjoining shall be open for you if you come, and you may preach if you list; but neither I nor any of mine shall hear you."

To preach to an empty church, or to a handful of country yokels, would not have answered the episcopal purpose; and Ridley was plainly losing his temper.

He hoped, he said, she would not refuse to hear God's word. The Princess answered with a scoff. She did not know what they now called God's word; she was sure it was not the same as in her father's time—to whom, it will be remembered, the Bishop had been chaplain.

The dispute was becoming heated. God's word, Ridley retorted, was the same at all times, but had been better understood and practised in some ages than in others. To this Mary replied by a186 personal thrust. He durst not, she told him, for his ears, have avowed his present faith in King Henry's time; then—asking a question to which she must have known the answer—was he of the Council? she demanded. The inquiry was probably intended as a reminder that his rights did not extend to interference with the King's sister, as well as to elicit, as it did, the confession that he held no such post.

"You might well enough, as the Council goeth nowadays," observed Mary carelessly; proceeding, at parting, to thank the Bishop for his gentleness in coming to see her, "but for your offering to preach before me I thank you never a whit."

In the presence of his hostess the discomfited guest appears to have kept his temper under control, but, having duly drunk of the stirrup cup presented to him by her steward, Sir Thomas Wharton, he gave free expression to his sentiments.

"Surely I have done amiss," he said, looking "very sadly," and explaining, in answer to Wharton's interrogation, that he had erred in having drunk under a roof where God's word was rejected. He should rather have shaken the dust off his feet for a testimony against the house and departed instantly, he told the listeners assembled to speed him on his way—whose hair, says Heylyn, in relating this story, stood on end with his denunciations.133

187 If scenes of this kind were not adapted to promote good feeling between belligerents in high places, neither was the spirit of the dominant party in the country one to conciliate opposition. It is not easy, as the figures of the English pioneers of Protestantism pass from time to time across the stage, in these years of their first triumph, to do them full justice. To judge a man by one period of his life, whether it is youth or manhood or old age, is scarcely fairer than to pronounce upon the colour and pattern of an eastern carpet, only one square yard of it being visible. The adherents of the new faith are here necessarily represented in a single phase, that of prosperity. At the top of the wave, they are seen at their worst, assertive, triumphant, intolerant and self-satisfied, the bull-dogs of the Reformation, only withheld by the leash from worrying their fallen antagonist. Thus, for the most part, they appear in Edward's reign. And yet these men, a year or two later, were many of them capable of an undaunted courage, an impassioned belief in the common Lord of Protestant and Catholic, and a power of endurance, which have graven their names upon the national roll-call of heroes.

Meantime, more and more, the King's precarious health was suggestive of disturbing contingencies. It may be that, as some assert, his uncle's death, once become irrevocable, had preyed upon his spirits—that he "mourned, and soon missed the life of his188 Protector, thus unexpectedly taken away, who, now deprived of both uncles, howsoever the time were passed with pastimes, plays and shows, to drive away dumps, yet ever the remembrance of them sat so near his heart that lastly he fell sick...."134 But though it is possible that, as his strength declined, matters he had taken lightly weighed upon his spirits, it is not necessary to seek other than natural and constitutional causes for a failure of health. That failure must have filled many hearts with forebodings.

There had been no attempt hitherto to ignore or deny the position occupied by Mary as next heir to the throne. When, at the New Year, she visited her brother, the honours rendered to her were a recognition of her rights, and the Northumberlands and Suffolks occupied a foremost place amongst the "vast throng" who rode with her through the city or met her at the palace gate and brought her to the presence-chamber of the King. Before the next New Year's Day came round Edward was to be in his grave; Mary would fill his place; and the little cousin Jane, now spending a gay Christmas with her father's nephews and wards, the young Willoughbys, at Tylsey, would be awaiting her doom in the Tower.

The shadow was already darkening over the King. It is said that the seeds of his malady had189 been sown by over-heating in his sports, during the progress of which he had sent so joyous an account to Fitzpatrick.135 Soon after his sister's visit he caught a bad cold, and unfavourable symptoms appeared. He had, however, youth in his favour, and few at first anticipated how speedy would be the end. Vague disquiet nevertheless quickly passed into definite alarm. In February the patient's condition was such that Northumberland, who of all men had most at stake, summoned no less than six physicians, desiring them to institute an examination and to declare upon their oath, first, whether they considered the King's disease mortal, and, if so, how long he was likely to live. The reply made by the doctors was that the malady was incurable, and that the patient might live until the following September.136 Northumberland had obtained his answer; it was for him to take measures accordingly.

In March Edward's last Parliament met and ended. "The King being a little diseased by cold-taking," recorded a contemporary chronicle,137 "it was not meet for his Grace to ride to Westminster in the air,"138 and on the 31st—it was Good Friday—the Upper House waited upon him at Whitehall, Edward in his royal robes receiving the Lords190 Spiritual and Temporal. At seven that evening Parliament was dissolved.

Many hearts, loyal and true and pitiful, will have grieved at the signs of their King's decay. But to Northumberland, watching them with the keenness lent by personal interest, personal ambition, and possibly by a consciousness of personal peril, they must have afforded absorbing matter of preoccupation. The exact time at which the designs by which the Duke trusted to turn the boy's death to his advantage rather than to his ruin took definite shape and form must remain to some extent undetermined—his plans were probably decided by the verdict given by the doctors in February; it is certain that in the course of the spring they were elaborated, and that in them Lady Jane Grey, ignorant and unsuspicious, was a factor of primary importance. She was to be the figure-head of the Duke's adventurous vessel.

The precise date of her birth is not known, but she was now in her sixteenth or seventeenth year—a sorrowful one for her and for all she loved. Childhood was a thing she had left behind; she was touching upon her brief space of womanhood; a few months later and that too would be over; she would have paid the penalty for the schemes and ambitions of others.

The eulogies of her panegyrists have, as a natural effect of extravagant praise, done in some sort an191 injury to this little white saint of the English Reformation. We do not readily believe in miracles; nor do infant prodigies either in the sphere of morals or attainments attract us. Yet, setting aside the tragedy of her end, there is something that appeals for pity in the very precocity upon which her contemporaries are fond of dwelling, testifying as it does to a wasted childhood, to a life robbed of its natural early heritage of carelessness and grace. To have had so short a time to spend on the green earth, and to have squandered so large a portion of it amongst dusty folios, and in the acquirement of learning; to have pored over parchments while sun and air, flowers and birds and beasts—all that should make the delight of a child's life, the pageant of a child's spring, was passed by as of no account; further, to have grown up versed in the technicalities of barren theological debate, the simple facts of Christ's religion overlaid and obscured by the bitterness of professional controversialists,—almost every condition of her brief existence is an appeal for compassion, and Jane, from her blood-stained grave, cries out that she had not only been robbed of life by her enemies, but of a childhood by her friends.

To a figure defaced by flattery and adulation, whose very virtues and gifts were made to minister to party ends, it is difficult to restore the original brightness and beauty which nevertheless belonged to it. But here and there in the pages of the192 Italian evangelist, Michel Angelo Florio, who was personally acquainted with her, pictures are to be found which, drawn with tender touches, set the girl more vividly before us than is done by the stilted commendations of English devotees or German doctors of theology. Many times, he says—times when it may be hoped she had forgotten that there were opponents to be argued with or heretics to be convinced or doctrinal subtleties to be set forth—she would speak of the Word of God and almost preach it to those who served her;139 and Florio himself, recounting the indignities and insults he had suffered by reason of his opinions, had seen her weep with pity, so that he well knew how much she had true religion at heart.140

Her attendants, too—in days when her melancholy end had caused each trifling incident to be treasured like a relic by those to whom she had been dear—related that she did not esteem rank or wealth or kingdom worth a straw in comparison with the knowledge God had granted to her of His only Son.141 It must be remembered that in no long time she was to give proof, by her fashion of meeting death, that these phrases were no repetition of a lesson learned by rote, no empty and conventional form of words, but the true and sincere confession of a living faith.

193

CHAPTER XV

1553

The King dying—Noailles in England—Lady Jane married to Guilford Dudley—Edward's will—Opposition of the law officers—They yield—The King's death.

The King was becoming rapidly worse, and as his malady increased upon him, strange suspicions were afloat amongst the people, their hatred to Northumberland giving its colour to their explanation of the situation. He himself, or those upon whom he could count, were ever with the sick boy, and hints were uttered—as was sure to be the case—of poison. For this, murmured the populace, had the King's uncles been removed, his faithful nobles disgraced; and the condition of public opinion caused the Duke, alarmed at its hostility, to publish it abroad that Edward was better.142

In May a rally appears to have in fact taken place, giving rise in some quarters to false hopes of recovery, and Mary wrote to offer her congratulations to her brother upon the improvement in his health. On May 13 the new French ambassador, Noailles, whose audience had been deferred from day to day, was informed by the Council that their master was194 so much better that he would doubtless be admitted to the royal presence in the course of a few days. The doctors told a different story, and Noailles believed the doctors. A diplomatist himself, he knew the uses of lying perhaps too well to condemn it severely. That the King was dying was practically certain, and though those whose object it was to conceal the fact lest measures should be concerted to ensure the succession of the rightful heir, might do their best to disguise the fact, the truth must become known before long.

Meantime the French envoy, in the interest of the reformed party in England—not by reason of their religion, but as opposed to Mary, the Emperor's cousin—was quite willing to play into Northumberland's hands, and to assist him in the work of spreading abroad the report that the King's malady was yielding to treatment. He and his colleagues were accordingly conducted to an apartment near to the presence-chamber, where they were left for a certain time alone, in order to convey the impression that they had been personally received by the sovereign. Some days later it was confessed, but as a peril past, that Edward had been seriously ill. He was then stated to be out of danger, and the ambassadors were admitted to his presence, finding him very weak, and coughing much.143

195 The rally had been of short duration. Hope of recovery had, in truth, been abandoned; and those it concerned so intimately were forced to face the situation to be created by his death. It was a situation momentous alike to men whose fortunes had been staked upon the young King's life, and to others honestly and sincerely solicitous regarding the welfare of the realm and the consequences to the new religion should his eldest sister succeed to the throne.

Every one of the Lords of the Council and officers of the Crown, with almost all the Bishops, save those who had suffered captivity and deprivation, had personal reasons for apprehension. Scarcely a single person of influence or power could count upon being otherwise than obnoxious to the heir to the crown. That most of them would be displaced from their posts was to be expected. Some at least must have felt that property and life hung in the balance. But it was Northumberland who, as he had most to lose, had most to fear. The practical head of the State, and wielding a power little less than that of Somerset, he had amassed riches and offices to an amount bearing witness to his rapacity. In matters of religion he had been as strong, though less sincere, in his opposition to the Church claiming Mary's allegiance as his predecessor. During the preceding autumn the iconoclastic work of destruction had been carried on196 in the metropolitan Cathedral; the choir, where the high altar had been accustomed to stand, had been broken down and the stone-work destroyed.144 Gardiner and Bonner, who, as prominent sufferers for the Catholic cause, would have Mary's ear, were in prison. For all this Northumberland, with the King's Council as aiders and abettors, was responsible. Not a single claim could be advanced to the liking or toleration of the woman presently to become head of the State. If safety was to be ensured to the advisers of her brother, steps must be taken at once for that purpose. Northumberland and Suffolk set themselves to do so.

It was on May 18 that Noailles and his colleagues had been at length permitted to pay their respects to the sick boy. On Whitsunday, the 23rd—the date, though not altogether certain, is probable—three marriages were celebrated at Durham House, the London dwelling-place of the Duke of Northumberland. On that day the eldest daughter of the Duke of Suffolk became the wife of Lord Guilford Dudley, the Duke of Northumberland's fourth and, some say, favourite son; her sister Katherine was bestowed upon Lord Herbert, the earl of Pembroke's heir—to be repudiated by him the following year—and Lady Katherine Dudley, Northumberland's daughter, was married to Lord Hastings.144

The object of the threefold ceremony was clear.197 The main cause of it, and of the haste shown in carrying it through, was a dying boy, whose life was flickering out a few miles distant at Greenwich. It behoved his two most powerful subjects, Northumberland

and Suffolk, to strengthen their position as speedily as might be, and by this means it was hoped to accomplish that object.

The place chosen for the celebration of the weddings might have served—perhaps it did—to host and guests as a reminder of the perils of those who climbed too high. Durham House, appropriated in his days of prosperity by Somerset—to the indignation of Elizabeth, who laid claim to the property—had been forfeited to the Crown upon his attainder, and was the dwelling of his more fortunate rival; and, as if to drive the lesson further home, the very cloth of gold and silver lent from the royal coffers to deck the bridal party had been likewise drawn from the possessions of the ill-starred Duke. The dead furnished forth the festal array of the living.

That day, with its splendid ceremonial—the marriages took place with much magnificence in the presence of a great assembly, including the principal personages of the realm—presents a grim and striking contrast to what was to follow. None were present, so far as we know, with the eyes of a seer, to discern the thin red ring foretelling the proximate fate of the girl who played the most prominent part in it, or198 to recognise in death the presiding genius of the pageant. Yet the destiny said in old days to dog the steps of those doomed to a violent death and to be present at their side from the cradle to the grave must have stood by many, besides the bride, who joined in the proceedings on that Whitsunday. Where would Northumberland be that day year? or Suffolk? or young Guilford Dudley? or, a little later, the Bishop who tied the knots?

How Jane played her part we can only guess, or what she had thought of the arrangement, hurriedly concluded, by which her future was handed over to the keeping of her boy husband. Whether willing or unwilling, she had no choice but to obey, to accept the bridegroom chosen for her—a tall, handsome lad of seventeen or nineteen, it is not clear which—and to make the best of it. Rosso indeed, deriving his information from Michele, Venetian ambassador in London, and Bodoaro, Venetian ambassador to Charles V., states that after much resistance, urged by her mother and beaten by her father, she had consented to their wishes. It may have been true; and, standing at the altar, her thoughts may have wandered from the brilliant scene around her to the room at Greenwich, where the husband proposed for her in earlier days was dying. She might have been Edward's wife, had he lived. She can scarcely have failed to have been aware of the hopes and designs of her father, of those of the199 dead Admiral, and of others; she had, in a measure, been brought up in the expectation of filling a throne. But the plan was forgotten now. Edward was to be the husband neither of Jane nor of that other cousin, not of royal blood, the daughter of his sometime Protector, whose father was dead and mother in the Tower; nor yet of the foreign bride, well stuffed and jewelled, of whom he had himself bragged. He was dying, like any other boy of no royal race, upon whose life no momentous issues hung. From his sick-bed he had taken a keen interest in what was going forward, appearing, says Heylyn, as forward in the marriages as if he had been one of the principals in the plot against him.145 He might be fond of Jane, but even had he loved her—which there is nothing to show—he was too far within the shadow of the grave to feel any jealousy in seeing her handed over to another bridegroom.

At the demeanour of the little victim of the Whitsun sacrifice we can but guess. Grave and serious we picture her, as it was her wont to be, with the steadfast face depicted by the painters of the day—far, in spite of Seymour's boast, from being "as handsome as any lady in England," but with a purity and simplicity, a stillness and repose, restful to those who looked into the quiet eyes and marked the tranquillity of the countenance. Did she, in her inward cogitations, divine that there was danger200 ahead? If so we can fancy she was ready to face it. Were it God's will, then let it come. Peril was the anteroom, death the portal, of the eternal city—the heavenly Jerusalem in which she believed.

Such was the image printed upon the time by the woman-child who was never to know maturity, as it lived in the tender and loving remembrance of her contemporaries, the delicately sculptured figure of a saint in the temples of the iconoclasts.

From an engraving by George Noble after a painting by Holbein.
LADY JANE GREY.

By the country at large the sudden marriages were regarded with suspicion. "The noise of these marriages bred such amazement in the hearts of the common people, apt enough in themselves to speak the worst of Northumberland, that there was nothing left unsaid which might serve to show their hatred against him, or express their pity for the King."146 Overbearing and despotic, the merciless "bear of Warwick," as he was nicknamed, was so detested that by some the failure of his scheme was afterwards ascribed rather to his unpopularity than to love for Mary. Yet it was Northumberland who, with the blindness born of a sanguine ambition, was to trust, six weeks later, to the populace to join with him in dispossessing the King's sister, for whom they had always shown affection, and in placing his daughter-in-law and her boy-husband upon the throne. So glaring a misapprehension of the situation demands explanation, and it is partly201 supplied by a French appreciation of the Duke's character. According to M. Griffet, he was more heedful to conceal his own sentiments than capable of discerning those of others; a man of ambition who neither knew whom to trust nor whom to suspect; who, blinded by presumption, was therefore easily deceived, and who nevertheless believed himself to possess to the highest degree the gift of deceiving all the world.147 Such as he was, he had deceived himself to his undoing.

Meantime Lady Jane's marriage had made for the moment little change in her manner of life. She had answered the purpose for which she was required, and was permitted temporarily to retire behind the scenes. It is said—and there is nothing unlikely in the assertion—that, the ceremony over and obedience having been rendered to her parents' behest, she entreated that she might continue with her mother for the present. She and her new husband were so young, she pleaded. Her request was granted. She was Guilford Dudley's wife, could be the wife of no other man, and that was, for the moment, sufficient.

There was much to think of, much to do. Measures had to be taken to keep the King's sisters at a distance, lest his old affection, for Elizabeth in particular, reawakening might frustrate the designs of those bent upon moulding events to their202 advantage. Above all, there was the pressing necessity of inducing the King to exclude them by will from their rightful heritage. On June 16 Noailles had again been conferring with the doctors, and had learnt that, in their opinion, Edward could not live till August. Ten days later Northumberland came from Greenwich to visit the envoy, and to prevent his going to Court. He then told the Frenchman that, nine days earlier, the King had executed his will in favour of the Duke's daughter-in-law, Lady Jane148—"qui est vertueuse, sage, et belle," reported the envoy to his master some three weeks later.149

Of the manner in which the will had been obtained full information is available. It was not out of love for Northumberland that Edward had yielded to his representations. The Throckmorton MS.150 asserts that Edward abhorred the Duke on account of his uncle's death. Sir Nicholas Throckmorton, in attendance on the King, should be a good authority; on the other hand, he was opposed to the Duke's designs. Whether or not the latter was personally distasteful to the boy, it was no difficult matter to represent the situation in a fashion to lead him to believe the sole alternative was the course suggested to him. Conscientious, pious, scrupulous to a fault, and worn by disease,203 the future of religion could be made to hang upon his fiat, and the thought of Mary, a devout Catholic, or even Elizabeth, who might marry a foreign prince, seated upon the throne, filled him with apprehensions for the welfare of a people for whom he felt himself responsible. Yet he, with little to love, had loved both his sisters, and the thought of the sick lad, torn between duty and affection, a tool in the hands of unprincipled and ambitious men who could play on his sensitive conscience and over-strained nerves at will, and turn his piety to their advantage, is a painful one.

The Duke's arguments lay ready to his hand. Religion was in danger, the Church set up by Edward in jeopardy; the work that he had done might be destroyed as soon as he was in his grave. How could he answer it before God were he, who was able to avert it, to permit so great an evil? The remedy was clear. Let him pass over his sisters, already pronounced severally illegitimate by unrepealed statutes of Parliament, and entail the crown upon those who, under his father's will, would follow upon Mary and Elizabeth, the descendants of Mary Tudor, known to be firm in their attachment to the reformed faith.

Edward yielded. Given the circumstances, the power exercised by the Duke over him, his physical condition, his fears for religion, he could scarcely have done less. With his own hand he204 drew up the draft of a will which, amended at Northumberland's bidding, left the crown in unmistakable terms to Lady Jane and her heirs male. It had now to be made law and accepted by the Council.

On June 11 Sir Edward Montagu, Chief Justice of the Common Pleas, Sir Thomas Bromley, another Justice of the same court, Sir Richard Baker, Chancellor of the Augmentations, and the Attorney- and Solicitor-General were called to Greenwich, and were introduced into the King's apartment, Northampton, Gates, and others being present at the interview. If what took place on this occasion and at the other audiences of the legal officers with the King, as recorded by themselves, is naturally, as Dr. Lingard has pointed out, represented in such a manner as to extenuate their conduct in Mary's eyes, there seems no reason to doubt that Montagu's account is substantially true.151

In his sickness, Edward told them, he had considered the state of the realm, and of the succession, should he die without leaving direct heirs; and, proceeding to point out the danger to religion and to liberty should his sister Mary succeed to the throne, he ordered them to "make a book with speed" of his articles.

The lawyers demurred, but the King, feverishly eager to put an end to the business, and conscious205 perhaps that if the thing were not done quickly it might not be done at all, refused to listen to the objections they would have urged, dismissing them with orders to carry out his pleasure with haste. For all his gentleness and piety, Edward was a Tudor, and no less peremptory than others of his race.

Two days later—it was June 14—having deliberated on the question, the men of law acquainted the Council with their decision. The thing could not be done. To make or execute the "devise" according to the King's instructions would be treason. The report was made to Sir William Petre at Ely Place; but the Duke of Northumberland was at hand, and came thereupon into the Council-chamber, "being in a great rage and fury, trembling for anger, and, amongst all his ragious talk called Sir Edward Montagu traitor, and further said he would fight any man in his shirt in that quarrel." It was plain that no technical or legal obstacles were to be permitted to turn him from his purpose.

The following day the law-officers were again called to Greenwich. Conveyed in the first place to a chamber behind the dining-room, they met with a chilling reception. "All the lords looked upon them with earnest countenances, as though they had not known them;" and, brought into the King's presence, Edward demanded, "with sharp words and angry countenance," why his book was not made?

Montagu, as spokesman for his colleagues, explained.206 Had the King's device been executed it would become void at the King's death, the Statute of Succession passed by Parliament being still in force. A statute could be altered by statute alone. On Edward's replying that Parliament should then shortly be called together, Montagu caught at the solution. The matter could be referred to it, and all perils saved. But this was not the King's meaning. The deed, he explained, was to be executed at once, and was to be afterwards ratified by Parliament. With growing excitement, he commanded the officers, "very sharply," to do his bidding; some of the lords, standing behind the King, adding that, did they refuse, they were traitors.

The epithet was freely bandied about in those days, yet it never failed to carry a menace; and Montagu, in as "great fear as ever he was in all his life before, seeing the King so earnest and sharp, and the Duke so angry the day before," and being an "old weak man and without comfort," began to look about for a method of satisfying King and Council without endangering his personal safety. In the end he gave way, consenting to prepare the required papers, on condition that he might first be given a commission under the great seal to draw up the instrument, and likewise a pardon for having done so. Northumberland had won the day.

It was afterwards reported that when the will was207 signed a great tempest arose, with a whirlwind such as had never been seen, the sky dark and fearful, lightning and infinite thunder; one of the thunderbolts accompanying that terrible storm falling upon the miserable church where heresy was first begotten.... "This accident was observed by many persons of sense and prudence, and was considered a great sign of the avenging justice of God."152

The Council, undeterred by the manifestations of divine wrath, were not backward in endorsing the deed. Overborne by the Duke, probably also influenced by the apprehension of a compulsory restoration of Church spoils should Mary succeed, they unanimously acquiesced in the act of injustice. To a second paper, designed by the Duke to commit his colleagues further, twenty-four councillors and legal advisers set their hands. By June 21 the official instrument had received the signatures of the Lords of the Council, other peers, judges, and officers of the Crown, to the number of 101. The Princesses had been set aside, and the fatal heritage, so far as it was possible, secured to Lady Jane. The King, at the direction of her nearest of kin, had in effect affixed his signature to her death-sentence.

When Northumberland was assured of success he gave a magnificent musical entertainment, to which the French ambassador was bidden. Three days earlier it had been reported to Noailles that208 Edward was at the point of death, and he was surprised at the merry-making and the good spirits prevalent. The affair, it was explained to him, was in honour of the convalescence of the King, who had been without fever for two days, and whose recovery appeared certain.153 The envoy doubtless expressed no incredulity, and congratulated the company upon the good tidings. He knew that Edward was moribund, and understood that the rejoicings were in truth to celebrate the approaching elevation to the throne of Northumberland's daughter-in-law.

Was she present? We cannot tell; but it was the Duke's policy to make her a prominent figure, and Noailles' description of her beauty and goodness implies a personal acquaintance.

It only remained for Edward to die. All those around him, with perhaps some few exceptions amongst his personal attendants, were eagerly awaiting the end. All had been accomplished that was possible whilst he was yet alive, and Northumberland and his friends were probably impatient to be up and doing. His sisters were at a distance, his uncles dead, Barnaby Fitzpatrick was abroad, and he was practically alone with the men who had made him their tool. The last scene is full of pathos. Three hours before the end, lying with his eyes shut, he was heard praying for the country which had been his charge.

209 "'O God,' he entreated, 'deliver me out of this miserable and wretched life, and take me among Thy chosen; howbeit not my will, but Thine, be done. Lord, I commend my spirit to Thee. O Lord, Thou knowest how happy it were for me to be with Thee. Yet, for Thy chosen's sake, send me life and health, that I may truly serve Thee. O my Lord God, bless Thy people and save Thine inheritance. O Lord God, save Thy chosen people of England. O Lord God, defend this realm from Papistry and maintain Thy true religion, that I and my people may praise Thy holy Name, for Jesus Christ His sake.'

"Then turned he his face, and seeing who was by him, said to them:

"'Are ye so nigh? I thought ye had been further off.'

"Then Doctor Owen said:

"'We heard you speak to yourself, but what you said we know not.'

"He then (after his fashion, smilingly) said, 'I was praying to God.'"154

The end was near.

"I am faint," he said. "Lord, have mercy upon me, and take my spirit"; and so on July 7, towards night, he passed away. On the following day Noailles communicated to his Court "le triste et piteux inconvénient de la mort" of Edward VI., last of the Tudor Kings.

210

CHAPTER XVI

1553

After King Edward's death—Results to Lady Jane Grey—Northumberland's schemes—Mary's escape—Scene at Sion House—Lady Jane brought to the Tower—Quarrel with her husband—Her proclamation as Queen.

A boy was dead. A frail little life, long failing, had gone out. That was all. Nevertheless upon it had hung the destinies of England.

Speculations and forecasts as to the consequences had Edward lived are unprofitable. Yet one wonders what, grown to manhood, he would have become—whether the gentle lad, pious, studious, religious, the modern Josiah, as he was often called, would have developed, as he grew to maturity, the dangerous characteristics of his Tudor race, the fierceness and violence of his father, the melancholy and relentless fanaticism of Mary, the absence of principle and sensuality of Elizabeth. Or would he have fulfilled the many hopes which had found their centre in him and have justified the love of his subjects, given him upon credit?

It is impossible to say. What was certain was that his part was played out, and that others were to take his place. Amongst these his little cousin Jane211 was at once the most innocent and the most unfortunate.

Hitherto she had looked on as a spectator at life. Her skiff moored in a creek of the great river, she had watched from a place of comparative calm the stream as it rushed by. Here and there a wave might make itself felt even in that quiet place; a wreck might be carried past, or she might catch the drowning cry of a swimmer as he sank. But to the young such things are accidents from participation in which they tacitly consider themselves exempted, regarding them with the fearlessness due to inexperience. Suddenly all was to be changed. Torn from her anchorage, she was to be violently borne along by the torrent towards the inevitable catastrophe.

As yet she was ignorant of the destiny prepared for her. Under her father's roof, she had pursued her customary occupations, and by some authorities her third extant letter to Bullinger—another tribute of admiration and flattery, and containing no allusion to current events—is believed to belong to the interval occurring between her marriage and the King's death. The allusion to herself as an "untaught virgin," and the signature "Jane Grey," seem to give it a date earlier in the year. The time was fast approaching when leisure for literary exercises of the kind would be lacking.

It would have been difficult to trace her movements212 precisely at this juncture were it not that she has left a record of them in a document—either directly addressed to Mary from her prison or intended for her eyes—in which she demonstrated her innocence.155 Notwithstanding the promise made by the Duchess of Northumberland at her marriage that she should be permitted to remain at home, she appears to have been by this time living with her husband's parents, and, upon Edward's death becoming imminent, she was informed of the fact by her father-in-law, who forbade her to leave his house; adding the startling announcement that, when it should please God to call the King to His mercy, she would at once repair to the Tower, her cousin having nominated her heir to the throne.

The news found her totally unprepared; and, shocked and partly incredulous, she refused obedience to the Duke's commands, continuing to visit her mother daily, in spite of the indignation of the Duchess of Northumberland, who "grew wroth with me and with her, saying that she was determined to keep me in her house; that she would likewise keep my husband there, to whom I should go later in any case, and that she would be under small obligation to me. Therefore it did not seem to me213 lawful to disobey her, and for three or four days I stayed in her house, until I obtained permission to resort to the Duke of Northumberland's palace at Chelsea." At this place—the reason of her preference for it is not given—she continued, sick and anxious, until a summons reached her to go to Sion House, there to receive a message from the King. It was Lady Sydney, a married daughter of the Duke's, who brought the order, saying, "with more gravity than usual," that it was necessary that her sister-in-law should obey it; and Lady Jane did not refuse to do so.

Sion House, where the opening scene of the drama took place, was another of the possessions of the Duke of Somerset, passed into the hands of his rival. A monastery, founded by Henry V. at Isleworth, it had been seized, with other Church property, in 1539, and had served two years later as prison to the unhappy child, Katherine Howard. The place had been acquired by Somerset in the days of his power, when the building of the great house, which was to replace the convent, was begun. The gardens were enclosed by high walls, a triangular terrace in one of their angles alone allowing the inmates to obtain a view of the country beyond.156 In 1552 it had, with most of the late Protector's goods and chattels, been confiscated, and during the following year, the year of the King's death, had214 been granted to Northumberland. It was to this place that Lady Jane was taken to receive the message said to be awaiting her from the King.

Her destination reached, Sion House was found empty; but it was not long before those who were pulling the strings arrived. The message from the King had been a fiction. Edward's gentle spirit was at rest, and he himself forgotten in the rush of events. There was little time for thought of the dead. The interests of religion and of the State, as some would call it, the ambition of unscrupulous and unprincipled men, as it would be named by others, demanded the whole attention of the steersmen who stood, for the moment, at the helm.

It had been decided to keep the fact of the King's death secret until measures should have been taken to ensure the success of the desperate game they were playing. To secure possession of the person of his natural successor was of the first importance; and a letter had been despatched to Mary when her brother was manifestly at the point of death which it was hoped would avail to bring her to London and would enable her enemies to fulfil their purpose. Stating that the King was very ill, she was entreated to come to him, as he earnestly desired the comfort of her presence.

Mary must have been well aware of the risk she would run in responding to the appeal; and it says much for her courage and her affection that she did215 not hesitate to incur it. A fortunate chance, however, frustrated the designs against her. Starting from Hunsdon, where the tidings had found her, she had reached Hoddesden on her way to Greenwich, when she was met by intelligence that determined her to go no further. The King was dead; nor was it difficult to discern in the urgent summons, sent too late to accomplish its ostensible purpose, a transparent attempt to induce her to place herself in the power of her enemies.

Opinions have differed as to the means by which Northumberland's scheme was frustrated. Some say that the news was conveyed to the Princess by the Earl of Arundel. Sir Nicholas Throckmorton also claims credit for the warning. According to this account of the matter, a young brother of his, in attendance upon Northumberland, had become cognisant of the intended treachery, and had come post-haste to report what was a-foot at his father's house. A few words spoken by Sir John Gates, visiting the Duke before he had risen, were all that had reached the young man's ears, but those words had been of startling significance, the state of affairs being what it was.

"What, sir," he had heard Gates say, "will you let the Lady Mary escape, and not secure her person?"

A consultation was hurriedly held at Throckmorton House, between the father and his three sons. Sir Nicholas, who had been present at the King's216 death, was too well aware of the circumstances to minimise the importance of his brother's story, and, summoning the Princess Mary's goldsmith, it was decided to entrust him with the duty of conveying a caution to his mistress, and stopping her journey. Sir Nicholas's metrical version of what followed may be given.157

> Mourning, from Greenwich did I straight depart,
> To London, to a house which bore our name.
> My brethren guessèd by my heavie hearte,
> The King was dead, and I confess'd the same:
> The hushing of his death I didd unfolde,
> Their meaning to proclaime Queene Jane I tolde.
> * * * * *
> Wherefore from four of us the newes was sent
> How that her brother hee was dead and gone;
> In post her goldsmith then from London went,
> By whom the message was dispatcht anon.
> Shee asked, "If wee knewe it certainlie?"
> Who said, "Sir Nicholas knew it verilie."

The first stroke hazarded by the conspirators had resulted in failure. Mary, after some deliberation, turned her face northwards, and escaped the snare laid for her by her enemies.

The next object of Northumberland and his friends was to obtain the concurrence of the City to the substitution of his daughter-in-law for the rightful heir. Various as were the views of the best means of ensuring success, all the Council were agreed on one point, namely, "that London was the hand which must reach Jane the crown."158 London was to217 be made to do it. On July 8 the Lord Mayor, with six aldermen, six "merchants of the staple, and as many merchant adventurers," were summoned to Greenwich, were there secretly informed of the King's death, and of his will by letters patent, "to which they were sworn and charged to keep it secret."

All this had been done before Lady Jane was summoned to Sion House. It was time for the stage Queen to make her appearance, and at Sion the facts were made known to her.159

Of her reception of the great news accounts vary. A graphic picture, painted in the first place by Heylyn, has been copied by divers other historians. The learned John Nichols, unable to trace it in any contemporary documents or records, has decided that it must be classed amongst "those dramatic scenes in which historical writers formerly considered themselves justified in indulging."160

He is probably right; yet an early and generally accepted tradition has a value of its own, and may be true to the spirit, if not to the letter, of what actually occurred. Mary herself afterwards told the envoy of Charles V. that she believed her cousin to have had no part in the Duke of Northumberland's218 enterprise; and, supposing her to have been ignorant, or only dimly cognisant, of the plot, the revelation of it may easily have occasioned her a shock. It has been constantly asserted that, in this first interview with those who, calling themselves her subjects, were practically the masters of her fate, she began by declining to be a party to their scheme; and if her letter, written at a later date, from the Tower to Mary, does not wholly confirm the assertion, it points to an attitude of reluctant assent. Her mother-in-law had given her hints of what was intended, but, like the announcement made by the Duke at Durham House of her approaching greatness, they were too incredible to be taken seriously; and the fact that when she was joined at Sion by the Dukes of Northumberland and Suffolk they did not at once make the matter plain, but confined the conversation for a time to indifferent subjects, seems to indicate a doubt upon their part of her pliability. There was, nevertheless, a change in their demeanour and bearing giving rise in her mind to an uneasy consciousness of a mystery she had not fathomed; whilst Huntingdon and Pembroke, who were present, treated her with even more incomprehensible reverence, and went so far as to bow the knee.

On the arrival of her mother, together with the Duchess of Northumberland, the explanation of the riddle took place. The tidings of the King's death219 and of her exaltation was broken to her, together with the reasons prompting Edward to set aside his sisters in her favour. The nobles fell upon their knees, took her formally for their Queen, and swore—it was shortly to be proved how little the oath was worth—to shed their blood in defence of her rights.

"Having heard which things," pursues Lady Jane in her apology, "with infinite grief of spirit, I call to witness those lords who were present that I was so stunned and stupefied that, overcome by sudden and unexpected sorrow, they saw me fall to the ground, weeping very bitterly. And afterwards, declaring to them my insufficiency, I lamented much the death of so noble a prince; and at the same time turned to God, humbly praying and beseeching Him that, if what was given me was in truth and legitimately mine, He would grant me grace and power to govern to His glory and service, and for the good of this realm."161

There is, as Dr. Lingard points out, nothing unnatural in this description of what had occurred; whereas the grandiloquent language attributed to her by some historians is most unlikely to have been used at a moment both of grief and excitement. According to these authorities, not only did she defend Mary's right, and denounce220 those who had conspired against it, but delivered a lengthy oration upon the fickleness of fortune. "If she enrich any, it is but to make them the subject of her sport; if she raise others, it is but to pleasure herself with their ruins. What she adored yesterday, to-day is her pastime. And if I now permit her to adorn and crown me, I must to-morrow suffer her to crush and tear me to pieces"—proceeding to cite Katherine of Aragon and Anne Boleyn as examples of those who had, to their own undoing, worn a crown. "If you love me sincerely and in good earnest," she is made to say, "you will rather wish me a secure and quiet fortune, though mean, than an exalted condition exposed to the wind, and followed by some dismal fall."

Poor little plaything of the fortune she is represented as anathematising, the designs of those who were striving to exalt her were due to nothing less than a sincere love. Any other puppet would have answered their purpose equally well, so that the excuse of royal blood was in her veins. But Jane, willing or unwilling, was to be made use of for their ends, and it was vain for her to protest.

On the following day, July 10, the Queen-designate was brought, following the ancient custom of Kings on their accession, to the Tower; reaching it at three o'clock, to be received at the gate by Northumberland, and formally presented with the keys in the presence of a great crowd who looked221 on at the proceedings in sinister silence and gave no sign of rejoicing or cordiality.

Shortly after, the Marquis of Winchester, in his capacity of Treasurer, brought the crown jewels, with the crown itself, "asking me," wrote Jane, "to put it on my head, to try whether it fitted me or not. Who knows well that, with many excuses, I refused. He not the less insisted that I should boldly take it, and that another should be made that my husband might be crowned with me, which I certainly heard unwillingly, and with infinite grief and displeasure."162

The idea that young Guilford Dudley, with no royal blood to make his claim colourable, was intended to share her dignity appears to have roused his wife, somewhat strangely, to hot indignation. She at least was a Tudor on her mother's side; but what was Dudley, that he should aspire so high? Had she loved her boy-husband she might have taken a different view of his pretensions; but there is nothing to show that she regarded him with any special affection, and she was disposed to use her authority after a fashion neither he nor his father would tolerate.

At first Guilford, taken by surprise, appeared inclined to yield the point, and in a conversation between the two, when Winchester had withdrawn, he agreed that, were he to be made King, it should222 be only by Act of Parliament. Thereupon, losing no time in setting the matter on a right footing, Jane sent for the Earls of Arundel and Pembroke, and informed them that, if she were to be Queen, she would be willing to make her husband Duke; "but to make him King I would not consent."

Though Arundel and Pembroke were probably quite at one with her on the question, that she should show signs of exercising an independent judgment was naturally exasperating to those to whom it was due that she was placed in her present position; and when the Duchess of Northumberland became aware of what was going forward she not only treated Lady Jane, according to her own account, very ill, but stirred up Guilford to do the like; the boy, primed by his mother, declaring that he would in no wise be Duke, but King, and, holding sulkily aloof from his wife that night, so that she was compelled, "as a woman, and loving my husband," to send the Earls of Arundel and Pembroke to bring him to her, otherwise he would have left in the morning, at his mother's bidding, for Sion. "Thus," ends the poor child, "I was in truth deceived by the Duke and Council, and badly treated by my husband and his mother."

The discussion was premature. Boy and girl were all too soon to learn that it was not to be a question of crowns for either so much as of heads to wear them. Whilst the wrangle had been carried223 on in the Tower, the first step had been taken towards bringing the disputants to the scaffold. The death of the King had been made public, together with the provisions of his will, and Jane had been proclaimed Queen in two or three parts of the City.

"The tenth day of the same month," runs the entry in the Grey Friar's Chronicle, "after seven o'clock at night, was made a proclamation in Cheap by three heralds and one trumpet ... for Jane, the Duke of Suffolk's daughter, to be Queen of England. But few or none said 'God save her.'"

There was a singular unanimity upon the subject amongst the citizens of London. It is said that upon the faces of the heralds forced to proclaim the new Queen their discontent was visible;163 and a curious French letter sent from London at the time states, after mentioning the absence of any acclamation upon the part of the people, that a moment afterwards they had broken out into lamentation, clamour, tears, sighs, sadness, and desolation impossible to describe.

Thus inauspiciously was Lady Jane's nine days' reign inaugurated. On a great catafalque in Westminster Abbey the dead boy-King was lying, guarded day and night by twelve watchers until he should be given sepulture. But there was little leisure to attend to his obsequies on the part of224 the men who had made him their tool, and had staked their lives and fortunes upon the success of their plot. For the present all had gone according to their hopes. "Through the pious intents of Edward, the religion of Mary, the ambition of Northumberland, the simplicity of Suffolk, the fearfulness of the judges, and the flattery of the courtiers"—thus Fuller sums up the causes to which the situation was due—"matters were made as sure as man's policy can make that good which in itself is bad." It was quickly to be seen to what that security amounted.

225

CHAPTER XVII

1553

Lady Jane as Queen—Mary asserts her claims—The English envoys at Brussels—Mary's popularity—Northumberland leaves London—His farewells.

To enter in any degree into the position of "Jane the Queen" during the brief period when she was the nominal head of the State, the time in which she lived, as well as the prevalent conception of royalty in England, must be taken into the reckoning.

In our own days she would not only have been a mere cipher—as indeed she was—but would have been content to remain such, so far as actual power was concerned. Royalty, stripped of its reality, is largely become a mere matter of show, a part of the pageant of State. In the case of a child of sixteen it would wear that character alone. But in the days of the Tudors a King was accustomed to govern; even in the hands of a minor a sceptre was not a mere symbolic ornament.

And Lady Jane was precisely the person to take a serious view of her duties. Thoughtful, conscientious, and grave beyond her years, she226 had no sooner found herself a Queen than she had asserted her authority in opposition to that of the man who had invested her with the dignity by announcing her intention of refusing to allow it to be shared by his son—already, it appears by letters from Brussels, recognised there as Prince Consort—and shut up in the gloomy fortress to which she had been taken she was occupied with the thought of her duty to the kingdom she believed herself to be called to rule over, of the necessity of providing for the wants of the nation, and more especially for the future of religion. Whilst, perhaps, all the time there lingered in her mind a misgiving, lifting its head to confront her from time to time with a paralysing doubt, torturing to a sensitive and scrupulous nature; was she indeed the rightful Queen of England?

Mary had lost no time in asserting her claims. On July 9—the day before that of Jane's proclamation—she had written a letter to the Council from Kenninghall in Norfolk, expressing her astonishment that they had neither communicated to her the fact of her brother's death, nor had caused her to be proclaimed Queen, and requiring them to perform this last duty without delay. The rebuke reaching London on the morning of January 11 "seemed to give their Lordships no other trouble than the returning of an answer,"164 which they did in terms227 of studied insult, reminding her of her alleged illegitimacy, and exhorting her to submit to her lawful sovereign, Queen Jane, else she should prove grievous unto them and unto herself. This unconciliatory document received the signature of every one of the Council, including Cecil, who was afterwards at much pains to explain his concurrence in the proceedings of his colleagues; and Northumberland, as he despatched it, must have felt with satisfaction that it would be difficult for those responsible for the missive to make their peace with the woman to whom it was addressed.

The terms in which the defiance was couched show the little importance attached to the chances that Henry VIII.'s eldest daughter would ever be in a position to vindicate her rights. Once again her enemies had failed to take into account the stubborn justice of the people. Though by many of them Mary's religion was feared and disliked, they viewed with sullen disapproval the conspiracy to rob her of her heritage. And Northumberland they hated.

The sinister rumours current during the last few years were still afloat; justified, as it seemed, by the course of recent events. It was said that the Duke had incited Somerset to put his brother to death, and had then slain Somerset, in order that, bereft of his nearest of kin, the young King might the more easily become his victim. The reports of foul228 play were repeated, and it was said that Edward had been removed by poison to make way for Northumberland's daughter-in-law. That he had not come by his death by fair means was indeed so generally believed that the Emperor, writing to Mary when she had defeated her enemies, counselled her to punish all those that had been concerned in it.165

The charge of poisoning was not so uncommon as to make it strange that it should be thought to have been instrumental in removing an obstacle from the path of an ambitious man. In Lady Jane's pitiful letter to her cousin she stated—doubtless in good faith—that poison had twice been administered to her, once in the house of the Duchess of Northumberland—when the motive would have been hard to find—and again in the Tower, "as I have certain evidence." What the poor child honestly believed had been attempted in her case, the angry people imagined had been successfully accomplished in the case of their young King, and his death was another item laid to the charge of the man they hated.

The news of what was going forward in England had by this time become known abroad. Though letters had been addressed by the Council to Sir Philip Hoby and Sir Richard Morysine, ambassadors at Brussels, announcing the King's death and his229 cousin's accession, the tidings had reached them unofficially before the arrival of the despatches from London. As the envoys were walking in the garden, they were joined by a servant of the Emperor's, Don Diego by name, who, making profession of personal good will towards their country, expressed his regret at its present loss, adding at the same time his congratulations that so noble a King—meaning, it would seem, Guilford Dudley—had been provided for them, a King he would himself be at all times ready to serve.

The envoys replied that the sorrowful news had reached them, but not the joyous—that they were glad to hear so much from him. Don Diego thereupon proceeded to impart the further fact of Edward's will in favour of Lady Jane. With the question whether the two daughters of Henry VIII. were bastards or not, strangers, he observed, had nothing to do. It was reasonable to accept as King him who had been declared such by the nobles of the land; and Diego, for his part, was bound to rejoice that His Majesty had been set in this office, since he was his godfather, and—so long as the Emperor was in amity with him—would be willing to shed his blood in his service.166

This last personal detail probably contained the explanation of Don Diego's approbation of an arrangement which could scarcely be expected to230 commend itself to his master, and likewise of the curiously subordinate part awarded to Lady Jane in his account of it. But whatever might be the opinion of foreigners, it had quickly been made plain in England that the country would not be content to accept either the sovereignty of Jane or of her husband without a struggle.

Of the temper of the capital a letter or libel scattered abroad, after the fashion of the day, during the week, is an example. In this document, addressed by a certain "poor Pratte" to a young man who had been placed in the pillory and had lost his ears in consequence of his advocacy of Mary's rights, love for the lawful Queen, and hatred of the "ragged bear," Northumberland, is expressed in every line. Should England prove disloyal, misfortune will overtake it as a chastisement for its sin; the Gospel will be plucked away and the Lady Mary replaced by so cruel a Pharaoh as the ragged bear. Her Grace—in marked contrast to the sentiments commonly attributed to the Duke—is doubtless more sorrowful for her brother than glad to be Queen, and would have been as glad of his life as the ragged bear of his death. In conclusion, the writer trusts that God will shortly exalt Mary, "and pluck down that Jane—I cannot nominate her Queen, for that I know no other Queen but the good Lady Mary, her Grace, whom God prosper." To those who would Mary to be Queen poor231 Pratte wishes long life and pleasure; to her opponents, the pains of Satan in hell.167

Such was the delirious spirit of loyalty towards the dispossessed heir, even amongst those who owed no allegiance to Rome. It was not long before the Council were to be taught by more forcible means than scurrilous abuse to correct their estimate of the situation and of the forces at work, strangely misapprehended at the first by one and all.

News was reaching London of the support tendered to Mary. The Earls of Sussex and of Bath had declared in her favour; the county of Suffolk had led the way in rising on her behalf; nobles and gentlemen, with their retainers, were flocking to her standard; it was becoming clearer with every hour that she would not consent to be ousted from her rights without a fierce struggle.

Measures for meeting the resistance of her adherents had to be taken without delay; and Northumberland, wisely unwilling to absent himself from the capital at a juncture so critical, had intended to depute Suffolk to command the forces to be led against her; to gain, if possible, possession of her person, and to bring her to London. This was the arrangement hastily made on July 12. Before nightfall it had been cancelled at the entreaty of the titular Queen.

232 It is not difficult to enter into the Lady Jane's feelings, threatened with the absence of her father on a dangerous errand. With her nervous fears of poison, her evident dislike of her mother-in-law, and ill at ease in new circumstances and surroundings, she may well have clung to the comfort and support afforded by his presence; nor is it incomprehensible that she had "taken the matter heavily" when informed of the decision of the Council. Her wishes might have had little effect if other causes had not conspired to assist her to gain her object, and it has been suggested that those of the lords already contemplating the possibility of Mary's success, and desirous of being freed from the restraint imposed by Northumberland's presence amongst them, may have had a hand in instigating her request, proffered with tears, that her father might tarry at home in her company. The entreaty was, at all events, in full accordance with their desires, and pressure was brought upon Northumberland to induce him to yield to her petition—leaving Suffolk in his place at the Tower, and himself leading the troops north.

Many reasons were urged rendering it advisable that the Duke should take the field in person. He had been the victor in the struggle with Kett, of which Norfolk had been the scene, and enjoyed, in consequence, a great reputation in that county, where it seemed that the fight with Mary and her233 adherents was to take place. He was, moreover, an able soldier; Suffolk was not. On the other hand, it was impossible for Northumberland to adduce the true motives prompting his desire to continue at headquarters; since chief amongst them was the wisdom and prudence of remaining at hand to maintain his personal influence over his colleagues and to keep them true to the oaths they had sworn. In the end he consented to bow to their wishes.

"Since ye think it good," he said, "I and mine will go, not doubting of your fidelity to the Queen's Majesty, which I leave in your custody."

More than the Queen's Majesty was left to their care. The safety, if not the life, of the man chiefly responsible for the conspiracy which had made her what she was, hung upon their loyalty to their vows, and Northumberland must have known it. But Lady Jane was to have her way, and the Council, waiting upon her, brought the welcome news to the Queen, who humbly thanked the Duke for reserving her father at home, and besought him—she was already learning royal fashions—to use his diligence. To this Northumberland, surely not without an inward smile, answered that he would do what in him lay, and the matter was concluded.

At Durham House, next day, the Duke's retinue assembled.168 In the forenoon he met the Council,234 taking leave of them in friendly sort, yet with words betraying his misgivings in the very terms used to convey the assurance of his confidence in their good faith and fidelity.

He and the other nobles who were to be his companions went forth, he told the men left behind, as much to assure their safety as that of the Queen herself. Whilst he and his comrades were to risk their lives in the field, their preservation at home, with the preservation of their children and families, was committed to those who stayed in London. And then he spoke some weighty words, the doubts and forebodings within him finding vent:

"If we thought ye would through malice, conspiracy, or dissension, leave us your friends in the briars and betray us, we could as well sundry ways forsee and provide for our own safeguards as any of you, by betraying us, can do for yours. But now, upon the only trust and faithfulness of your honours, whereof we think ourselves most assured, we do hazard and jubarde [jeopardize] our lives, which trust and promise if ye shall violate, hoping thereby of life and promotion, yet shall not God count you innocent of our bloods, neither acquit you of the sacred and holy oath of allegiance made freely by you to this virtuous lady, the Queen's Highness, who by your and our enticement is rather of force235 placed therein than by her own seeking and request." Commending to their consideration the interests of religion, he again reiterated his warning. "If ye mean deceit, though not forthwith, yet hereafter, God will revenge the same," ending by assuring his colleagues that his words had not been caused by distrust, but that he had spoken them as a reminder of the chances of variance which might grow in his absence.

One of the Council—the narrator does not give his name—took upon him to reply for the rest.

"My Lord," he answered, "if ye mistrust any of us in this matter your Grace is far deceived. For which of us can wipe his hands clean thereof? And if we should shrink from you as one that is culpable, which of us can excuse himself as guiltless? Therefore herein your doubt is too far cast."

It was characteristic of times and men that, far from resenting the suspicion of unfaith, the sole ground upon which the Duke was asked to base a confidence in the fidelity of his colleagues was that it would not be to their interest to betray him.

"I pray God it may be so," he answered. "Let us go to dinner."

After dinner came an interview with Jane, who bade farewell to the Duke and to the lords who were to accompany him on his mission. Everywhere we are confronted by the same heavy atmosphere of impending treachery. As the chief236 conspirator passed through the Council-chamber Arundel met him—Arundel, who was to be one of the first to leave the sinking ship, and who may already have been looking for a loophole of escape from a perilous situation. Yet he now prayed God be with his Grace, saying he was very sorry it was not his chance to go with him and bear him company, in whose presence he could find it in his heart to shed his blood, even at his foot.

The words, with their gratuitous and unsolicited asseveration of loyal friendship, must have been remembered by both when the two met again. It is nevertheless possible that, moved and affected, the Earl was sincere at the moment in his protestations.

"Farewell, gentle Thomas," he added to the Duke's "boy," Thomas Lovell, taking him by the hand, "Farewell, gentle Thomas, with all my heart."

The next day Northumberland took his departure from the capital. As he rode through the city, with some six hundred followers, the same ominous silence that had greeted the proclamation of Lady Jane was preserved by the throng gathered together to see her father-in-law pass. The Duke noticed it.

"The people press to see us," he observed gloomily, "but not one sayeth God speed us."

When next Northumberland and the London crowd were face to face it was under changed circumstances.

237

CHAPTER XVIII

1553

Turn of the tide—Reaction in Mary's favour in the Council—Suffolk yields—Mary proclaimed in London—Lady Jane's deposition—She returns to Sion House.

Northumberland was gone. The weight of his dominant influence was removed, and many of his colleagues must have breathed more freely. In the Tower Lady Jane, with those of the Council left in London, continued to watch and wait the course of events. It must have been recognised that the future was dark and uncertain; and whilst the lords and nobles looked about for a way of escape should affairs go ill with the new government, the boy and girl arbitrarily linked together may have been drawn closer by the growing sense of a common danger. Guilford Dudley did not share his father's unpopularity. Young and handsome, he is said to have been endowed with virtues calling forth an unusual amount of pity for his premature end,169 and Heylyn declared that of all Dudley's brood he had nothing of his father in him.170 "He was," says Fuller, adding238 his testimony, "a goodly and (for aught I find to the contrary) a godly gentleman, whose worst fault was that he was son to an ambitious father."171 The flash of boyish ambition he had evinced in his determination to be content with nothing less than kingship must have been soon extinguished by the consciousness that life itself was at stake.

For quicker and quicker came tidings of fresh triumphs for Mary, each one striking at the hopes of her rival's partisans. News was brought that Mary had been proclaimed Queen first in Buckinghamshire; next at Norwich. Her forces were gathering strength, her adherents gaining courage. Again, six vessels placed at Yarmouth to intercept her flight, should she attempt it, were won over to her side, their captains, with men and ordnance, making submission; whereat "the Lady Mary"—from whose mind nothing had been further than flight—"and her company were wonderful joyous."

This last blow hit the party acknowledging Jane as Queen hard; nor were its effects long in becoming visible. In the Tower "each man began to pluck in his horns," and to cast about for a manner of dissevering his private fortunes from a cause manifestly doomed to disaster. Pembroke, who in May had associated himself with Northumberland by marrying his son to Katherine Grey, was one of the foremost in considering the possibility of quitting the Tower, so239 that he might hold consultation with those without; but as yet he had not devised a means of accomplishing his purpose. Each day brought its developments within the walls of the fortress, and beyond them. On the Sunday night—not a week after the crown had been fitted on Jane's head—when the Lord Treasurer, then officiously desirous of adding a second for her husband, was leaving the building in order to repair to his own house, the gates were suddenly shut and the keys carried up to the mistress of the Tower. What was the reason? No one knew, but it was whispered that a seal had been found missing. Others said that she had feared some packinge [sic] in the Treasurer. The days were coming when it would be in no one's power to keep the Lords of the Council at their post under lock and key.

That Sunday morning—it was July 16—Ridley had preached at Paul's Cross before the Mayor, Aldermen, and people, pleading Lady Jane's cause with all the eloquence at his command. Let his hearers, he said, contrast her piety and gentleness with the haughtiness and papistry of her rival. And he told the story of his visit to Hunsdon, of his attempt to convince Mary of her errors, and of its failure, conjuring all who heard him to maintain the cause of Queen Jane and of the Gospel. But his exhortations fell on deaf ears.

And still one messenger of ill tidings followed240 hard upon the heels of another. Cecil, with his natural aptitude for intrigue, was engaging in secret deliberations with members of the Council inclined to be favourable to Mary, finding in especial the Lord Treasurer, Winchester, the Earl of Arundel, and Lord Darcy, willing listeners, "whereof I did immediately tell Mr. Petre"—the other Secretary—"for both our comfort."172 Presently a pretext was invented to cover the escape of the lords from the Tower. It was said that Northumberland had sent for auxiliaries, and that it was necessary to hold a consultation with the foreign ambassadors as to the employment of mercenaries.173 The meeting was to take place at Baynard's Castle, Arundel observing significantly that he liked not the air of the Tower. He and his friends may indeed have reflected that it had proved fatal to many less steeped in treason than they. To Baynard's Castle some of the lords accordingly repaired, sending afterwards to summon the rest to join them, with the exception of Suffolk, who remained behind, in apparent ignorance of what was going forward.

In the consultation, held on July 19, the deathblow was dealt to the hopes of those faithful to the nine-days' Queen. Arundel was the first to declare himself unhesitatingly on Mary's side, and to denounce241 the Duke, from whom he had so lately parted on terms of devoted friendship. He boasted of his courage in now opposing Northumberland—a man of supreme authority, and—as one who had little or no conscience—fond of blood. It was by no desire of vengeance that Arundel's conduct was prompted, he declared, but by conscience and anxiety for the public welfare; the Duke was actuated by a desire neither for the good of the kingdom nor by religious zeal, but purely by a desire for power, and he proceeded to hold him up to the reprobation of his colleagues.

Pembroke made answer, promising, with his hand on his sword, to make Mary Queen. There were indeed few dissentient voices, and, though some of the lords at first maintained that warning should be sent to Northumberland and a general pardon obtained from Mary, their proposals did not meet with favour, and they did not press them.

A hundred men had been despatched on various pretexts, and by degrees, to the Tower, with orders to make themselves masters of the place, in case Suffolk would not leave it except upon compulsion; but the Duke was not a man to lead a forlorn hope. Had Northumberland been at hand a struggle might have taken place; as it was, not a voice was raised against the decision of the Council, and with almost incredible rapidity the face of affairs underwent a change, absolute and complete. Suffolk, so soon242 as the determination of the lords was made known to him, lost no time in expressing his willingness to concur in it and to add his signature to the proclamation of Mary, already drawn up.174 He was, he said, but one man; and proclaiming his daughter's rival in person on Tower Hill, he finally struck his colours; going so far, as some affirm, as to share in the demonstration in the new Queen's honour in Cheapside, where the proclamation was read by the Earl of Pembroke amidst a scene of wild enthusiasm contrasting vividly with the coldness and apathy shown by the populace when, nine days earlier, they had been asked to accept the Duke of Northumberland's daughter-in-law as their Queen.

"For my time I never saw the like," says a news-letter,175 "and by the report of others the like was never seen. The number of caps that were thrown up at the proclamation were not to be told.... I saw myself money was thrown out at windows for joy. The bonfires were without number, and, what with shouting and crying of the people and ringing of the bells, there could no one hear almost what another said, besides banquetings and singing in the street for joy."

Arundel was there, as well as Pembroke, with Shrewsbury and others, and the day was ended with evensong at St. Paul's.

243 And whilst all this was going on outside, in the gloom of the Tower, where the air must have struck chill even on that July day, sat the little victim of state-craft—"Cette pauvre reine," wrote Noailles to his master, "qui s'en peut dire de la féve"—a Twelfth Night's Queen—in the fortress that had seen her brief exaltation, and was so soon to become to her a prison. As the joy-bells echoed through the City and the shouting of the

83

people penetrated the thick walls she must have wondered what was the cause of rejoicing. Presently she learnt it.

That afternoon had been fixed for the christening of a child born to Underhyll—nicknamed, on account of his religious zeal, the Hot-Gospeller—on duty as a Gentleman Pensioner at the Tower. The baby was highly favoured, since the Duke of Suffolk and the Earl of Pembroke were to be his sponsors by proxy and Lady Jane had signified her intention of acting as godmother, calling the infant Guilford, after her husband.

Lady Throckmorton, wife to Sir Nicholas, in attendance on Jane,176 had been chosen to represent her mistress at the ceremony; and, on quitting the Tower for that purpose, had waited on the Queen and received her usual orders, according to royal244 etiquette. Upon her return, the baptism over, she found all—like a transformation scene at the theatre—changed. The canopy of state had been removed from Lady Jane's apartment, and Lady Jane herself, divested of her sovereignty, was practically a prisoner.177

During the absence of the Lady-in-waiting, Suffolk, his part on Cheapside played, had returned to the Tower, to set matters there on their new footing. Informing his daughter, as one imagines with the roughness of a man smarting under defeat, that since her cousin had been elected Queen by the Council, and had been proclaimed, it was time she should do her honour, he removed the insignia of royalty. The rank she had possessed not being her own she must make a virtue of necessity, and bow to that fortune of which she had been the sport and victim.

Rising to the occasion, Jane, as might be expected, made fitting reply. The words now spoken by her father were, she answered, more becoming and praiseworthy than those he had uttered on putting her in possession of the crown; proceeding to moralise the matter after a fashion that can only be attributed to the imaginative faculties of the narrator of the scene. This done she, more naturally, withdrew into her private apartments with her mother and other ladies and gave way, in spite245 of her firmness, to "infinite sorrow."178 A further scene narrated by the Italian, Florio, on the authority of the Duke of Suffolk's chaplain—"as her father's learned and pious preacher told me"—represents her as confronted with some at least of the men who had betrayed her, and as reproaching them bitterly with their duplicity. Without vouching for the accuracy of the speech reported, touches are discernible in it—evidences of a very human wrath, indignation, and scorn—unlikely to have been invented by men whose habit it was to describe the speaker as the living embodiment of meekness and patience, and it may be that the evangelist's account is founded on fact.

"Therefore, O Lords of the Council," she is made to say, "there is found in men of illustrious blood, and as much esteemed by the world as you, double dealing, deceit, fickleness, and ruin to the innocent. Which of you can boast with truth that I besought him to make me a Queen? Where are the gifts I promised or gave on this account? Did ye not of your own accord drag me from my literary studies, and, depriving me of liberty, place me in this rank? Alas! double-faced men, how well I see, though late, to what end ye set me in this royal dignity! How will ye escape the infamy following upon such deeds?" How were broken246 promises, violated oaths, to be coloured and disguised? Who would trust them for the future? "But be of good cheer, with the same measure it shall be meted to you again."

With this prophecy of retribution to follow she ended. "For a good space she was silent; and they departed, full of shame, leaving her well guarded."179

Her attendants were not long in availing themselves of the permission accorded them to go where they pleased. The service of Lady Jane was, from an honour, become a perilous duty; and they went to their own homes, leaving their nine-days' mistress "burdened with thought and woe." The following morning she too quitted the Tower, returning to Sion House. It was no more than ten days since she had been brought from it in royal state.

247

CHAPTER XIX

1553

Northumberland at bay—His capitulation—Meeting with Arundel, and arrest—Lady Jane a prisoner—Mary and Elizabeth—Mary's visit to the Tower—London—Mary's policy.

The unanimous capitulation of the Council, in which he was by absence precluded from joining, sealed Northumberland's fate. The centre of interest shifts from London to the country, whither he had gone to meet the forces gathering round Mary. The ragged bear was at bay.

Arundel and Paget had posted northwards on the night following the revolution in London to inform the Queen of the proceedings of the Council and to make their peace with the new sovereign; Paget's success in particular being so marked that the French looker-on reported that his favour with the Queen "etait chose plaisante à voir et oir." The question all men were asking was what stand would be made by the leader of the troops arrayed against her. That Northumberland, knowing that he had sinned too deeply for forgiveness, would yield without a blow can scarcely have been contemplated by the most sanguine of his opponents, and the singular248 transmutation taking place in a man who hitherto, whatever might have been his faults or crimes, had never been lacking in courage, must have taken his enemies and what friends remained to him by surprise.

"Bold, sensitive, and magnanimous," as some one describes him,180 he was to display a lack of every manly quality only explicable on the hypothesis that the incessant strain and excitement of the last three weeks had told upon nerves and spirits to an extent making it impossible for him to meet the crisis with dignity and valour.

Hampered with orders from the Council framed in Mary's interest and with the secret object of delaying his movements until her adherents had had time to muster in force, he did not adopt the only course—that of immediate attack—offering a possibility of success, and had retreated to Cambridge when the news that Mary had been proclaimed in London reached him. From that instant he abandoned the struggle.

On the previous day the Vice-Chancellor of the University, Doctor Sandys, had preached, at his request, a sermon directed against Mary. Now, Duke and churchman standing side by side in the market-place, Northumberland, with the tears running down his face, and throwing his cap into the air, proclaimed her Queen. She was a merciful woman, he told Sandys, and all would doubtless share in her249 general pardon. Sandys knew better, and bade the Duke not flatter himself with false hopes. Were the Queen ever so much inclined to pardon, those who ruled her would destroy Northumberland, whoever else were spared.

The churchman proved to have judged more accurately than the soldier. An hour later the Duke received letters from the Council, indicating the treatment he might expect at their hands. He was thereby bidden, on pain of treason, to disarm, and it was added that, should he come within ten miles of London, his late comrades would fight him. Could greater loyalty and zeal in the service of the rising sun be displayed?

Fidelity was at a discount. His troops melted away, leaving their captain at the mercy of his enemies. In the camp confusion prevailed. Northumberland was first put under arrest, then set again at liberty upon his protest, based upon the orders of the Council that "all men should go his way." Was he, the leader, to be prevented from acting upon their command? Young Warwick, his son, was upon the point of riding away, when, the morning after the scene in the market-place, the Earl of Arundel arrived from Queen Mary with orders to arrest the Duke.

What ensued was a painful spectacle, Northumberland's bearing, even in a day when servility on the part of the fallen was so common as to be almost a250 matter of course, being generally stigmatized as unworthy of the man who had often given proof of a brave and noble spirit.181 As the two men met, it may be that the Duke augured well from the Queen's choice of a messenger. If he had, he was to be quickly undeceived. Arundel was not disposed to risk his newly acquired favour with the sovereign for the sake of a discredited comrade, and Northumberland might have spared the abjectness of his attitude; as, falling on his knees, he begged his former friend, for the love of God, to be good to him.

"Consider," he urged, "I have done nothing but by the consents of you and all the whole Council."

The plea was ill-chosen. That Arundel had been implicated in the treason was a reason the more why he could not afford to show mercy to a fellow-traitor; nor was he in a mood to discuss a past he would have preferred to forget and to blot out. It is the unfortunate who are prone to indulge in long memories, and the Earl had just achieved a success which he was anxious to render permanent. Disregarding Northumberland's appeal, he turned at once to the practical matter in hand. He had been sent there by the Queen's Majesty, he told the Duke; in her name he arrested him.

Northumberland made no attempt at resistance. He obeyed, he answered humbly; "and I beseech251 you, my Lord of Arundel, use mercy towards me, knowing the case as it is."

Again Arundel coldly ignored the appeal to the past.

"My lord," he replied, "ye should have sought for mercy sooner. I must do according to my commandment," and he handed over his prisoner forthwith to the guards who stood near.

For two hours, denied so much as the services of his attendants, the Duke paced the chamber wherein he was confined, till, looking out of the window, he caught sight of Arundel passing below, and entreated that his servants might be admitted to him.

"For the love of God," he cried, "let me have Cox, one of my chamber, to wait on me!"

"You shall have Tom, your boy," answered the Earl, naming the lad, Thomas Lovell, of whom, a few days earlier, he had taken so affectionate a leave. Northumberland protested.

"Alas, my lord," he said, "what stead can a boy do me? I pray you let me have Cox." And so both Lovell and Cox were permitted to attend their master. It was the single concession he could obtain.182

Thus Northumberland met his fate.

The Queen's justice had overtaken more innocent victims. Lady Jane's stay at Sion House had not252 been prolonged. By July 23, not more than three days after she had quitted the Tower, she returned to it, not as a Queen, but as a captive, accompanied by the Duchess of Northumberland and Guilford Dudley, her husband. More prisoners were quickly added to their number. Northumberland was brought, with others of his adherents, from Cambridge. Northampton, who had hurried to Framlingham, where Mary then was, to throw himself upon her mercy, arrived soon after; with Bishop Ridley, who, notwithstanding his recent declamations against the Queen, had resorted with the rest to Norfolk, had met with an unfriendly reception from Mary, and was sent back to London "on a halting horse."183

It is singular that to the Duke of Suffolk, prominent amongst those who had been arrayed against her, the new Queen showed unusual indulgence. So far as actual deeds were concerned, he had been second in guilt only to Northumberland; though there can be little doubt that he was led and governed by the stronger will and more soaring ambition of his confederate. Lady Jane being, besides, his daughter, and not merely married to his son, it would have been natural to expect that he would have been called to a stricter account than Dudley. He was, as a matter of course, arrested and consigned to the Tower; but when a convenient attack253 of illness laid him low—a news-letter reporting that he was "in such case as no man judgeth he could live"184—and his wife represented his desperate condition to her cousin the Queen, adding that, if left in the Tower, death would ensue, Mary appears to have made no difficulty in granting her his freedom, merely ordering him to confine himself to his house, rather as restraint than as chastisement.185

Mary could afford to show mercy. On August 3 she made her triumphal entry into the capital which had proved so loyal to her cause, riding on a white horse, with the Earl of Arundel bearing before her the sword of state, and preceded by some thousand gentlemen in rich array.

Elizabeth was at her side—Elizabeth, who had learnt wisdom since the days, nearly five years ago, when she had compromised herself for the sake of Seymour. During the crisis now over, she had shown both prudence and caution, playing in fact a waiting game, as she looked on at the contest between her sister and Northumberland, and carefully abstaining from taking any side in it, until it should be seen which of the two would prove victorious. To her, as well as to Mary, a summons had been sent as from her dying brother; more wary than her sister, she detected the snare, and remained at Hatfield, whilst Mary came near to falling a prey to her enemies. At Hatfield she continued during254 the ensuing days, being visited by commissioners from Northumberland, who offered a large price, in land and money, in exchange for her acquiescence in Edward's appointment of Lady Jane as his successor. If Elizabeth loved money, she loved her safety more; and returned an answer to the effect that it was with her elder sister that an agreement must be made, since in Mary's lifetime she herself had neither claim nor title to the succession. Leti,186 representing her as regarding Lady Jane as a jeune étourdie—the first and only time the epithet can have been applied to Suffolk's grave daughter—states that she indignantly expostulated with Northumberland upon the wrong done to herself and Mary. She is more likely to have kept silence; and it is certain that an opportune attack of illness afforded her an excuse for prudent inaction. When Mary's cause had become triumphant she had recovered sufficiently to proceed to London, meeting her sister on the following day at Aldgate, and riding at her side when she made her entry into the capital.

From a photo by Emery Walker after a painting attributed to F. Zuccaro.
QUEEN ELIZABETH.

The two presented a painful contrast: Mary prematurely aged by grief and care, small and thin, "unlike in every respect to father or mother," says Michele, the Venetian ambassador, "with eyes so piercing as to inspire not only reverence, but fear"; Elizabeth, now twenty, tall and well made, though possessing more grace than beauty, with fine eyes,255 and, above all, beautiful hands, "della quale fa professione"—which she was accustomed to display.

Her entry into the City made, Mary proceeded, according to ancient custom, and as her unwilling rival had done three weeks before, to the Tower, where a striking scene took place. On her entrance she was met by a group of those who, imprisoned during the two previous reigns, awaited her on their knees. Her kinsman, Edward Courtenay, was there—since he was ten years old he had known no other home—and the Duchess of Somerset, widow of the Protector, with the old Duke of Norfolk, father to Surrey, Tunstall, the deprived Bishop of Durham, and Gardiner, Bishop of Winchester. In Mary's eyes some of these were martyrs, suffering for their fidelity to the faith for which she had herself been prepared to go to the scaffold; for others she felt the natural compassion due to captives who have wasted long years within prison walls; and, touched and overcome by the sight of that motley company, she burst into tears.

"These are my prisoners," she said, as she bent and kissed them.

Their day was come. By August 11 Gardiner was reinstated in Winchester House, which had been appropriated to the use of the Marquis of Northampton, now perhaps inhabiting the Bishop's quarters in the Tower. The Duke of Norfolk, the Duchess of Somerset, Courtenay, were all at liberty. Bonner256 was once more exercising his functions as Bishop of London. But their places in the old prison-house were not left vacant: fresh captives being sent to join those already there. Report declared—prematurely—that sentence had been passed on Northumberland, Huntingdon, Gates, and others. Pembroke, notwithstanding the zealous share he had taken in proclaiming Mary Queen, as well as Winchester and Darcy, were confined to their houses.

All necessary measures had been taken for the security of the Government. It was time to think of the dead boy lying unburied whilst the struggle for his inheritance had been fought out. In the arrangements for her brother's funeral Mary displayed a toleration that must have gone far to raise the hopes of the Protestant party, awaiting, in anxiety and dread, enlightenment as to the course the new ruler would pursue with regard to religion. Permitting her brother's obsequies to be celebrated by Cranmer according to the ritual prescribed by the reformed Prayer-book, she caused a Requiem Mass to be sung for him in the Tower in the presence of some hundreds of worshippers, notwithstanding the fact that, according to Griffet, "this was not in conformity with the laws of the Roman Church, since the Prince died in schism and heresy."187

It was the moment when Mary, the recipient, as she told the French ambassador, of more graces than257 any living Princess; the object of the love and devotion of her subjects; her long years of misfortune ended; her record unstained, should have died. But, unfortunately, five more years of life remained to her.

The presage of coming trouble was not absent in the midst of the general rejoicing, and the first notes of discord had already been struck. Emboldened by the Requiem celebrated in the Tower, a priest had taken courage, and had said Mass in the Church of St. Bartholomew in the City. It was then seen how far the people were from being unanimous in including in their devotion to the Queen toleration for her religion. "This day," reports a news-letter of August 11, "an old priest said Mass at St. Bartholomew's, but after that Mass was done, the people would have pulled him to pieces."188 "When they saw him go up to the altar," says Griffet, "there was a great tumult, some attempting to throw themselves upon him and strike him, others trying to prevent this violence, so that there came near to being blood shed."189

Scenes of this nature, with the open declarations of the Protestants that they would meet the re-establishment of the old worship with an armed resistance, and that it would be necessary to pass over the bodies of twenty thousand men before a258 single Mass should be quietly said in London, were warnings of rocks ahead. That Mary recognised the gravity of the situation was proved by the fact that, after an interview with the Mayor, she permitted the priest who had disregarded the law to be put into prison, although taking care that an opportunity of escape should shortly be afforded him.190

A proclamation made in the middle of August also testified to some desire upon the Queen's part, at this stage, to adopt a policy of conciliation. In it she declared that it was her will "that all men should embrace that religion which all men knew she had of long time observed, and meant, God willing, to continue the same; willing all men to be quiet, and not call men the names of heretick and papist, but each man to live after the religion he thought best until further order were taken concerning the same."191

Though the liberty granted was only provisional and temporary, there was nothing in the proclamation to foreshadow the fires of Smithfield, and it was calculated to allay any fears or forebodings disquieting the minds of loyal subjects.

259

CHAPTER XX

1553

Trial and condemnation of Northumberland—His recantation—Final scenes—Lady Jane's fate in the balances—A conversation with her.

The great subject of interest agitating the capital, when the excitement attending the Queen's triumphal entry had had time to subside, was the approaching trial of the Duke of Northumberland and his principal accomplices. On August 18 the great conspirator, with his son, the Earl of Warwick, and the Marquis of Northampton, were arraigned at Westminster Hall, the Duke of Norfolk, lately himself a prisoner, presiding, as High Steward of England, at the trial.

Its issue was a foregone conclusion. If ever man deserved to suffer the penalty for high treason, that man was Northumberland. His brain had devised the plot intended to keep the Queen out of the heritage hers by birth and right; his hand had done what was possible to execute it. He had commanded in person the forces arrayed against her, and had been taken, as it were, red-handed. He must have recognised the fact that any attempt at a260 defence would be hopeless. Two points of law, however, he raised: Could a man, acting by warrant of the great seal of England, and by the authority of the Council, be accused of high treason? And further, could he be judged by those who, implicated in the same offence, were his fellow-culprits?

The argument was quickly disposed of. If, as Mr. Tytler supposes,192 the Duke's intention was to appeal to the sanction of the great seal affixed to Edward's will, the judges preferred to interpret his plea, as most historians have concurred in doing, as referring to the seal used during Lady Jane's short reign; and, thus understood, the authority of a usurper could not be allowed to exonerate her father-in-law from the guilt of rebellion. As to his second question, so long as those by whom he was to be judged were themselves unattainted, they were not disqualified from filling their office. Sentence was passed without delay, the Duke proffering three requests. First, he asked that he might die the death of a noble; secondly, that the Queen would be gracious to his children, since they had acted by his command, and not of their own free will; and thirdly, that two members of the Council Board might visit him, in order that he might declare to them matters concerning the public welfare.

261 The trial had been conducted on a Friday. The uncertainty prevailing as to the condition of public sentiment in the city may be inferred from the fact, that, when the customary sermon was to be preached at Paul's Cross on the following Sunday, it was considered expedient to have the preacher chosen by the Queen surrounded by her guards, lest a tumult should ensue. The state of feeling in the capital must have been curiously mixed. Mary was the lawful sovereign, and had been brought to her rights amidst universal rejoicing. Northumberland was an object of detestation to the populace. Yet, whilst the Queen was undisguisedly devoted to a religion to which the majority of her subjects were hostile, the Duke was regarded as, with Suffolk, the chief representative and support of the faith they held and the Church as by law established. If his adherence to Protestant doctrine, as was now to appear, had been a matter of policy rather than of conviction, it had been singularly successful in imposing upon the multitude; though, according to the story which makes him observe to Sir Anthony Browne that he certainly thought best of the old religion, "but, seeing a new one begun, run dog, run devil, he would go forward," he had been at little pains to conceal his lack of genuine sympathy with innovation.193 When the speech was made, suspicion of Catholic262 proclivities would have been fatal to his position and his schemes. The case was now reversed. He was about to forfeit, by the fashion of his death, the solitary merit he had possessed in the eyes of a large section of his countrymen; to throw off the mask, however carelessly it had been worn; and to give the lie, at that supreme moment, to the professions of years.

It is said that, in consequence of the request he had preferred at his trial that he might be visited by some members of the Council, he was granted an interview with Gardiner and another of his colleagues, name unknown; that the Bishop of Winchester subsequently interceded with the Queen on his behalf, and was sanguine of success; but that, in deference to the Emperor's advice, Mary decided in the end that the Duke must die.194 To Arundel, in spite of the little encouragement he had received at Cambridge to hope that the Earl would prove his friend, Northumberland wrote, begging for life, "yea, the life of a dog, that he may but live and kiss the Queen's feet."195 All was in vain. Prayers, supplications, entreaties, were useless. He was to die.

Of those tried together with him, two shared his sentence—Sir Thomas Palmer and Sir John Gates. Monday, August 21, had been fixed for the executions, Commendone, the Pope's agent, delaying his263 journey to Italy at Mary's request that he might be present on the occasion.196 For some unexplained reason, they were deferred. It was probably in order to leave Northumberland time to make his recantation at leisure; for he had expressed his desire to renounce his errors "and to hear Mass and to receive the Sacrament according to the old accustomed manner."197

The account of what followed has been preserved in detail. At nine in the morning the altar in the chapel was prepared; and thither the Duke was presently conducted by Sir John Gage, Constable of the Tower, four of the lesser prisoners being brought in by the Lieutenant. Dying men, three of them, and the rest in jeopardy, it was a solemn company there assembled as the officiating priest proceeded with the ancient ritual. At a given moment the service was interrupted, so that the Duke might make his confession of faith and formally abjure the new ways he had followed for sixteen years, "the which is the only cause of the great plagues and vengeance which hath light upon the whole realm of England, and now likewise worthily fallen upon me and others here present for our unfaithfulness; ... and this I pray you all to testify, and pray for me."

264 After which, kneeling down, he asked forgiveness from all, and forgave all.

90

"Amongst others standing by," says the narrator of the scene, "were the Duke of Somerset's sons," Hertford and his brother, boys scarcely emerged from childhood; watching the fallen enemy of their house, and remembering that to him had been chiefly due their father's death.

Other spectators were some fourteen or fifteen merchants from the City, bidden to the chapel that they might witness the ceremony and perhaps make report of the Duke's recantation to their fellows.

The news of what was going forward must have spread through the Tower, partly palace, partly dungeon, partly fortress; and men must have looked strangely upon one another as they heard that the leader principally responsible for all that had happened in the course of the last month, to whom the safety of the Protestant faith had been war-cry and watchword, had abjured it as the work of the devil. Where was truth, or sincerity, or pure conviction to be found?

Of Lady Jane, during this day, there is but one mention. The limelight had been turned off her small figure, and she had fallen back into obscurity. Yet we hear that, looking through a window, she had seen her father-in-law led to the chapel, where he was, in her eyes, to imperil his soul. But265 whether she had been made aware of what was in contemplation we are ignorant.

The final scene took place on the succeeding day. At nine o'clock the scaffold was ready, and Sir John Gates, with young Lord Warwick, were brought forth to receive Communion in the chapel ("Memorandum," says the chronicler again, "the Duke of Somerset's sons stood by"). By one after the other, their abjuration had been made, and the priest present had offered what comfort he might to the men appointed to die.

"I would," he said, "ye should not be ignorant of God's mercy, which is infinite. And let not death fear you, for it is but a little while, ye know, ended in one half-hour. What shall I say? I trust to God it shall be to you a short passage (though somewhat sharp) out of innumerable miseries into a most pleasant rest—which God grant."

As the other prisoners were led out the Duke and Sir John Gates met at the garden gate. Northumberland spoke.

"Sir John," he said, "God have mercy on us, for this day shall end both our lives. And I pray you, forgive me whatsoever I have offended; and I forgive you, with all my heart, although you and your counsel was a great occasion thereof."

"Well, my Lord," was the reply, "I forgive you, as I would be forgiven. And yet you and your authority was the only original cause of all together.266 But the Lord pardon you, and I pray you forgive me."

So, not without a recapitulation of each one's grievance, they made obeisance, and the Duke passed on. Again, "the Duke of Somerset's sons stood thereby"—the words recur like a sinister refrain.

The end had come. Standing upon the scaffold, the Duke put off his damask gown; then, leaning on the rail, he repeated the confession of faith made on the previous day, begging those present to remember the old learning, and thanking God that He had called him to be a Christian. With his own hands he knit the handkerchief about his eyes, laid him down, and so met the executioner's blow.

Gates followed, with few words. Sir Thomas Palmer, having witnessed the ghastly spectacle, came last. That morning, whilst preparations for the executions were being made, he had been walking in the Lieutenant's garden, observed, says that "resident in the Tower" in whose diary so many incidents of this time have been preserved, to seem "more cheerful in countenance than when he was most at liberty in his lifetime"; and when the end was at hand, he met it, as some men did meet death in those days, with undaunted courage, and with a heroism not altogether unaffected by dramatic instinct.

267 Though apparently implicitly included amongst the prisoners who had made their peace with the Church, he is not recorded to have taken any prominent part in the affair, and his dying speech dealt with no controversial matters, but with eternal verities confessed alike by Catholic and Protestant. At his trial he had denied that he had ever borne arms against the Queen; though, charged with having been present when others did so, he acknowledged his guilt. He now passed that matter over, with a brief admission that his fate had been deserved at God's hands: "For I know it to be His divine ordinance by this mean to call me to His mercy and to teach me to know myself, what I am, and whereto we are all subject. I thank His merciful goodness, for He has caused me to learn more in one little dark corner in yonder Tower than ever I learned by any travail in so many places as I have been." For there he had seen God; he had seen himself; he had seen and known what the world was. "Finally, I have seen there what death is, how near hanging over every man's head, and yet how uncertain the time, and how unknown to all men, and how little it is to be feared. And why should I fear death, or be sad therefore? Have I not seen two die before mine eyes, yea, and within the hearing of mine ears? No, neither the sprinkling of the blood, or the shedding thereof, nor the bloody axe itself, shall not make me afraid."

Taking leave of all present, he begged their268 prayers, forgave the executioner, and, master of himself to the last, kneeling, laid his head upon the block.

"I will see how meet the block is for my neck," he said, "I pray thee, strike me not yet, for I have a few prayers to say. And that done, strike in God's name. Good leave have thou."

So the scene came to an end. The three rebels whose life Mary had taken—no large number—had paid the forfeit of their deed. That night the Lancaster Herald, a dependant of the Duke of Northumberland, more faithful to old ties and memories than those in higher place, sought the Queen, and begged of her his master's head, that he might give it sepulture. In God's name, Mary bade him take his lord's whole body and bury him. By a curious caprice of destiny the Duke was laid to rest in the Tower at the side of Somerset.198 There, in the reconciliation of a common defeat, the ancient rivals were united.

The three chief victims had thus paid the supreme penalty. The rest of the participators in Northumberland's guilt, if not pardoned, were suffered to escape with life. Young Warwick had shared his father's condemnation, and, finding that the excuse of youth was not to be allowed to avail in so grave a matter, had contented himself with begging that, out of his269 goods, forfeited to the Crown, his debts might be paid. Returning to the Tower, he had afterwards followed his father's example in abjuring Protestantism, and had listened, with the older victims, to the words addressed by the priest to the men appointed to die. Whether or not he had been aware that he was to be spared, Mass concluded, he had been taken back to his lodging and had not shared the Duke's fate.

Northampton's defence had been a strange one. He had, he said, forborne the execution of any public office during the interregnum and, being intent on hunting and other sports, had not shared in the conspiracy. The plea was not allowed to stand, but though he, like Warwick, was condemned, he was likewise permitted to escape with life. As Warwick's youth may have made its appeal to Mary, so she may have remembered that Northampton was the brother of her dead friend, Katherine Parr, and have allowed that memory to save him.

Lady Jane's fate had hung in the balances. By some she was still considered a menace to the stability of her cousin's throne. Charles V.'s ambassadors, representing to the Queen the need of proceeding with caution in matters of religion, urged the necessity of executing punishment upon the more guilty of those who had striven to deprive her of her crown, clemency being used towards the rest. In which class was Jane to be included? The270 determination of that question would decide her fate. At an interview between Mary and Simon Renard, one of the Emperor's envoys, it was discussed, the Queen declaring that she could not make up her mind to send Lady Jane to the scaffold; that she had been told that, before her marriage with Guilford Dudley, she had been bestowed upon another man by a contrat obligatoire, rendering the subsequent tie null and void. Mary drew from this hypothetical fact the inference that her cousin was not the daughter-in-law of the Duke of Northumberland's, adding that she had had no share in his undertaking, and that, as she was innocent, it would be against her own conscience to put her to death.

Renard demurred. He said, what was probably true, that it was to be feared that the alleged contract of marriage had been invented to save Lady Jane; and it would be necessary at the least to keep her a prisoner, since many inconveniences might be expected were she set at liberty. To this Mary agreed, promising that her cousin should not be liberated without all precautions necessary to ensure that no ill results would follow.199

This interview must have taken place shortly before Northumberland's death; for on August 23 the Emperor, to whom it had been duly reported, was replying by a reiteration of his opinion that271 all those who had conspired against the Queen, as well as any concerned in Edward's death, should be chastised without mercy. He advised that the executions should take place simultaneously, so that the pardon of the less guilty should follow without delay. If Mary was unable to resolve to put "Jeanne de Suffolck" to death, she ought at least to relegate her to some place of security, where she could be kept under supervision and rendered incapable of causing trouble in the realm.

That Mary had decided upon this course is clear, and there is no reason to believe that Lady Jane would have suffered death had it not been for her father's subsequent conduct. In the meantime, she remained a prisoner in the Tower, and on August 29, eleven days after the executions on Tower Hill, she is shown to us in one of the rare pictures left of her during the time of her captivity. On that day—a Tuesday—the diarist in the Tower, admitted to dine at the same table as the royal prisoner, placed upon record an account of the conversation.

Besides Lady Jane, who sat at the end of the board, there was present the narrator himself, one Partridge,200 and his wife—it was in "Partridge's house," or lodging within the Tower, that the guests met—with Lady Jane's gentlewoman and272 her man. Her presence had been unexpected by the diarist, as he was careful to explain, excusing his boldness in having accepted Partridge's invitation on the score that he had not been aware that she dined below.

Lady Jane did not appear anxious to stand on her dignity. Desiring guest and host to be covered, she drank to the new-comer and made him welcome. The conversation turned, naturally enough, upon the conduct of public affairs, of which Lady Jane was inclined to take a sanguine view.

"The Queen's Majesty is a merciful Princess," she observed. "I beseech God she may long continue, and send His merciful grace upon her."

Religious matters were discussed, Lady Jane inquiring as to who had been the preacher at St. Paul's the preceding Sunday.

"I pray you," she asked next, "have they Mass in London?"

"Yea, forsooth," was the answer, "in some places."

"It may be so," she said. "It is not so strange as the sudden conversion of the late Duke. For who would have thought he would have so done?" negativing at once and decidedly the suggestion made by some one present that a hope of escaping his imminent doom and winning pardon from the Queen might supply an explanation of his change of front.

273 "'Pardon?' repeated the dead man's daughter-in-law. 'Woe worth him! He hath brought me and our stock into most miserable calamity and misery by his exceeding ambition. But for the answering that he hoped for life by his turning, though other men be of that opinion, I utterly am not. For what man is there living, I pray you, although he had been innocent, that would hope of life in that case; being in the field against the Queen in person as general, and, after his taking, so hated and evil spoken of by the commons? and at his coming into prison so wondered at as the like was never heard by any man's time? Who was judge that he should hope for pardon, whose life was odious to all men? But what will ye more? Like as his life was wicked and full of dissimulation, so was his end thereafter. I pray God I, nor no friend of mine, die so. Should I who [am] young and in my fewers [few years?] forsake my faith for the love of life? Nay, God forbid, much more he should not, whose fatal course, although he had lived his just number of years, could not have long continued. But life was sweet, it appeared; so he might have lived, you will say, he did [not] care how. Indeed the reason is good, he that would have lived in chains, to have had his life, by like would leave no other means attempted. But God be merciful to us, for He saith, whoso denyeth Him before men, He will not know in His Father's Kingdom.'"

274 The conviction of Northumberland's daughter-in-law that his recantation had not been a mere device designed to lengthen his days may be allowed in some sort to weigh in favour of the man she hated; and it is also fair to remember that if his first abjuration may be accounted for by a lingering hope that it might purchase life, any such expectation must have been abandoned before the final repetition of it upon the scaffold. In Lady Jane's eyes, however, there seems to have been little to choose between a sham apostacy and a genuine reversion to his older creed.

"With this and much like talk the dinner passed away," and with exchange of courtesies the little company separated. The brief shaft of light throwing Lady Jane's figure into relief fades and leaves her once more in the shadow—a shadow that was to deepen above her till the end. It was early days of captivity still. Yet one discerns something of the passionate longing of the prisoner for freedom in her wonder that life in chains could be accounted worth any sacrifice.

275

CHAPTER XXI

1553

Mary's marriage in question—Pole and Courtenay—Foreign suitors—The Prince of Spain proposed to her—Elizabeth's attitude—Lady Jane's letter to Hardinge—The coronation—Cranmer in the Tower—Lady Jane attainted—Letter to her father—Sentence of death—The Spanish match.

To Mary there were at present matters of more personal and pressing moment than the fate of her ill-starred cousin. It was essential that the kingdom should be provided as quickly as possible with an heir whose title to the throne should admit of no question. Mary was no longer young and there was no time to lose. The question in all men's minds was who was to be the Queen's husband. Amongst Englishmen, Pole, who, though a Cardinal, was not in priest's orders, and Courtenay, the prisoner of the Tower, were both of royal blood, and considered in the light of possible aspirants to her hand. The first, however, was soon set aside, as disqualified by age and infirmity. Towards Courtenay she appeared for a time not ill-disposed. His unhappy youth, his long captivity, may have told in his favour in the eyes of a woman herself the victim of injustice and misfortune. He was276 young, not more than twenty-seven, handsome—called by Castlenau "l'un des plus beaux entre les jeunes seigneurs de son âge"—and the Queen cherished a special affection for his mother. He had been restored to the forfeited honours of his family, had been made Earl of Devonshire and Knight of the Bath. Gardiner also, whose opinion carried weight, was an advocate of the match. But on his enfranchisement from prison the young man had not used his liberty wisely. His head turned by the position already his, and the chance of a higher one, he had started his household on a princely scale, inducing many of the courtiers to kneel in his presence. Follies such as these Mary might have condoned, although the fact that she directed her cousin to accept no invitations to dinner without her permission indicates the exercise of a supervision somewhat like that to be kept over an emancipated schoolboy. But at a moment when he was aspiring to the highest rank to be enjoyed by any subject, his moral misconduct was matter of public report and sufficient to deter any woman from becoming his wife. He was also headstrong and self-willed, "so difficult to guide," sighed Noailles, "that he will believe nobody; and as one who has spent his life in a tower, seeing himself now in the enjoyment of entire liberty, cannot abstain from its delights, having no fear of those things which may be placed before him."

277 To these causes, rather than to the romantic passion for Elizabeth attributed to Courtenay by some other writers, Dr. Lingard attributes Mary's refusal to entertain the idea of becoming his wife. "In public she observed that it was not for her honour to marry a subject, but to her confidential friends she attributed the cause to the immorality of Courtenay."201

Her two English suitors disposed of, it remained to select a husband from amongst foreign princes—the King of Denmark, the Prince of Spain, the Infant of Portugal, the Prince of Piedmont, being all under consideration. A few months ago Mary had been a negligible quantity in the marriage market; she had now become one of the most desirable matches in Europe. She was determined to follow in her choice the advice of the Emperor; and the Emperor had hitherto abstained from proffering it, contenting himself with negativing the candidature of the son of the King of the Romans. It was not until September 20 that, in answer to her repeated inquiries, he instructed his ambassadors to offer her the hand of his son; requesting that the matter should be kept secret, even from her ministers of State, until he had been informed whether she was inclined to accept his suggestion.202 The contents of the Emperor's despatch278 must have been communicated to the Queen immediately before her coronation on September 30; but not being as yet made public there was nothing to interfere with the loyal rejoicings of the people, to whom the very idea of the Spanish match would have been abhorrent.

Meantime the attitude of Elizabeth was increasing the desire of the Catholic party that a direct heir should be born to the Catholic Queen. The nation was insensibly dividing itself into two camps, and the Protestant and Catholic parties eyed one another with suspicion, each looking to the sister who shared its faith for support. The enthusiasm displayed towards Elizabeth by a section of the people was not conducive to the continuance of affectionate relations between the Queen and the next heir to the throne,

Pope Julius describing the younger sister as being in the heart and mouth of every one. Elizabeth was in a position of no little difficulty. She desired to continue on good terms with the Queen; she was not willing to relinquish her chief title to honour in Protestant eyes; and it is possible that genuine religious sentiment, a sincere preference for the creed she professed, may have added to her embarrassment. It may have been due to conviction that she declined to bow to her sister's wishes by attending Mass, refusing so much as to be present at the ceremonial which created Courtenay Earl of Devonshire. It was satisfactory to know that279 Protestant England looked on and applauded. It was less pleasant to hear that some of the Queen's hot-headed friends, interpreting her refusal as an act of disrespect to their mistress, had demanded—though vainly—her arrest; and though on September 6 Noailles reported to his master that on the previous Saturday and Sunday the Princess had proved deaf to the arguments of preachers and the solicitations of Councillors, and had gone so far as to make a rude reply to the last, she suddenly changed her tactics, fell on her knees, weeping, before Mary, and begged that books and teachers might be supplied to her, so that she might perhaps see cause to alter the faith in which she had been brought up. The expectation seems to have been promptly realised. On September 8 she accompanied the Queen to Mass, and, expressing an intention of establishing a chapel in her house, wrote to the Emperor to ask permission to purchase the ornaments for it in Brussels.

It was a season of sudden conversions. Elizabeth was not the only person who saw the wisdom of conforming in appearance or in sincerity to the standard set up by the Queen. Hardinge, a chaplain of the Duke of Suffolk's—he must have succeeded to the post of the worthy Haddon—had recognized his errors; and it is believed that to him a letter of Lady Jane's—though signed with her unmarried name—was addressed. Printed in English, and280 abroad, perhaps through the instrumentality of her former tutor, Aylmer, it is an epistle of expostulation, reproof, and warning, couched in the violent language of the time. To her "noble friend, newly fallen from the truth" she writes, marvelling at him, and lamenting the case of one who, once the lively member of Christ, was now the deformed imp of the devil, and from the temple of God was become the kennel of Satan—with much more in the same strain. It has not been recorded what effect, if any, the missive produced upon the delinquent to whom it was addressed.

Elizabeth, for her part, had effectually made her peace with her sister. The coronation, on October 10, found their relations restored to a pleasant footing, and Elizabeth's proper place at the ceremony was assured to her. To Mary, a sad and lonely woman, the reconciliation must have been welcome. To Elizabeth the material advantages of standing on terms of affection with the Queen will have appealed more strongly than motives of sentiment; and that her attitude was surmised by those about her would seem to be shown by a curious incident reported in the despatches of the imperial ambassador.

As the younger sister bore the crown to be placed upon Mary's head, she complained to M. de Noailles, who stood near, of its weight. It was heavy, she said, and she was weary.

281 The Frenchman replied with a flippant jest, overheard by Charles's ambassador, though Noailles himself, perhaps convicted of indiscretion, makes no mention of it in his account of the day's proceedings. Let Elizabeth have patience, he replied. When the crown should shortly be upon her own head it would appear lighter.203

Outwardly all was as it should be. Mary held her sister's hand in an affectionate clasp, assigning to her the place of honour next her own at the ensuing banquet, and court and nation looked on and were edified.

Gardiner, now not only Bishop of Winchester but Lord Chancellor, had performed the rites of the coronation, in the absence of the Archbishops, both in confinement. The Tower had been once more opening its hospitable doors, and a fortnight earlier its resident diarist had noted Cranmer's arrival. "Item, the Bishop of Canterbury was brought into the Tower as prisoner, and lodged in the Tower over the gate anenst the water-gate, where the Duke of Northumberland lay before his death."

Nor was Cranmer the only churchman to find a lodging there. Doctor Ridley had preceded him to the universal prison-house, and on the same day that the Archbishop took up his residence in it "Master Latimer was brought to the Tower prisoner; who at his coming said to one Rutter,282 a warder there, 'What, my old friend, how do you? I am now come to be your neighbour again,' and was lodged in the garden in Sir Thomas Palmer's lodging."

Ominous quarters both! It was a day when the great fortress received, and discharged, many guests.

If Cranmer had drawn his imprisonment upon himself, the imprudence to which it was due did him honour. He had at first been treated by Mary with an indulgence the more singular when it is remembered that he had been the instrument of her mother's divorce, and a strenuous supporter of Lady Jane. Prudence would have dictated the adoption on his part of a policy of silence; but, confined to his house at Lambeth, and regarding with the bitterness inevitable in a man of his convictions the steps in course of being taken for the restoration of the ancient worship, the news that Mass had been once again celebrated in Canterbury Cathedral, and that it was commonly reported that it had been done with his consent and connivance, was too much for him. Feeling the need of clearing himself from what he regarded as a damaging imputation, he wrote and spread abroad a declaration of his faith and opinions, adding to it a violent attack upon the rites of the Catholic Church. By Mary and her advisers the challenge could scarcely have been ignored;283 and it was this document, read to the people in the streets, which was the cause of the Archbishop being called before the Council and committed to the Tower on a charge of treason accompanied by the spreading abroad of seditious libels.204

The Tower continued to be, in some sort, the centre of all that was going forward. On September 27, two days before the coronation, Mary had again visited the fortress whither she had so nearly escaped being brought in quite another character and guise. Elizabeth came with her, and she was attended by the whole Council—just as they had, not three months before, attended upon Jane, the innocent usurper. And somewhere in the great dark building the little Twelfth-night Queen must have listened to the pealing of the joy-bells and to the acclamations of the people who had kept so ominous a silence when she herself had made her entry. Perhaps young Guilford Dudley too, who a week or two before had been accorded "the liberty of the leads on Beacham's Tower," may have stood above, catching a glimpse of the show, and remembering the day when he and his wife had their boy-and-girl quarrel, because she would not make him a King.

The two questions of the hour were those relating to the Queen's marriage and to matters of religion. When Parliament met on October 5,284 the news of the Spanish match had not been announced, and the bills of chief interest passed were one dealing with the important point of the validity of Katherine of Aragon's marriage, and a second, which, avoiding any discussion of the Papal supremacy, the only thoroughly unpopular article of the Catholic creed, cancelled recent legislation on ecclesiastical matters, and restored the ritual in use during the last year of Henry's reign. The other important measure carried in this session was the attainder of Cranmer, Lady Jane and her husband, and Sir Ambrose Dudley.

So far as Lady Jane was concerned the step was purely formal, intended to serve as a warning to her friends, and it was understood on all hands that a pardon would be granted to the guiltless figure-head of the conspiracy. Yet to a nervous child, not yet seventeen, there may well have been something terrifying in the sentence hanging over her, and it seems to have been about this time that she addressed a letter to her father which could scarcely have been otherwise conceived had she expected in truth to suffer the penalty due to treason.

From an etching by W. Hollar.
Photo by W. A. Mansell & Co.
THE TOWER OF LONDON.

"If I may without offence rejoice in mine own mishap," she wrote, "meseems in this I may account myself blessed, that washing mine hands with the innocency of my fact, my guiltless blood may cry before the Lord, mercy, mercy to the innocent. And yet I must acknowledge that being285 constrained, and, as you wot well enough, continually assailed, in taking upon me I seemed to consent, and therein offended the Queen and her laws, yet do I assuredly trust that this mine offence towards God is much the less, in that being in so royal an estate as I was, mine enforced honour never agreed with mine innocent heart."205

The trial was held on November 13, on which day Cranmer, with Guilford, and his brother, and Lady Jane, were all conducted on foot to the Guildhall to answer the charge of treason.

The Archbishop led the way, followed by young Dudley. After them came Lady Jane, a childish figure of woe, dressed in black, with a French hood, also black, a book bound in black velvet hanging at her side, and another in her hand.

Her condemnation was a foregone conclusion, and, pleading guilty, she was sentenced to death, by the axe or by fire, according to the old brutal law dealing with a woman convicted of treason. As she returned to the Tower a demonstration took place in her honour, not unlikely to be productive of some uneasiness to those in power, and little calculated to serve her cause.

The London populace were more favourably disposed towards her in misfortune, than in her brief period of prosperity. The sight of the forlorn pair, still no more than boy and girl,286 touched and moved the multitude, and crowds accompanied them to their place of captivity. It is said that this was the solitary occasion upon which she and Guilford Dudley met during their imprisonment.

Another cause, besides simple pity, was perhaps responsible for the tenderness displayed towards the Queen's rival. A week or two before the trial the news of the Spanish match had been made known to the public, and may have had the effect of suggesting doubts as to the wisdom of the enthusiastic welcome given to Mary. At the beginning of November the affair had been undecided, and Gardiner was telling the Emperor's envoy candidly that, if the Queen asked his advice, he would counsel her to choose an Englishman for her husband. The nation, he added, was deeply prejudiced against foreign domination, especially in the case of Spaniards, and the proposed union would also produce war with France.

Mary's mind, however, was made up, nor had she any intention of being swayed by Gardiner's advice. On the night of October 30 she took the singular step of summoning the ambassador, Simon Renard, to her apartment; when, in the presence of the Blessed Sacrament, and after repeating on her knees the Veni Creator, she gave him her promise to wed the Prince of Spain. In the face of the curious determination thus shown287 to

98

bind herself by a contract irrevocable in her own eyes, it is strange to find historians attributing to her a continued leaning towards Courtenay.

When the fact got abroad that the Emperor's son was destined to become the Queen's husband, London thrilled with indignation; whilst Parliament made its sentiments plain by means of a deputation which, in an address containing an entreaty that she would marry, expressed a hope that her choice would fall upon an Englishman. But Mary was a Tudor. Dispensing with the customary medium of the Chancellor, she gave her reply in person. Thanking the petitioners for their zeal, she declared herself disposed to act upon their advice and to take a husband. It was, however, for herself alone to select one, according to her inclination, and for the good of her kingdom.

Simon Renard, reporting the scene, observed that her speech had been applauded by the nobles present, Arundel informing the Chancellor in jest that he had been deprived of his office, since the Queen had undertaken the functions belonging to it. In the pleasantry the Emperor's envoy detected a warning that should Gardiner continue his opposition to the match he would not long retain his present post.206

The Bishop yielded. He may have agreed with Renard. At all events, the Queen being determined,288 and recognising that he was unable to deter her from the measure upon which she had decided, he took the prudent step of putting himself on her side. His opposition removed, Renard was able to inform his master, on December 17, that Mary had received him in open daylight, had informed him that the necessity for secrecy was at an end, and that she regarded her marriage as a thing definitely and irrevocably fixed.207

289

CHAPTER XXII

1553-1554

Discontent at the Spanish match—Insurrections in the country—Courtenay and Elizabeth—Suffolk a rebel—General failure of the insurgents—Wyatt's success—Marches to London—Mary's conduct—Apprehensions in London, and at the palace—The fight—Wyatt a prisoner—Taken to the Tower.

When the year 1553 drew towards its close there was nothing to indicate that any catastrophe was at hand. The crisis appeared to be past and no further danger to be apprehended. Northumberland and his principal accomplices had paid the penalty of their treason. Suffolk, with lesser criminals, had been allowed to escape it; the rest of the confederates had been practically pardoned. If some were still in confinement it was understood to be without danger to life or limb. In the Tower Lady Jane and her husband lay formally under sentence of death, but the conditions of their captivity had been lightened; on December 18 Lady Jane was accorded "the liberty of the Tower," and was permitted to walk in the Queen's garden and on the hill; Guilford and his brother—Elizabeth's Leicester—were allowed the liberty of the leads in the Bell Tower. Both290 Northampton and young Warwick—who did not long survive his enfranchisement—had been released. No further chastisement seemed likely to be inflicted in expiation of the late attempt to keep Mary out of her rights.

Yet discontent was on the increase. As early as November steps had been taken to induce Courtenay to head a new conspiracy. He was timid and faint-hearted, and urged delay, and nothing had, so far, come of it. It would be well, he said, advocating a policy of procrastination, to wait to be certain that the Queen was determined upon the Spanish match before taking hazardous measures to oppose it.208

Thus Christmas had found the country ostensibly at peace, and the prisoners in the Tower with no reason to fear any change for the worse in their condition. On the following day the thunder of the cannon discharged as a welcome to the Emperor's ambassadors sounded in their ears, and was, though they were ignorant of it, the prelude of their destruction. The arrival of envoys expressly charged with the marriage negotiations put the matter beyond doubt; nor was England in a mood to submit passively to a union it hated and feared.

By January 2 the Counts of Egmont and Laing and the Sieur de Corriers had reached the capital; landing at the Tower, where they were greeted291 with a salute from the guns, and met by the Earl of Devonshire, who escorted them through the City. "The people, nothing rejoicing, held down their heads sorrowfully." When on the previous day the retinue of the Spanish envoys had ridden through the town, more forcible expression had been given to public opinion, and they had been pelted with snowballs.209

Matters were pressed quickly on. By January 13 the formal announcement of the unpopular arrangement, with its provisions, was made by Gardiner in the Presence-chamber at Westminster to the lords and nobles there assembled; hope could no longer be entertained that the Queen would be otherwise persuaded. "These news," adds the Tower diarist, "although they were not unknown to many and very much disliked, yet being now in this wise pronounced, was not only credited, but also heavily taken of sundry men; yea, and almost each man was abashed, looking daily for worse matters to grow shortly after."

They did not look in vain. The unpopularity of the Spanish match was the direct cause of the insurrections which soon broke out. Indirectly it was the cause of the death of Lady Jane Grey.

Wild tales were afloat, rousing the passions of the angry people to fever-heat. Some reports stated that Edward was still alive; others asserted that292 the tower and the forts were to be seized and held by an imperialist army; abuse of every kind was directed against the Prince of Spain and his nation. Mary was said to have given her pledge that she would marry no foreigner, and by the breach of this promise she was declared to have forfeited the crown. Fresh schemes were set on foot for a rising in the spring. It does not appear that the substitution of Lady Jane for her cousin was again generally contemplated. That plan had resulted in so complete a failure that it had probably been tacitly admitted that the arrangement would not work. But the eyes of many were turning towards Elizabeth. She was to wed Courtenay, and they were jointly to occupy the throne. The two principally concerned were not likely to have refused to fall in with the project had it seemed to offer a fair chance of success, and France was in favour of it.

"By what I hear," wrote Noailles, "it will be by my Lord Courtenay's own fault if he does not marry her, and she does not follow him to Devonshire,"—the selected centre of operations—"but the misfortune is that the said Courtenay is in such fear that he dares undertake nothing. I see no reason that prevents him save lack of heart."

Courtenay was in truth not the stuff of which conductors of revolutions are made. Gratitude and loyalty would not have availed to keep him true to Mary, and in able hands he might293 have become the instrument of a rebellion. But Gardiner found no difficulty in so playing on his apprehensions as to lead him to divulge the plots that were on foot; and his revelations, or betrayals, whichever they are to be called, precipitated the action of the conspirators. If their enterprise was to be attempted, no time must be lost.210

On January 20 it became known that Devonshire was in arms, "resisting the King of Spain's coming," and that Exeter was in the hands of the insurgents. By the 25th the Duke of Suffolk, with his two brothers, Lord John and Lord Leonard Grey, had fled from his house at Sheen, and gone northwards to rouse his Warwickshire tenants to insurrection. It was currently reported that he had narrowly escaped being detained, a messenger from the Queen having arrived as he was on the point of starting, with orders that he should repair to Court.

"Marry," said the Duke, "I was coming to her Grace. Ye may see I am booted and spurred ready to ride, and I will but break my fast and go."

Bestowing a present upon the messenger, he gave him drink, and himself departed, no one then knew whither.

That same day tidings had reached the Council that Kent had risen, Sir Thomas Wyatt at its head, with Culpepper, Cobham, and others, alleging, as their sole motives, resistance to the Prince of Spain,294 and the removal of certain lords from the Council Board. Sir John Crofts had proceeded to Wales to call upon it to join the insurrectionary movement.

The country being thus in a turmoil the two persons who should have taken the lead and upon whom much of the success of the insurgents depended were playing a cautious game. Courtenay was at Court, and Elizabeth remained at Ashridge to watch the event, no doubt prepared to shape her course accordingly. A letter addressed to her by her partisans, counselling her withdrawal to Dunnington, as to a place of greater safety, had been intercepted by the authorities; and she had received an invitation, or command, to join her sister at St. James's, where, it was significantly added, she would be more secure than either at Ashridge or Dunnington. On the score of ill-health she disobeyed the summons, fortifying the house, and assembling around it some numbers of armed retainers.

From a photo by Emery Walker after a painting by Joannes Corvus in the National Portrait Gallery.

HENRY GREY, DUKE OF SUFFOLK, K.G.

The hopes built by the insurgents upon the general discontent throughout the country were doomed to disappointment. It was one thing to disapprove of the Queen's choice; it was quite another to take up arms against her. Devonshire proved cold; most of the leaders there were seized, or compelled to make their escape to France; Crofts had been pursued to Wales, and was arrested before he had time to rally any support in the principality.

295 Suffolk had done no better in the Midlands. Authorities are divided as to his intentions. By Dr. Lingard it is considered uncertain whether he meant to press Elizabeth's claims or to revive those of his daughter. With either upon the throne the dominance of the Protestant religion would have been ensured, and, unlike Northumberland, Suffolk was sincere and honest in his attachment to the principles of the Reformation. Other writers, however, assert categorically that he caused Lady Jane to be proclaimed at his halting-places as he went north; and the sequel seems to make it probable that she had been once more forced into a position of dangerous prominence.

Whatever may have been the exact nature of the scheme he propounded, the country made no response to his appeal; after a skirmish near Coventry he gave up hopes of any immediate success, disbanded his followers, and, betrayed by a tenant upon whose fidelity he had believed he could count, fell into the hands of those in pursuit of him. By February 10 he had gone to swell the numbers of the prisoners in the Tower.

The rising in Kent had alone answered in any degree to the expectations of its promoters. Drawn into the conspiracy, if his own assertions are to be credited, by Courtenay, Wyatt had become the most conspicuous leader of the insurrection known by his name. He was well296 fitted for the post. Brave, skilful, and secret, he was, says Noailles, "un gentilhomme le plus vaillant et assuré que j'ai jamais ouï parler"; and whether or not he had been deserted by the man to whom it was due that he had taken up arms, he was not disposed to submit to defeat without a struggle.

Fixing his headquarters at Rochester, he had gathered together a body of some fifteen thousand men, and was there found by the Duke of Norfolk, sent at the head of the Queen's forces against him. The utmost enthusiasm prevailed amongst the insurgents, and when a herald arrived in Rochester commissioned by the Duke to proclaim a pardon for all who would consent to lay down arms, "each man cried that they had done nothing wherefore they should need any pardon, and that quarrel which they took they would die and live in it."211 Sir George Harper was in fact the sole rebel who accepted the proffered boon.

Worse was to follow. At the first encounter of the royal troops with the Kentish men Captain Bret, leading five hundred Londoners, went over to the rebels, explaining in a spirited speech the grounds for his desertion, the miseries which might be expected to befall the nation should the Spaniards bear rule over it, and expressing his determination to spend his blood "in the quarrel of this worthy captain, Master Wyatt."212

297 It was an ominous beginning to the struggle, and at the applause greeting Bret's announcement, the Duke of Norfolk, the Earl of Ormond, and Jerningham, Captain of the Guard, fled. Wyatt, taking instant advantage of the situation, rode in amongst the Queen's troops, crying out that any who desired to join him should be welcome and that those who wished might depart.

Most of the men accepted the alternative of throwing in their lot with Wyatt and his company, leaving their leaders to return without them to London. "Ye should have seen," adds the diarist, from whom these details and many others of this episode are taken, "some of the Guard come home, their coats turned, all ruined, without arrows or string in their bow, or sword, in very strange wise; which discomfiture, like as it was very heart-sore and displeasing to the Queen and Council, even so it was almost no less joyous to the Londoners and most part of others."

With the capital in this temper, the juncture was a critical one. Wyatt was marching on London, and who could say what reception he would meet with at the hands of the discontented populace? The fact that he was encountered at Deptford by a deputation from the Council, sent to inquire into his demands, is proof of the apprehensions entertained. The interview did not end amicably. Flushed with victory, Wyatt was not disposed to be moderate.298 To Sir Edward Hastings, who asked the reason why, calling himself a true subject, he played the part of a traitor, he answered boldly that he had assembled the people to defend the realm from the danger of being overrun by strangers, a result which must follow from the proposed marriage of the Queen.

Hastings temporised. No stranger was yet come who need be suspected. Therefore, if this was their only quarrel, the Queen would be content they should be heard.

"To that I yield," returned Wyatt warily, "but for my further surety I would rather be trusted than trust."

In carrying out this principle of caution it was reported that he had pressed his demand for confidence so far as to require that the custody of the Tower, and the Queen's person within it, should be conceded to him. If this was the case, he can scarcely have felt much surprise that the negotiations were brought to an abrupt conclusion, Hastings replying hotly that before his traitorous conditions should be granted, Wyatt and twenty thousand with him should die. And thus the conference ended.213

London was in a ferment. Mayor, aldermen, and many of the citizens went about in armour, "the lawyers pleaded their causes in harness," and when Dr. Weston said Mass before the Queen on299 Ash Wednesday he wore a coat of mail beneath his vestments. There had been no need to bid the Spanish ambassadors to depart, those gentlemen having prudently decamped as speedily as possible. Upon February 2 Mary in person proceeded to the Guildhall, and, there meeting the chief amongst the citizens, made them a speech which was an admirable combination of appeal and independence, and showed that if outwardly she bore no resemblance to father or sister the Tudor spirit was alive in her. She had come, she said, to tell them what they already knew—of the treason of the Kentish rebels, who demanded the possession of her person, the keeping of the Tower, and the placing and displacing of her counsellors.

That day marked the crisis in the progress of the insurrection. Mary's visit to the Guildhall had taken place on February 2. When on the following day Wyatt, leaving Deptford, marched to Southwark the tide had turned. His followers were falling away; no other part of the country was in arms to support him; and his position was becoming desperate. His daring, nevertheless, did not fail. A price had been put upon his head, and, aware of the proclamation, he caused his name to be "fair written," and set it on his cap. The act of bravado was characteristic of the spirit of the popular leader.

Meantime the measures to be taken against him300 were anxiously discussed. On the 4th Sir Nicholas Poynings, on duty at the Tower, waited upon the Queen to receive her orders, and to learn whether the ordnance was to be directed upon Southwark, and the houses knocked down upon the heads of Wyatt and his men, quartered in that district.

Mary, to her honour, refused to authorise the drastic mode of attack.

"Nay," she replied, "that were pity; for many poor men and householders are like to be undone there and killed. For, God willing, they shall be fought with to-morrow."

The innocent were not to be involved in the destruction of the guilty. Her decision was unwelcome at the Tower. The night before Sir John Bridges had expressed his surprise to the sentinel on duty that the rebels had not yet been fought.

"By God's mother," he added, "I fear there is some traitor abroad, that they be suffered all this while. For surely if it had been about my sentry [or beat] I would have fought with them myself, by God's grace."

Wyatt, strangely enough, was no less pitiful than the Queen. Although she had refused permission for the discharge of the guns, they had been directed by those responsible for them upon the spot where the rebel body was stationed; and, in terror of a cannonade, the inhabitants, men and women, approached the insurgent leader "in most lamentable301 wise," setting forth the danger his presence was bringing upon them, and praying him for the love of God to have pity. The appeal was not made in vain.

"At which words he, being partly abashed, stayed awhile, and then said these, or much like words, 'I pray you, my friends, content yourselves a little, and I will soon ease you of this mischief. For God forbid that you, or the least child here, should be hurt or killed on my behalf,' and so in most speedy manner marched away."

A meeting was to have taken place before sunrise with some of the disaffected in the City. By this means it had been hoped that a surprise might be contrived. But a portion of Kingston Bridge, where the river was to be crossed, had been destroyed; time was lost in repairing it, and the assignation at Ludgate was missed. The scheme had supplied Wyatt's last chance and failure was staring him in the face. Rats were leaving the sinking vessel. The Protestant Bishop of Winchester, who had hitherto lent the countenance of his presence in the camp to the insurgents, fled beyond seas; Sir George

Harper, having rejoined Wyatt's forces, deserted for the second time, and made his way to St. James's to give warning to the Court of the approach of the rebel leader.

Such being the condition of things, it is singular to find that at the palace something like a panic302 was prevailing. Mary was entreated by her ministers to seek safety at the Tower; and, though deciding in the end to remain at her post, she appears at first to have been inclined to act upon the suggestion. A plan of action was determined upon in a hurried consultation. Wyatt, it was agreed, was to be permitted to reach the City, with a certain number of his followers, and having been thus detached from the main body of his troops it was hoped that he would be trapped and seized.

In the meantime arrangements were made for the defence of the Queen and the palace. Edward Underhyll, the Hot-Gospeller for whose child Lady Jane had stood godmother six months earlier, and who was on duty as a gentleman-pensioner at St. James's, has left a graphic account of the scene there that night, and of the terror of the Queen's ladies when the pensioners, armed with pole-axes, were placed on guard in their mistress's apartments. The breach of etiquette appears to have struck them as an earnest of the peril to which it was owing. Was such a sight ever seen, they cried, wringing their hands, that the Queen's chamber should be full of armed men?

Underhyll, for his part, soon received his dismissal. As the usher charged with the duty looked at the list of the pensioners before calling them over, his eye was caught by the well-known name of the Hot-Gospeller.

303 "By God's Body," he said, "that heretic shall not watch here!" and Underhyll, taking his men with him, and professing satisfaction at his exemption from duty, went his way.

By the morning he had reconsidered the matter, and thought it well to ignore his rebuff and return to his post. For the present, he joined company with one of the Throckmortons, who had just left the palace after reporting there the welcome tidings of the capture of the Duke of Suffolk at Coventry, the two proceeding together to Ludgate, intending to pass the remainder of the night in the City. The gate, however, was found to be fast locked, and those on guard within explained, with much ill-timed laughter, to the tired wayfarers outside, that they were not entrusted with the keys, and could give admittance to none.

It was disconcerting intelligence to men in search of a lodging and repose; and Throckmorton, in especial, fresh from his hurried journey, felt that he was hardly treated.

"I am weary and faint," he complained, "and I wax now cold." No man would open his door in this dangerous time, and he would perish that night. Such was his piteous lament.

Underhyll, a man of resource, had a plan to propose.

"Let us go to Newgate," he suggested. He thought himself secure of an entrance there into304 the city. At the worst, he had acquaintances within the prison—like most men at that day—having recently been in confinement there. The door of the keeper of the gaol was without the gate, and Underhyll entertained no doubts of finding a hospitable reception in his old quarters. Throckmorton, it was true, declared at first that he would almost as soon die in the street as seek so ill-omened a refuge; but in the end the two proceeded thither, and, a friend of Underhyll's being fortunately in command of the guard placed outside the gate, the wanderers were permitted to enter the City.

Whilst consternation and alarm were felt at the palace at the tidings of Wyatt's approach, the rebel leader himself must have been aware that the game had been played and lost. Yet he kept up a bold front, and refused to acknowledge that he was beaten.

"Twice have I knocked, and not been suffered to enter," he was reported to have said. "If I knock the third time I will come in, by God's grace."

They were brave words. An incident of his march to Kingston nevertheless sounds the note of a consciousness of impending defeat. Meeting, as he went, a merchant of London who was known to him, he charged him with a greeting to his fellow-citizens. "And say unto them from me that when liberty and freedom was offered them they would not accept305 it, neither would they admit me within their gates, who for their freedom and the disburthening of their griefs and oppression by strangers would have frankly spent my blood in that their cause and quarrel; ... therefore they are the less to be bemoaned hereafter when the miserable tyranny of strangers shall oppress them."

It may be that by some amongst the men to whom the message was sent his words were remembered thereafter.

Still the insurgents pushed on. By nine in the morning Knightsbridge was reached. Disheartened, weary, and faint for lack of food, they were in no condition to stand against the Queen's troops. But the mere fact of their vicinity was disquieting to those in no position to form a correct estimate of their strength or weakness, and when Underhyll returned to the palace he found confusion and turmoil there.

His men were stationed in the hall, which was to be their special charge. Sir John Gage, with part of the guard, was placed outside the gate, the rest of the guard were within the great courtyard; the Queen occupying the gallery by the gatehouse, whence she could watch what should befall.

This was the disposition of the defenders, when suddenly a body of the rebels made their way to the very gates of the palace. A struggle took place; Gage and three of the judges who had been with306 him retreated hurriedly within the gates, Sir John, who was old, stumbling in his haste and falling in the mire. Within all was in disorder. The gates had clanged to behind Gage, his soldiers, and the men of law, as they gained the shelter of the courtyard. Without the rebels were using their bows and arrows. The guard stationed in the outer court, attempting to make good their entrance to the hall, were forcibly ejected by the gentlemen pensioners in charge of it. Poor Gage—"so frighted that he could not speak to us"—and the three judges, also in such terror that force would have been necessary to keep them out, were alone admitted to the comparative safety it afforded.

There was in truth little reason for alarm. The manœuvre decided upon during the night had been executed. The Queen's troops, Pembroke at their head, had deliberately permitted Wyatt to break through their lines, and, with some hundreds of his men, to proceed eastward. Behind him the enemy had closed up, and he was separated from the main body of the rebels, thus left leaderless to be engaged by the royal forces. The Queen's orders had been successfully carried out. But to the anxious watchers in the palace the affair may have worn the aspect of a defeat, if not of a treason, and there were not wanting those who suspected Pembroke of a betrayal of his trust. A shout was raised that all was lost.

307 "Away, away! a barge, a barge!—let the Queen be placed in safety!" was the cry.

Again Mary was to show that she was a Tudor. She would not beat a retreat before rebels. Where, she inquired, was the Earl of Pembroke? and receiving the answer that he was in the field, "Well then," she said, "fall to prayer, and I warrant you that we shall have better news anon, for my lord will not deceive me, I know well. If he would, God will not, in Whom my chief trust is, Who will not deceive me."

Though it was well to have confidence in God, men with arms in their hands would have liked to use them, and the pensioners entreated Sir Richard Southwell, in authority within the palace, to have the gates opened that they might try a fall with the enemy; else, they threatened, they would break them down. It was too much shame that the doors should be shut upon a few rebels.

Southwell was quite of the same mind; and, interceding with Mary, obtained her leave for the pensioners to have their way, provided they would not go out of her sight, since her trust was in them—a command she reiterated as, the gates being thrown open, the band marched under the gallery, where she still kept her place. It was not long before her confidence in the commander of the royal troops was justified, and news was brought that put an end to all fear. Wyatt was taken.

308 At the head of that body of his men who had been allowed to clear the enemy's lines, he had ridden on towards the City, had passed Temple Bar and Fleet Street, till Ludgate was reached. There he halted. He had kept his tryst, fulfilled the pledge he had given, and knocked, as he had promised, at the gate. Let them open to him; Wyatt was there—successful so long, he may have thought there was magic in the name—Wyatt was there; the Queen had granted their requests.

The City remained unmoved; and, in terms of insult, Sir William Howard refused him entrance.

"Avaunt, traitor," he said, barring the way, "thou shalt not come in here."

It was the last blow. The poor chance that the City might have lent its aid had constituted the single remaining possibility of a retrieval of the fortunes of the insurrection. That vanished, the end was inevitable. London had blustered, had expressed its detestation for the Spanish match, had paraded its Protestantism; it was now plain that it had not meant business, and the man who had taken it at its word was doomed.

A strange little scene followed—a scene forming an interlude, as it were, in the tumult and excitement of the hour. It may be that the effects of the strain and fatigue of the last weeks, of the hopes and fears that had filled them, of the march of the night before, unlightened by any genuine309 anticipation of victory, were suddenly felt by the man who had borne the burden and heat of the day. At any rate, turning without further parley, he made his way back to the Bel Savage Inn, and there "awhile stayed, and, as some say, rested him upon a seat." Sitting there, trapped by his enemies, in "the shirt of mail, with sleeves very fair, velvet cassock, and the fair hat of velvet with broad bone-work lace" he had worn that day, he may have looked on and seen the future bounded by a scaffold. Then, rousing himself, he rose, and returned by the way he had come, until Temple Bar was reached.

Though the combat was there renewed, all must have known that further resistance was vain, and at length, yielding to a remonstrance at the shedding of useless blood, Wyatt consented to acknowledge his defeat and to yield himself a prisoner to Sir Maurice Berkeley. He had fought the battle of many men who had taken no weapon in hand to support him. When false hopes had at one time been entertained of his success "many hollow hearts rejoiced in London at the same." But scant sympathy will have been shown to the vanquished.

It remained to consign the captives to the universal house of detention. By five o'clock in the afternoon, as the spring day was closing in, Wyatt and five of his comrades had been conducted to the Tower by Jerningham. They arrived by310 water, and were met at the bulwark by Sir Philip Denny, who greeted the prisoners with words of fierce upbraiding.

"Go, traitor," he said, as Wyatt passed by, "there was never such a traitor in England."

Wyatt turned upon him.

"I am no traitor," he answered. "I would thou should well know thou art more traitor than I; and it is not the part of an honest man to call me so."

He was right; but courtesy to the defeated was no article of the code of the day. At the Tower Gate Sir John Bridges, the Lieutenant, stood, likewise ready to receive and to revile his prisoners. To each in turn he addressed some varied form of abuse, taking Wyatt, who came last, by the collar "in very rigorous manner," and shaking him.

"'Thou villain and unhappy traitor,' he cried, ... 'if it were not that the law must justly pass upon thee, I would strike thee through with my dagger.'

"To whom Wyatt made no answer, but, holding his arms under his side, and looking grievously with a grim look upon the said Lieutenant, said, 'It is no mastery now,' and so they passed on."

Thus ended Wyatt's rebellion. Together with her father's treason, it had sealed Lady Jane's fate, and that of the boy-husband who shared her captivity.

311

CHAPTER XXIII

1554

Lady Jane and her husband doomed—Her dispute with Feckenham—Gardiner's sermon—Farewell messages—Last hours—Guilford Dudley's execution—Lady Jane's death.

Those anxious days when the fortunes of England and its Queen appeared once more to hang in the balance had sealed the fate of the prisoners in the Tower. They must die. Mary had been warned that the clemency shown to her little cousin was unwise; she had struggled against the counsellors who had striven to convince her that the usurper, so long as she lived, was a menace to the peace of the realm, and the stability of her government. Their warnings had been justified, and Jane must pay the penalty.

What was to be done was to be done quickly. It was perhaps feared that, with leisure to reconsider the matter, the Queen would even now retract her consent to deliver up the victim; nor was there any excuse for delay. The boy and girl already lay under sentence of death; it was only necessary to carry it into effect. So far as this life was concerned Lady Jane's doom was fixed.

312 It remained to take thought for her soul. With death staring them in the face, many had been lately found willing to conform their faith to the Queen's. Why should it not be so with the Queen's cousin? To compass this object Mary's chaplain, Dr. Feckenham, the new Dean of St. Paul's, was sent to plead with the captive, and to strive to reconcile her with God and the Church before she went hence.

The ambassador was well chosen. Learned and devout, he had been bred a Benedictine, and had, under Henry VIII., suffered imprisonment on account of his faith; until Sir Philip Hoby, in his own words, "borrowed him of the Tower." Since then it had been his habit to hold disputations, "earnest yet modest," according to Fuller, in defence of his religion, and was honoured by Mary and Elizabeth alike. This was the man to whom was entrusted the difficult task of convincing Lady Jane of her errors. It was scarcely to be anticipated that he would succeed, but he seems to have performed the thankless duty laid upon him with gentleness and good feeling.

Arrived at the Tower—his whilom place of captivity—Feckenham, after some preliminary courtesies, disclosed the object of his visit, adding certain persuasive arguments, to which the prisoner made reply that he had delayed too long, and time was over-short to allow her to give attention to these matters. The answer, in whatever sense it313 was meant, was sufficiently ambiguous to afford a sanguine and anxious man grounds for hope that, with leisure for discussion, he might win a favourable hearing; considering his proposed convert "in very good dispositions," he went to seek the Queen; and, describing his interview, had no difficulty in inducing her to grant a three-days' reprieve. Friday, February 9, had been at first appointed for the execution, and when—for reasons undisclosed to the public—it was deferred until the following Monday, the change may have given rise in some quarters to expectations unwarranted by the event. There were those determined to hold Mary to her purpose.

On Sunday, the 11th, Gardiner preached before the Queen, dealing first with the doctrine of free will; secondly, with the institution of Lent; thirdly, with the necessity of good works; and fourthly, with Protestant errors. After which he came to the practical question in all men's minds. He asked a boon of the Queen's Highness—that, like as she had beforetime extended her mercy, particularly and privately, so through her lenity and gentleness much conspiracy and open rebellion were grown, according to the proverb, nimia familiaritas parit contemptum, which he brought in for the purpose that she would now be merciful to the body of the Commonwealth and conservation thereof, which could not be unless the rotten and314 hurtful members thereof were cut off and consumed. "And thus he ended soon after, whereby all the audience did gather there should shortly follow sharp and cruel execution."214

Whether or not Gardiner's discourse was directed against a tendency to waver in her intention on the part of his mistress, it was proved that there was nothing in that direction to be apprehended. Meantime, armed with the boon he had obtained, Feckenham had returned to the Tower, to beg the captive to make use of the reprieve for the salvation of her soul.

Lady Jane's reply was not encouraging. She had not, she told him, intended her words to be repeated to the Queen; she had already abandoned worldly things, had no thought of fear, and was prepared to meet death patiently in whatsoever form might please the Queen. To the flesh it was indeed painful, but her soul was joyful at quitting this darkness, and rising, as by God's mercy she hoped to rise, to eternal light.215

It was not to be expected that the priest, a good man, full of zeal for his religion and of solicitude for the dying culprit, would consent to relinquish, without an effort, the attempt to utilise the respite he had been granted. Of what followed accounts vary, according to the theological proclivities315 of the narrator of the scene, an early pamphlet asserting that Feckenham, finding himself, in reasoning, "in all holy gifts so short of [Lady Jane's] excellence that he acknowledged himself fitter to be her disciple than teacher, thereupon humbly besought her to deliver unto him some brief sum of her faith which he might hereafter keep, and as a faithful witness publish to the world; to which she willingly condescended, and bade him boldly question her in what points of religion soever it pleased him."216

The attitude ascribed to Queen Mary's chaplain would seem more likely to be due to imagination than to fact. It appears, however, that a species of "catechising argument" did in truth take place in the presence of witnesses, an account of which was set down in writing, and received Lady Jane's signature. The only result of the discussion was the strengthening rather than shaking of her convictions; and though it was not until she stood upon the scaffold that the last farewells of the disputants were taken, Feckenham must soon have been aware that his efforts would be made in vain. It may be hoped that to the imagination of the chronicler is again to be ascribed the manner of the parting of the two on this first occasion, when, feeling himself to be worsted in argument, Feckenham is said to have "grown into316 a little choler," and used language unsuitable to his gravity, received with smiles and patience by the cause of his irritation. It is further stated that to a final speech of her visitor, to the effect that he was sorry for her obstinacy, and was certain that they would meet no more, Lady Jane, not altogether with the meekness attributed to her, retorted that his words were indeed most true, since, unless he should repent, he was in a sad and desperate case, and she prayed God that, as He had given him His great gift of utterance, He might open his heart to His truth.217

So the days passed, and the fatal one was at hand. On Saturday, February 10, the Duke of Suffolk, with his brother, Lord John Grey, had been brought prisoners to the Tower; but it does not appear that any meeting took place between father and daughter, and Lady Jane's leave-taking was made in writing; sentences of farewell being inscribed by her and her husband in a manual of prayers belonging, as is conjectured, to the Lieutenant of the Tower, and used by her on the scaffold. In this volume three sentences were written.

"Your loving and obedient son," wrote Guilford, "wisheth unto your Grace long life in this world,317 with as much joy and comfort as ever I wished to myself, and in the world to come joy everlasting.

G. Duddeley."

Jane's farewell followed:

"The Lord comfort your Grace, and that in His word wherein all creatures only are to be comforted. And though it has pleased God to take away two of your children, yet think not, I most humbly beseech your Grace, that you have lost them, but trust that we, by leaving this mortal life, have won an immortal life. And I, for my part, as I have honoured your Grace in this life, will pray for you in another life.

"Your Grace's humble daughter,

"Jane Duddeley."

The same book bears another inscription addressed to the Lieutenant of the Tower, Bridges, apparently at his own request.

"Forasmuch as you have desired," Jane wrote, "so simple a woman to write in so worthy a book, good Master Lieutenant, therefore I shall as a friend desire you, and as a Christian require you, to call upon God to incline your heart to His laws, to quicken you in His way, and not to take the word of truth utterly out of your mouth. Live still to die, that by death you may purchase eternal life, and remember the end of Methuselah, who, as318 we read in the Scriptures, was the longest liver that was of a man, died at the last; for as the preacher saith, there is a time to be born and a time to die, and the day of death is better than the day of our birth. Yours, as the Lord knoweth, as a friend,

"Jane Duddeley."

Such an admonition to the Lieutenant, written when death was very near, is characteristic. It was ever Lady Jane's custom to use her pen, and the habit clung to her. Tradition asserts that three sentences, the one in Greek, the other in Latin, and the third in English, were written by her in yet another book; and though it has been argued that she would have been in no condition to compose epigrams in the dead languages at a moment when death was staring her in the face, there is nothing improbable in the story, unsupported as it is by evidence. As a man lives, he dies; and Jane had been a scholar and a moralist from her cradle.

"If justice dwells in my body"—thus the sentences are said to have run—"my soul will receive it from the mercy of God.—Death will pay the penalty of my fault, but my soul will be justified before the Face of God.—If my fault merited chastisement, my youth, at least, and my imprudence, deserved excuse. God and posterity will show me grace."

319 A letter of exhortation addressed to her sister Katherine likewise remains, another proof of her desire to impress upon others the lessons life had taught her. Having been reading, the night before her death, in "a fair New Testament in Greek," she found, on closing it, some few leaves of clean paper, unwritten, at the end of the volume, and made use of them to convey her final farewell to the sister she was leaving behind, giving it in charge to her servant as a token of love and remembrance. As might have been expected, with the thought of the morrow before her, death was the recurrent burden of her theme. "Live still to die," she told little Katherine, as she had told the Lieutenant of the Tower, "and that by death you may purchase eternal life; and trust not that the tenderness of your age shall lengthen your life ... for as soon will the Lord be glorified in the young as in the old.... Once more let me entreat thee to learn to die.... Desire with St. Paul to be dissolved and to be with Christ, with whom even in death there is life.... As touching my death, rejoice as I do ... that I shall be delivered of this corruption and put on incorruption; for I am assured that I shall, for losing of a mortal life, win one that is immortal, joyful, and everlasting."

Another composition is extant, said to belong to this last period, and showing the writer, it320 may be, in a more pathetic light than that thrown upon her by disputes with controversialists, or exhortations to those she left behind. This is a prayer, exhibiting not so much the premature woman as the child—a child, it is true, facing death with steadfast faith and resignation, but nevertheless frightened, unhappy, "unquieted with troubles, wrapped in cares, overwhelmed with miseries, vexed with temptations ... craving Thy mercy and help, without the which so little hope of deliverance is left that I may utterly despair of my liberty."218

Of liberty it was, in truth, time to despair. It is said that for two hours on this last night two bishops, with other divines, made a vain attempt to accomplish the conversion that Feckenham had failed to effect218; after which we may hope that, worn out and exhausted, the prisoner forgot her troubles in sleep. And so the night passed away.

In another part of the great fortress young Guilford Dudley was also preparing for the end. It is said219 that, "desiring to give his wife the last kisses and embraces," he begged for an interview, but that she refused the request—not disallowed by Mary— replying that, could sight have given souls comfort, she would have been very willing; that since it would only increase the misery of each, and bring greater grief, it would be best to put off321 their meeting, since soon they would see each other in another place and live joined for ever by an indissoluble tie. If the story is true, there is something a little inhuman—or perhaps only belonging to the coldness of a child—in the wisdom which, at that moment, could weigh and balance the disadvantages of a leave-taking and refuse it. It is not, however, out of character.

It had been at first intended that the two should suffer together on Tower Hill. Fearing the effect upon the populace, the order was cancelled, and it was decided that, whilst Guilford's execution should take place as originally arranged, Lady Jane should meet her death within the precincts of the Tower itself. As the lad, led to his doom, passed below her window, the two looked upon each other for the last time. Young Dudley met the end bravely. Taking Sir Anthony Browne, John Throckmorton and others by the hand, he asked their prayers; then, attended by no priest or minister, he knelt to pray, "holding up his eyes and hands to God many times," before the executioner did his work and he went to join the father who was responsible for his fate, "bewailed with lamentable tears" even by those of the spectators who till that day had never seen him.220

A ghastly incident, variously recorded, followed. His body thrown into a cart, and his head wrapped322 in a cloth, he was brought into the Tower chapel, where Lady Jane, having probably left her apartments on her way to her own place of execution, encountered the cart and those in charge of it, seeing the husband who had passed beneath her window a few minutes earlier living, taken from it a corpse—a sight to her, says the chronicler, no less than death. It "a little startled her," observes another narrator, "and many tears were seen to descend and fall upon her cheeks, which her silence and great heart soon dried."221 According to a third account, she addressed the dead.

"Oh, Guilford, Guilford," she is made to exclaim, "the antepast that you have tasted and I shall soon taste, is not so bitter as to make my flesh tremble; for all this is nothing to the feast that you and I shall partake this day in Paradise."

It had been ten o'clock when Guilford had left his prison. By the time that the first act of the tragedy was over, a scaffold had been erected upon the green over against the White Tower, and led by the Lieutenant, the chief victim was brought forth, "her countenance nothing abashed, neither her eyes moisted with tears,"222 as she moved onwards, a book in her hand—the same she gave afterwards to Sir John Bridges—from which she prayed all323 the way until the scaffold was reached. With her were her two gentlewomen, Elizabeth Tylney and Eleyn, who both "wonderfully wept" as they accompanied their mistress; and Feckenham was also present, her kindly opponent, perhaps even now hoping against hope that success might crown his efforts. As the two stood together at the place of execution, she took him by the hand, and, embracing him, bade him leave her—desiring, it may be, to spare him the sight of what was to follow. Might God our Lord, she said, give him all his desires; she was grateful for his company, although it had given her more disquiet than, now, the fear of death.223

Like most of her fellow-sufferers she had come prepared with a speech. That her sentence was lawful she admitted, but reasserted the absence on her part of any desire for her elevation to the throne, "touching the procurement and desire thereof by me or my half, I do wash my hands in innocency before God and the face of you, good Christian people, this day," and therewith she wrung her hands, in which she had her book; proceeding to make confession of the faith in which she died, owning that she had neglected the word of God, and loved herself and the world, and thereby merited her punishment. "And yet I thank God that He hath thus given me time and respite to324 repent. And now, good people, while I am alive, I pray you to assist me with your prayers."

After this, kneeling down, she turned to Feckenham, who had not availed himself of her suggestion that he should leave her.

"Shall I say this psalm?" she asked him; and on his assenting repeated the Miserere in English, before, rising again, she prepared for the end, giving her book to Bridges, brother to the Lieutenant, who stood by, and her gloves and handkerchief to one of her ladies. With her own hands she untied her gown, rejecting the aid of the executioner, and, turning to her maids for assistance, removed her "frose paast"—probably some kind of head-dress—let down her hair, throwing it over her eyes, and knit a "fair handkerchief" about them.

After kneeling for her forgiveness, the executioner directed her to take her place on the straw.

"Then she said,

"'I pray you despatch me quickly.'

"Then she kneeled down, saying,

"'Will you take it off before I lay me down?'

"And the hangman answered her,

"'No, madame.'"

The handkerchief was bound about her eyes, blinding her.

"What shall I do?" she said, feeling for the block. "Where is it?"

Then, as some one standing near guided her,325 she laid down her head, and saying, "Lord, into Thy hands I commend my spirit," met the blow of the executioner.

Thus died Lady Jane Grey, most guiltless of traitors; who, to quote Fuller's panegyric, possessed, at sixteen, the innocency of childhood, the beauty of youth, the solidity of middle, and the gravity of old, age; who had had the birth of a princess, the learning of a clerk, the life of a saint, and the death of a malefactor.

326

INDEX

113

Printed by Hazell, Watson & Viney, Ld., London and Aylesbury.

FOOTNOTES

1 Hall's Chronicle.

2 Martin Hume, The Wives of Henry VIII., p. 447.

3 Ellis's Original Letters, Series III., vol. iii., p. 203.

4 Grey Friar's Chronicle (Camden Society), p. 44.

5 Martin Hume, Wives of Henry VIII., p. 344.

6 Holinshed.

7 Strype's Memorials of Archbishop Cranmer.

8 Hall's Chronicle.

9 Spanish Chronicle of Henry VIII., translated by Martin Hume.

10 Hayward's Life of Edward VI.

11 Sir H. Ellis, Original Letters.

12 Calendar, Henry VIII., vol. xviii., p. 1.

13 Speed.

14 Chronicle of Henry VIII., translated by Martin Hume.

15 Martin Hume, Wives of Henry VIII., p. 438.

16 Heylyn's Reformation.

17 Heylyn's Reformation.

18 Andrew Bloxam.

19 Calendar of State Papers (Venetian), p. 346.

20 It is stated in the Dictionary of National Biography that Lady Jane was attached to the Queen's household in 1546, but I am unable to discover any proof of the fact. Speed, in his chronicle, makes two or three mentions of her, from which other biographers have concluded that she was in close attendance on Katherine Parr during the King's lifetime. But it seems clear that he made a confusion between Lady Jane, the King's great-niece, and Lady Lane, Katherine's cousin, born Maud Parr, who was at that time a member of her household.

21 Naunton.

22 Foxe, Acts and Monuments.

23 Grey Friars' Chronicle (Camden Society), p. 50.

24 G. Leti, Vie d'Elizabeth, Reine d'Angleterre, t. i., p. 153.

25 Grey Friars' Chronicle (Camden Society), p. 51.

26 Ellis's Original Letters, Series II., vol. ii., p. 176.

27 Lord Herbert of Cherbury, Life of Henry VIII., p. 537.

28 N. D., quoted, with disapproval, by Speed.

29 Lingard, History, vol. v., p. 200.

30 Foxe, Acts and Monuments.

31 Dr. Lingard, quoting the narrative attributed to Anne, credits neither it nor the addition for which Foxe is responsible, stating that there is no other instance of a woman being subjected to torture, that a written order from the Lords of the Council was necessary before it could be inflicted, and that it was not customary for either the Chancellor or his colleagues to be present on these occasions.—History, vol. v., p. 201.

32 Foxe, Acts and Monuments.

33 Life of Henry VIII., p. 561.

34 Speed, and Miss Strickland following him, read the name "Jane."

35 Acts and Monuments, Speed's Chronicle, Lord Herbert of Cherbury, etc.

36 Bapst, Deux Gentilshommes Poëtes, p. 275.

37 Bapst, Deux Gentilshommes Poëtes, p. 287.

38 Lord Herbert of Cherbury, Life of Henry VIII., p. 564.

39 Ibid., p. 563.

40 Chronicle of King Henry VIII. of England (translated by Martin Hume), p. 182.

41 Chronicle of Henry VIII. (tr. by Martin Hume), p. 152.

42 Bapst, Deux Gentilshommes Poëtes, p. 346.

43 Grey Friars' Chronicle, p. 52.

44 Chronicle of Henry VIII. (tr. by Martin Hume), p. 147.

45 Chronicle of Henry VIII. (tr. by Martin Hume), p. 148.

46 Foxe, Acts and Monuments, vol. v., p. 689.

47 History of the World.

48 Chronicle of Henry VIII. (tr. by Martin Hume), p. 152.

49 Acts and Monuments, vol. v., p. 689.

50 Acts and Monuments, vol. v., p. 691.

51 Literary Remains of Edward VI., Roxburgh Club, ed. Nichols.

52 Hayward's Life of Edward VI., p. 82.

53 Leti, Vie de la Reine Elizabeth, p. 166.

54 Haynes, State Papers. It is difficult to distinguish between statements relating to the negotiations with regard to Lady Jane carried on at this date, and those taking place eighteen months later.

55 Tytler, England under Edward VI. and Mary, vol. i.

56 Fuller's Worthies.

57 Leti, Vie de la Reine Elizabeth, p. 163.

58 Chronicle of Henry VIII., p. 158.

59 Leti, Vie de la Reine Elizabeth, p. 170.

60 Haynes, State Papers.

61 An Historical Account of Sudeley Castle.

62 Quoted by Strype.

63 Chronicle of Henry VIII., p. 156.

64 Hayward, Life of Edward VI., p. 82.

65 Heylyn's Reformation, p. 71.

66 Haynes, State Papers.

67 Ibid.

68 Haynes, State Papers.

69 State Papers. Quoted in Strickland's Queens of England, vol. iii., p. 272.

70 Haynes, State Papers.

71 Haynes, State Papers.

72 Leti is responsible for it.

73 Haynes, State Papers, p. 96.

74 Tytler, Edward and Mary, vol. i., p. 70.

75 Haynes, State Papers, p. 61.

76 Ibid.

77 Quoted Remains of Edward VI.

78 Tytler, Edward and Mary, vol. i.

79 Haynes, State Papers, pp. 103, 104.

80 Miss Strickland, Queens of England, vol. iii., p 281.

81 Haynes, State Papers, pp. 77, 78.

82 Haynes, State Papers, pp. 78, 79.

83 Tytler, Edward VI. and Mary, vol. i., p. 134.

84 Haynes, State Papers, p. 76.

85 Ibid., pp. 79, 80.

86 Chronicle of King Henry VIII., p. 163.

87 Haynes, State Papers, p. 89.

88 Haynes, State Papers.

89 Haynes, State Papers, p. 109.

90 Haynes, State Papers, p. 98.

91 Haynes, State Papers, p. 108.

92 Haynes, State Papers, p. 71.

93 Haynes, State Papers, p. 106.

94 Latimer's Sermons, quoted by Lingard, History, vol. v., p. 279.

95 Leti, Vie de la Reine Elizabeth.

96 Lingard, History, vol. v., p. 293.

97 Strype's Ecclesiastical Memorials, vol. ii., p. 2.

98 Tytler, Edward VI. and Mary, vol. i., p. 174.

99 Holinshed, vol. iii., p. 1014.

100 Chronicle of King Henry VIII., p. 187.

101 See Tytler, Edward VI. and Mary, vol. i., p. 241. Dr. Lingard expresses doubts as to the document upon which Tytler relies, and Froude acquits the Council of treachery.

102 Tytler, Edward VI. and Mary, vol. i., p. 242.

103 Chronicle of King Henry VIII., p. 192.

104 Foxe, Acts and Monuments, vol. vi., pp. 351, 352.

105 Ascham describes her as fifteen—a manifest error.

106 Roger Ascham, The Schoolmaster, bk. ii.

107 Ascham, The Schoolmaster, bk. i.

108 Zurich Letters, Parker Society.

109 Ibid.

110 Zurich Letters, vol. ii., Parker Society, p. 399.

111 Ibid., p. 427.

112 Zurich Letters, vol. ii., p. 430.

113 Zurich Letters, p. 433.

114 There is little mention of Lady Jane's mother in contemporary records. But the nature of the woman, and her heritage of Tudor blood, is sufficiently indicated by the fact that not a fortnight after her husband had been executed, and about a month after Lady Jane's death she bestowed herself in marriage upon her equerry.

115 Becon's Jewel of Joy, Parker Society.

116 Zurich Letters, p. 103.

117 Zurich Letters, vol. i., p. 5.

118 Zurich Letters, vol. i., p. 72.

119 Zurich Letters, vol. i., pp. 76, 77.

120 Church History, vol. i., p. 338.

121 Church History, vol. i., p. 340.

122 Zurich Letters, vol. ii., p. 441.

123 Fuller's Church History, vol. i., p. 341.

124 Ellis's Original Letters, Series III., vol. i., p. 216.

125 Heylyn's Reformation, vol. ii., p. 7.

126 Soranzo's Report (Venetian Calendar), p. 535.

127 Strype's Ecclesiastical Memorials, vol. ii., p. 2.

128 Venetian Calendar, p. 535.

129 Fuller's Church History, vol, i., p. 345.

130 Zurich Letters, vol. ii., p. 466. Meaning that Cranmer, who had already been married some years, had brought his wife from Germany, and owned her openly. See Strype.

131 Two victims were burnt for heresy, Joan Bocher and a Dutch surgeon, named Pariss. A priest is also stated by Wriothesley to have been hanged and quartered, July 7, 1548.

132 Zurich Letters, pp. 281 et seq.

133 Foxe, Acts and Monuments, vol. vi., pp. 354-5. Heylyn's Reformation.

134 Speed's Chronicle, p. 1122.

135 Heylyn's Reformation, vol. i., p. 291.

136 Rosso, Succesi d'Inghilterra, p. 5.

137 Wriothesley's Chronicle, vol. ii., p. 82.

138 Ibid.

139 Florio's Life, p. 27.

140 Ibid., p. 28.

141 Ibid.

142 Heylyn's Reformation, p. 297.

143 Ambassades de Noailles; Griffet, Nouveaux Éclaircissements sur l'Histoire de Marie.

144 Wriothesley's Chronicle, vol. ii., p. 79.

145 Reformation, vol. i., p. 294.

146 Heylyn's Reformation, vol. i., p. 294.

147 Griffet, Éclaircissements, etc., p. 16.

148 Ambassades de Noailles, vol. i., p. 49.

149 Ibid., p. 57.

150 Quoted in Strickland's Queen Mary.

151 Fuller's Church History, vol. i., pp. 369 et seq.

152 Rosso, Succesi d'Inghilterra.

153 Griffet's Éclaircissements, etc.

154 Foxe's Acts and Monuments, vol. vi., p. 352.

155 The paper is only to be found in two Italian histories, Pollini's Istoria Ecclesiastica della Rivoluzione d'Inghilterra and Raviglio Rosso's account of the events following upon Edward's death, stated to be partly drawn from the despatches of Bodoaro. The discrepancies here and there in the translation point to both having had access to an English version.

156 History of Syon Monastery, Aungier.

157 Chronicle of Queen Jane (Camden Society), p. 2.

158 Speed's Chronicle, p. 1127.

159 Heylyn makes Durham House the scene of the announcement. In this he seems clearly to be mistaken, as it is stated in the Grey Friar's Chronicle that she was brought down the river from Richmond to Westminster, and so to the Tower.

160 The Chronicle of Queen Jane and Queen Mary (Camden Society), p. 3.

161 Letter from Jane to Mary, Pollini's Istoria Ecclesiastica della Rivoluzione d'Inghilterra, pp. 355-8.

162 Rosso, Succesi d'Inghilterra, p. 13.

163 Rosso, Succesi d'Inghilterra, p. 9.

164 Heylyn's Reformation.

165 Griffet, Nouveaux Éclaircissements.

166 Strype's Memorials.

167 Chronicle of Queen Jane and Queen Mary, ed. John Nichols (Camden Society), App., pp. 116-121.

168 The foregoing details are mostly taken from Stowe's Chronicle. At this point The Chronicle of Queen Jane and Queen Mary by a Resident in the Tower (Camden Society), takes up the tale. The anonymous author plainly speaks from personal knowledge, and is the principal authority for this period.

169 Grafton's Chronicle.

170 Heylyn's Reformation.

171 Fuller's Worthies.

172 Tytler's Edward and Mary, vol. ii., p. 202.

173 Rosso's Succesi.

174 Rosso's Succesi.

175 Quoted in Chronicle of Queen Jane and Queen Mary, p. 11.

176 This fact, together with Sir Nicholas's subsequent trial, seems to throw doubt upon the veracity of his versified account of the services he had rendered to Mary.

177 Biog. Brit. Quoted in Lady Jane Grey's Literary Remains.

122

178 L'Istoria Ecclesiastica della Rivoluzione d'Inghilterra. Pollini, pp. 274, 275. Rosso's Succesi, p. 20.

179 M. A. Florio, Vita, pp. 58, 59.

180 Dictionary of National Biography.

181 Rosso, Succesi, p. 23.

182 Chronicle of Queen Jane, etc., pp. 10, 11.

183 Foxe, Acts and Monuments.

184 Chronicle of Queen Jane, etc. p. 16.

185 Rosso.

186 Vie d'Elizabeth, p. 198.

187 Griffet, Nouveaux Éclaircissements, p. 23.

188 Chronicle of Queen Jane and Queen Mary, p. 16.

189 Griffet, Nouveaux Éclaircissements, p. 25.

190 Griffet, Nouveaux Éclaircissements, pp. 26, 27.

191 Chronicle of Queen Jane and Queen Mary, p. 24.

192 Edward and Mary, vol. ii., p. 224.

193 Peerage of England (1799), vol. ii., p. 406. Quoted in Strickland's Queens of England.

194 Lingard, History, vol. v., pp. 390, 391.

195 Ibid., p. 391.

196 Tytler, Edward and Mary, vol. ii., p. 227.

197 Chronicle of Queen Jane and Queen Mary, from which the following details of the execution are mostly taken.

198 Peerage of England (1709), vol. ii., p. 406. Quoted in Miss Strickland's Queens.

199 Griffet, Nouveaux Éclaircissements, p. 55.

200 Dr. Nichols suggests that Partridge may have been Queen Mary's goldsmith of that name, apparently resident in the Tower during the following year.

201 Lingard, History, vol. v., p. 393.

202 Griffet, Nouveaux Éclaircissements, p. 65.

203 Griffet, Nouveaux Éclaircissements, p. 60.

204 Lingard, History, vol. v., p. 401.

205 Speed's Chronicle.

206 Griffet, Nouveaux Éclaircissements, pp. 125-6.

207 Griffet, Nouveaux Éclaircissements, p. 127.

208 Lingard, History, vol. v., p. 411.

209 Chronicle of Queen Jane and Queen Mary, p. 34.

210 Griffet, Nouveaux Éclaircissements, p. 118.

211 Chronicle of Queen Jane and Queen Mary, p. 38 et seq.

212 Ibid.

213 Speed's Chronicle, p. 1133.

214 Chronicle of Queen Jane and Queen Mary, p. 54.

215 Rosso, Succesi d'Inghilterra, p. 53.

216 Life and Death of Lady Jane Grey, 1615, p. 22.

217 It will be seen that the bearing of the two opponents on the scaffold would seem to give the lie to this account of their interview; unless, the heat of argument over, both should have regretted what had passed.

218 Life and Death of Lady Jane Grey, 1615, p. 25.

219 Rosso, Succesi, etc., p. 57.

220 Chronicle of Queen Jane and Queen Mary.

221 Life and Death of Lady Jane Grey, 1615, p. 30.

222 Chronicle of Queen Jane and Queen Mary, pp. 54-6. The author, "resident in the Tower," was doubtless an eye-witness of the scene.

223 Rosso, Succesi d'Inghilterra, etc., pp. 57, 58.